BLACK
RAINBOW

BLACK RAINBOW

Barbara Michaels

SOUVENIR PRESS

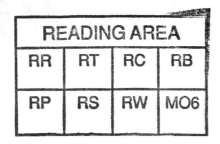
Copyright © 1982 by Barbara Michaels

First published in the U.S.A. by
Congdon & Weed Inc., New York

First British Edition published 1984 by
Souvenir Press Ltd, 43 Great Russell Street London WC1B 3PA

ISBN 0 285 62598 5

Printed and bound in Great Britain by
A. Wheaton & Co. Ltd, Exeter

M

For
Erika
Schmid

CONTENTS

FOREWORD

As AN admirer of cats, particularly Siamese, I am of course familiar with the tradition that the first Siamese cats in England were brought to that country by Owen Gould, British Consul-General at Bangkok, in 1884. I have felt at liberty to introduce a fictitious member of the breed at an earlier date, since it seems to me quite possible that unrecorded examples may well have existed.

Like the cat, all the characters in this book are entirely fictitious and bear no resemblance to any persons living or dead.

BLACK
RAINBOW

Book One

MEGAN

Chapter
One

SCIENTISTS ASSERT that it is a wholly natural phenomenon —child of storm cloud and full moon, as its bright sister of day is the offspring of sunlight and rain. Megan was not superstitious, but when she reached the top of the ridge and saw the black rainbow framing the huddled towers of Grayhaven Manor, her first impulse was to pick up her wet, clinging skirts and retreat at full speed back down the slope she had so laboriously ascended.

The rainsquall that had drenched her during her walk passed as quickly as it had come, and as the weary girl paused to rest, the full moon burst free of the clouds. The rainbow's hues ranged from palest silver-gray to a black deeper than the moonlit vault of the sky—an ominous portent for a traveler whose destination was the old house under that sinister arc.

It lay in a little cup of hills, whose slopes must be green and pleasant by daylight. The moon robbed them of color, as it did all other objects in view; the trees were sable plumes, the lawns pale as snow, the little stream a silver ribbon. The scene had an eerie beauty, but Megan found herself wishing she had not beguiled her weeks of enforced idleness by reading so many of the Gothic romances then in fashion, with their abundance of specters, vampires, and haunted castles. Not that she had had much choice; her landlady's small library consisted entirely of such volumes, and she had not had the money to join a circulating library.

At first glance the ancient walls and towers of Grayhaven appeared to be a perfect setting for one of Mrs. Radcliffe's tales of imperiled maidens and Black Monks. Subsequent glances gave quite a different impression. Sheltered by the enclosing hills, the house clung to the earth like a curled-up cat, blinking yellow windows of eyes in smug content. The suggestion of warmth and light in those amber squares was most welcome to a wet and weary traveler.

Still Megan lingered, tempted to rest awhile before proceeding. They had told her at the station that it was only four miles to the house. The distance had seemed at least twice that long. She had eaten nothing since breakfast, and her wet skirts felt heavy as lead. The ground was damp, and she shivered in the sharp breeze that had arisen to scatter the clouds. The moon rode high above the last wrack of the storm, a silver ball rolling up an invisible path across the sky —chariot of the goddess Diana, virgin huntress of the Romans.

Megan was better educated than most of her class, she knew her Latin and even a little Greek; but she had not learned of pagan gods from the nuns who had provided her formal schooling. Her father had been half a pagan himself; from his tales, and from the books he somehow managed to obtain, wherever their travels led them, she had learned of Zeus and Apollo, grim Pluto and his stolen bride, and the other immortals of Olympus. Under the spell of the black rainbow she remembered things she would rather have forgotten. The black-and-silver landscape was no place for bright Apollo or the harmless nymphs of grove and stream;

but what a night for Diana the huntress, whose other persona is the witch goddess Hecate, and whose pack hunts human prey. Megan's skin prickled as she heard a frenzied distant howling. Another sound, closer at hand, made her glance fearfully over her shoulder. Surely it had been the soft patter of hooves. A harmless deer—or a ghostly stag? The horse of a human traveler—or a great black stallion spurred on by one of the grim, inhuman heroes so popular with the lady authors of the romances . . . dark hair flowing back from a high, noble forehead, grave brown eyes fixed on the horizon . . . ?

Megan gave herself a shake and returned to the real world of wet shoes, soggy garments, and aching limbs. The face of the imaginary rider had not been a product of fiction-induced fancy, it had a living model; and common sense told her to stop dreaming. Edmund Mandeville was her employer. He could never be anything else. She forced herself to stoop and pick up the heavy bag, which she had dropped when she reached the summit of the hill.

She had more strength of character than her fragile form and delicate features suggested. Though the weight of the bag dragged painfully at her weary muscles, she was about to proceed when she saw something that made her breath catch in her throat. Her wild fancies had not been imagination after all—or else they had given solid form to something that should never have existed in the real world. On a great boulder beside the path perched a small bowed hump of a figure. The moonlight glinted off a helmet of sleek dark hair and showed the curve of a pale cheek; there was no dismissing the object as a natural formation.

Megan's half-suppressed cry was heard. The dwarfish creature bounded up. Balancing atop the boulder, it turned to face the girl.

In the bright moonlight it lost its goblin air and took on a kindlier aspect—that of a brownie or dwarf, one of the Little People who haunt the remote hills and are said, on occasion, to grant wishes to humans. It was muffled in a dark cloak,

BR–B

whose hood had fallen back to display human features, but it was of diminutive size—though, as Megan was to learn, not so tiny as her startled imagination had made it seem.

At first its round homely face mirrored her own shock. Wide eyes glinted palely.

"Who are you?" The two voices blended in an impromptu duet.

The little woman was the first to relax. Her mouth opened in a wide smile and she broke out laughing.

"You gave me such a start! I thought myself quite alone, and for a moment you had a look of. . . . But I had better not tell you what peculiar notions were passing through my mind, or you will think me entirely mad instead of slightly eccentric."

Megan had realized that her "brownie" was only a human female of unusually short stature; but her second theory, that the humbly dressed woman must be one of the servants from the manor below, was negated by the voice and speech, which were those of a lady.

Gratefully she responded to the friendly smile and cordial voice. "If you are eccentric to be out on such a night, then so am I. But anyone might be fascinated by so strange a sight. That is—you did see it, did you not?"

"The black rainbow?" The little woman let out another peal of laughter. "I assure you, it is quite a natural phenomenon. My old nurse saw it once when she was a girl, but it is very rare, and I never expected I would have the good fortune to behold it myself." She fell silent; her smile faded into a look of dreamy wonder, and in a softer, altogether different voice she murmured, "Dark child of falling water and full moon, the road on which the Huntress rides. . . ."

Megan started at hearing her own fantasy echoed by a stranger, though, she assured herself, anyone educated in the classics might think in such terms. However, the little lady's altered look made her uncomfortable, and she said rather sharply, "I suppose the common people hereabouts have invented ignorant superstitions about it."

"To be sure." The other woman's voice returned to normal. "Nurse quite curdled my infant blood with her tales about it; her sister died thirteen months later, and she was convinced the black rainbow was a sign of approaching death. It was partly to dispel my childish terrors about it that I was prompted to inquire into the origin of the phenomenon. But this is an odd conversation for two strangers met in such a place, and so late at night. Have you lost your way? This road leads nowhere except to the house."

"If it be, as I suppose, Grayhaven Manor, I have not lost my way. That is my destination."

"Indeed?"

She said no more; only the rising tone of her voice requested an explanation. Megan appreciated her courtesy, but the fact that the woman was obviously ignorant of her identity made her heart sink down into her sodden boots.

"Am I correct in assuming that you are Miss Mandeville?" she asked.

"You are."

"I am Megan O'Neill."

The same look of polite curiosity met this statement.

"Oh, dear," Megan said, unable to keep her voice steady. "You did not know of my coming? He did not tell you?"

"He? Ah—I think I am beginning to understand. You speak of my brother?"

"Yes, Mr. Edmund Mandeville. It was he who hired me. He assured me he would write in case, as he rather expected, he was delayed in London and I arrived before him. . . ."

Her voice failed her as a great lump seemed to block her throat. It had been bad enough to find herself abandoned at the railway station, like an unwanted parcel, but this was worse than she had imagined. No wonder Miss Mandeville had looked at her questioningly. Indeed, she had received more consideration than she had any right to expect; Miss Mandeville must have taken the bedraggled wanderer for a beggar—or worse. Shame and embarrassment were not the only emotions that struck Megan dumb. Most painful of all

7

was the realization that she had meant so little to Edmund Mandeville that he had not even bothered to notify the household of her existence.

"My brother hired you?" Miss Mandeville said, after a prolonged silence. "For what position?"

"Governess. I . . . he said there was a child."

"His ward. She is three years old."

"So young as that? Mr. Mandeville did not mention—"

"He may have forgotten," Miss Mandeville said drily. "He has scarcely seen her since she was an infant. Well, but this is not a suitable time or place for conversation. The night grows cold, and you are shivering. Come along."

Gathering up her skirts she jumped from the rock and started down the graveled drive that descended the slope into the valley. Mutely Megan followed. Her head ached and she had the sensation of walking not on solid earth but on some boggy surface that dragged at her feet.

After a few strides Miss Mandeville stopped and waited for her companion to catch up. "I beg your pardon, I did not mean to run away from you. I was thinking of Edmund. It is not like him to be so thoughtless. I only pray he has not had a relapse. He was ill, you know—very ill."

Megan hastened to give what reassurance she could. "He looked in good health when I saw him two days ago. A little thin and pale, but in excellent spirits. Was he in the Crimea? I did not like to ask."

"Yes. At Inkerman. It was not his wound that brought him so near death, but the typhoid, which he caught while in hospital. It is a mercy he was spared."

"From what I saw of him I am sure you have no cause for present concern."

"It is good of you to reassure me. I suppose we must forgive him an occasional lapse, after all his troubles. But my dear Miss O'Neill, you were most unwise to set out alone, on foot, and in the rain. Was there no one at the station whom you could have hired to drive you?"

Megan did not want to tell her the truth—that she lacked

the money to hire transportation. Not only would this force the further disclosure that she had been abruptly dismissed from her last post, without a reference, but it would reflect further on Mr. Mandeville. She had hoped he would give her an advance on her salary, or at least the price of her fare, but he had not offered—perhaps because he had never been in the position of having only a few shillings in his pocket. Men could not be expected to think of such trivial matters. And men, Megan devoutly thanked Heaven, were more apt than women to forget about such trivialities as references.

She realized that her companion was awaiting an answer, and said quickly, "It was not raining when I set out; and the porter assured me it was only a short walk. After the cramped hours in the train, I looked forward to the exercise. I left my trunk at the station—"

"I should hope so! That bag looks very heavy; if you wish to leave it here by the gate, I will send one of the footmen to fetch it."

"Thank you, I can manage. I hope, Miss Mandeville, that you will accept my apologies for—"

"Nonsense. Apologies are due you, not me. Enough of that; once you are warm and comfortable, we will talk."

She said no more during the remainder of the walk, for which Megan was grateful; she concentrated on dragging one heavy foot after the other. They squelched with each step and felt as if they weighed fifty pounds apiece. She was vaguely aware of the bulk of the house looming up before her and of a great central tower, whose crenellated roofline stood out blackly against the sky. Miss Mandeville marched up to the front door and flung it open. A flood of warmth, light, and comfort clasped Megan in supporting arms.

The arms were actually those of a stout old woman wearing the neat black gown and ruffled cap of a servant. Her face was as wrinkled as a withered apple, but her arms had a blacksmith's strength; they had propelled the dazed girl up a flight of stairs and along a lighted corridor before she came fully to her senses.

Megan muttered something—she scarcely knew what—and attempted to demonstrate that she could walk unassisted. The brawny arms only tightened their hold.

"Don't fret yourself, poor child," the old woman crooned. "Lizzie will take care of you; you came all over queer just now, and small wonder, wet and tired as you are. It's a shame, it is, but just like Master Edmund, he always was a careless lad—handsome as a little lord, but never thinking. . . ."

Megan had not the inclination nor the strength to resist. Her wet garments were removed and she was helped into a bath filled with steaming water. Drowsy and content, she was carried back to a time when other hands had tended her and other voices had murmured soothingly. Nurse. . . . She had forgotten the name, but the once-loved face was clear in her mind—apple-cheeked and smiling, framed by snowy white frills. And another face, dimmer and less distinct—a pearly oval and a drift of sunny bright hair, a light laughing voice crooning endearments in that language that makes any sound like music.

Lizzie plucked her out of the bath and wrapped her in a dressing gown, and gradually Megan began to take account of her surroundings. It seemed to her, in her confused state, that the room was filled with people; but in fact there were only three others—two young girls, dressed like housemaids, who were emptying the copper tub, and the old woman, who had begun unpacking her bag, her lips pursed critically as she shook out the wrinkled garments.

Lit by a number of lamps as well as by the firelight, the room was of considerable size, its high ceiling hidden by shifting shadows. The furnishings were dark and heavy; conspicuous among them was the bed, a carved four-poster with tester and hangings of blue velvet. Except for a few rugs, the floor was bare; its surface, reflecting the dancing flames, shimmered like brown honey.

For the past two years, since her father's death had forced her to seek the only employment for which she was fitted, Megan had seen several fine mansions, but only as an outsider allowed to admire from afar. A governess's position was peculiar. Almost everyone else in the class-conscious society had a proper place in the caste system, based on such factors as wealth, ancestry, and occupation. The place might be lowly and abject, but it was defined; one knew where one stood and what was expected of one. A governess's education and birth might be as good as or better than that of the people who employed her. In this sense she was not a servant, but she was definitely not one of the ruling class. In consequence she was usually looked down on by both servants and masters, and her comfort depended solely on the goodwill of those she served.

Megan's physical surroundings had reflected this ambivalence. Her own room had been little better than a servant's, furnished with cast-offs and neglected by the busy chambermaids; but, unlike the maids, she was occasionally summoned to the drawing room if her employer required music or reading aloud or some other service. She had become familiar with the latest fashions in architecture and furnishings, and thus was able to see the deficiencies in her present surroundings.

This room, and everything in it, was old. It was perilously clean; there was not a speck of dust on any surface, and even the fenders shone with strenuous polishing. But the blue velvet hangings of the bed had faded to a grayish azure, and the bed itself must be a hundred years old; the wood was black with age.

But who was she to be critical? This faded grandeur was too fine for her; it must be a temporary accommodation only. Miss Mandeville seemed very kind, for all her peculiarities; she had ordered the inconveniently collapsing governess to be carried to the nearest comfortable room, but next day Megan would be relegated to her proper place in the nursery wing—if she was not summarily ejected.

She can't dismiss me, Megan thought. But she has great influence with her brother; he spoke of her with such affection and admiration, he said she was the mistress of the house. . . . And the child only three! She needed a nursemaid, not a governess. Some ambitious parents started their sons on Latin grammar and the use of the globes when they were little older, but who would bother with a girl? They were considered overeducated and unfeminine if they acquired more than the conventional ladylike skills—music, drawing, a little French.

Megan's hands clenched. The room might be shabby, but it had a graciousness the newer mansions lacked, and an air of warmth and welcome they would never attain. I want to stay, she thought childishly. Holy Mother, let me stay; Blessed Virgin, give me sanctuary—just for a while, I am so tired.

The door opened to admit Miss Mandeville, followed by a servant carrying a tray. Megan's nostrils quivered. She had not realized how hungry she was until she smelled the tantalizing odors emanating from the covered platters. At Miss Mandeville's direction the food was placed on a low table convenient to Megan's reach, and then the servants were dismissed. The last to leave was the stout old woman, whom Miss Mandeville addressed familiarly as Lizzie.

Megan added her thanks, but did not venture to use the familiar name; she had learned by painful experience that servants such as cooks and housekeepers were sensitive about the honorable title of "Mrs." and did not brook familiarity from a mere governess. In fact, she was puzzled by Lizzie's role. Her garments were exceedingly old-fashioned, like those of a nursery- or housemaid of half a century before, yet the young maids had scurried to obey her orders.

Megan was curious enough to ask a direct question. Miss Mandeville responded with a smile that rounded her cheeks and reduced her eyes to twinkling slits. In her simple gray wool gown, with her brown hair tugged into an unfashionable knob at the back of her neck, she resembled one of the maids instead of the mistress, and her feet dangled several inches clear of the floor.

"Lizzie considers herself the housekeeper, but in fact she is empress of Grayhaven, and a great tyrant. She has bullied all of us since she was nannie to me and Edmund. But please eat, while the food is hot. I know what railway food is like —limp and lumpy and snatched from the hands of other frantic passengers while the train hoots from the platform. I dined some time ago, but I will have a glass of wine to keep you company."

The wine was a Burgundy with a fine bouquet and brilliant color. It went down as smoothly as water, warming Megan's chilled limbs. Her face reflected her appreciation, and her companion said with a smile, "You know good wine, Miss O'Neill. This is my brother's choice; if your other qualifications are as outstanding I am not surprised Edmund was impressed with you."

"Being half French, I suppose I might claim to have a natural appreciation of wine," Megan said. "But in fact it was my father who cultivated my taste—not a particularly suitable taste for a young lady, I am afraid."

"Your father was Irish?"

The seemingly casual question dispelled the euphoria induced by warmth, food, and wine. Megan braced herself for a task which, but for the lady's kindness, she would have faced long before. She hated exposing her history to strangers, but it had to be done; a prospective employer was entitled to know who and what she was.

"My mother was a French lady. My father was Irish—the youngest son of a Lord Connacht, of Kerry. I see by your expression that you understand the implications; Irish younger sons are notoriously poor, are they not? It was a sizable family; when all possible connections had been exploited, to procure positions for the others, my father was left without a means of earning a living."

Megan paused. Mistaking her motive, her companion

gestured hospitably toward the food, as if to say, "Your story can wait until you are satisfied."

But the roast beef, which had been so tasty moments before, had lost its appeal. This was the part of the story Megan dreaded most; she had adopted the habit of glossing over it when she described her father to other employers. What demon, or angel of truth, moved her tongue to candor on this occasion she did not then understand.

She put down her fork and drank more wine, to fortify her courage. "He gambled," she said. "Among other things . . . I never knew what means he used to keep us, he was careful not to let us know. There were periods of affluence, when he wrapped my mother in furs and bought me expensive toys; and periods when we lived for days on bread and cheap wine. My mother died when I was five. Instead of handing me over to an aunt or cousin, my father kept me with him in his travels. He made sure I was educated—"

"A convent school?"

The question caught Megan by surprise. She had meant to keep this part of her history secret.

"How did you know?" she gasped.

Miss Mandeville indicated a nearby table, where Lizzie had placed Megan's personal belongings. Prominent among them was the shining gilt shape of the crucifix, which was normally hidden under the bodice of her high-necked frocks.

"Knowing you were of Irish and French blood, I would have suspected you were Roman Catholic," Miss Mandeville said.

There was some excuse for Megan's consternation. Since Henry the Eighth had broken with Rome over three hundred years earlier, Catholics had been persecuted, reviled, and barred from the full privileges of British citizenship. Only in recent years had the laws preventing non-Anglicans from holding public office been repealed, and even yet Catholics were not allowed to hold professorships at the two great universities. In 1850, scarcely five years before, angry mobs had smashed the windows of Catholic-owned shops and the Pope had been burned in effigy in countless towns. Anglicans and Protestant dissenters, differing on so many articles of faith, were united in common warfare against "Papist superstition."

"The—the trinket was my mother's," Megan stammered. "I wear it for sentimental reasons . . . I no longer practice her faith."

"I am sorry to hear it," was the amazing reply. "Unless honest conviction brought about your conversion. But I suspect that was not the case."

Tears of self-pity and rage flooded Megan's eyes. How could this woman speak so complacently about honest conviction and imply that expediency had led her to commit an ignoble act? What did she know of the struggle to earn a living, or of the compromises demanded by that struggle? She was tempted to let her tears flow, but something in Miss Mandeville's calm regard warned her that device would not be effective. She conquered her weakness, but not her anger. At least she would have the satisfaction of venting some long-built-up rage before she was dismissed.

"Honesty is not a virtue, Miss Mandeville; it is a luxury reserved for the well-to-do. For a woman in my position the choices are few—if I cannot obtain honest work, I must choose death or dishonor, or the grudging hand of charity, which is worse than either. What do you know of hunger —not a healthy zest for food, but aching emptiness, with not even a crust of bread on the larder shelf? What do you know of the lure of the dark river, which promises peace and safety to the homeless wanderer? More than once I have looked into those cold depths and yearned to end the struggle."

Several times Miss Mandeville had tried to interrupt, but had been prevented by Megan's impassioned oratory. When the latter was finally forced to pause for breath, Miss

Mandeville said mildly, "You have a very forceful style of speaking, Miss O'Neill. Have you, perhaps, a fondness for sensational novels?"

Megan did not bother to answer this satirical question. Drained of feeling by her outburst, she shrugged defiantly and reached for the wine. It was her second glass, had she but known; and a faint smile touched the corners of Miss Mandeville's mouth as she watched.

"However," she went on, "I am well aware of the conditions to which you refer and of the fact that no description overstates the case. There are households in this country where your religion might be a bar to employment; and I suspect your appearance is another handicap. You look very young."

"I am eighteen," Megan said dully.

"So old as that? And you are very pretty, in that fragile, delicate fashion that brings out the bully in certain people. Do you know, when I first saw you, in your green cloak, with your hair streaming in the wind, I thought you were one of the People of the Hills, come to carry me off to fairyland."

"And I thought you were a pixie or a brownie."

She had not meant to say that; something seemed to have loosened the connection between her tongue and her brain. Miss Mandeville was not offended. Swinging her little feet, she laughed heartily.

"I have been called worse things. It seems we both have uncontrolled imaginations, Miss O'Neill. Perhaps we can overcome that weakness together."

The words, so casually spoken, were slow to penetrate Megan's increasing drowsiness. "But," she faltered, "you do not intend I should stay on—after what I told you."

"I couldn't dismiss you if I wanted to," said her companion coolly. "That is my brother's prerogative. But if I could, you have told me nothing that would give me cause to do so. In my opinion, little Caroline is not ready for a governess; she is a sweet child, but not clever, and I do not believe in forcing children into learning prematurely. However, there is no reason why she should not begin to have a few simple, pleasant lessons, and you seem to me a gentle person who would do her good."

The last words blended into an unintelligible murmur, and the walls of the room began to waver like scenes painted on thin paper. Megan was dimly aware of being helped from her chair and into the bed.

"I am only a little tired," she murmured. "Not faint . . ."

"No, no." Miss Mandeville's face appeared above her; grinning broadly, it seemed to hang disembodied in midair. "You are not faint; only a little tipsy."

Her laughter was the last sound Megan heard as sleep enveloped her.

Chapter
Two

THE ART of overindulgence was one skill Megan had not learned from her father, though he had certainly been qualified to teach it. She was unpleasantly surprised to find herself wide awake in the pre-dawn hours, with an aching head and a mouth that felt like sawdust. Water was her first thought. The fire had died to embers, but by groping she found the water bottle on the nearby table and quenched her thirst.

Refreshed, she lay back against the pillows, but was unable to woo sleep. The memory of her behavior made her cheeks flame with embarrassment. She *must* have been tipsy; nothing else could explain such lack of control. With a groan she turned her aching head into the cool linen of the pillow.

But Miss Mandeville had not been angry. She had laughed. What a strange little woman she was, dressed like a well-to-do farmer's daughter and speaking like a lady of quality. For all her dignified airs, she could not be much older than Megan herself.

Remembering that lady's last speech, Megan forgot her embarrassment in gratitude and relief. She would not have to leave. She had found sanctuary; and for this night, at least, she could enjoy the comfort of a quiet room to herself. The sheets smelled like lavender, and the air was fresh and cool. She might be lying in a summer garden under an open night sky, for the dying fire left the walls shrouded in darkness.

Her thoughts wandered in the half-world between sleep and waking. Sanctuary . . . the room and the house had that sort of feeling. Sheer age, perhaps—centuries of peaceful living had woven a spell of safety around the ancient walls. The old castle in Ireland, which she had last seen shortly after her mother's death, had the same atmosphere, though it had been half in ruins for years. The O'Neills were a noble family, but there was not much money. There was an abundance of Irish ghosts, however, if her father's tales could be believed—the White Lady, the headless coachman driving a spectral team, the family banshee, whose howl warned of imminent death. . . . Megan smiled drowsily. This room had no ghosts. It was as friendly and welcoming as a nursery.

She was almost asleep when she was jolted upright by the most appalling sound she had ever heard—a long, undulating howl that wavered up and down the scale in an ecstasy of anguish. It sounded like a damned soul bewailing the loss of Heaven and the torment of Hell.

Megan dragged the bedclothes up to her nose and stared wildly into the darkness. If the howl was that of a banshee —and what else could it be?—her father's description had fallen far short of the mark. Something rustled at the open window, and she squeezed her eyes shut for fear of seeing the fiery red eyes of the Bean Si glaring in at her.

The cry came again—not from the window, but from beyond her closed door. This was reassuring. The O'Neill banshee never entered the castle, it hung from the eaves like a huge gray bat, its long hair streaming. Also, Megan remembered that there was a child in the house, and that

that child was now her responsibility. If the howling had frightened her, what would it do to a baby of three? Barefoot, not stopping to find a wrap, she ran to the door and flung it open.

The wailing cry broke out again. Unmuted by the thick panels of the door, it was even more appalling, but her courage was strengthened by light streaming out from the open door of an adjoining room. There were voices as well —human voices that seemed not so much frightened as impatient and angry. One of them rose in a triumphant shriek; then, at the dark end of the corridor, there appeared the form of a small child clutching something in her arms. She was an angelic infant, with rumpled yellow curls, wearing a long white nightgown. Seeing Megan silhouetted against the light, she called out, "I have her, Auntie. Here she is!"

Footsteps from the other direction heralded the approach of Miss Mandeville, carrying a lamp in one hand. Her tousled hair and long brown robe gave her the look of a sleepy gnome.

The little girl stopped near Megan. "You aren't my Aunt Jane," she said.

"This is Miss O'Neill," said Miss Mandeville. "She is a new friend, who will help you learn."

"How do you do, Miss O'Neill." The child made a grave little curtsy, imperiling her grasp on the object she clutched. It wriggled and snarled.

Megan had begun to suspect that the creature Caroline held had been the source of the unearthly cries, though it seemed impossible that anything so small could emit such monumental woe. Her doubts were put to rest when it opened a mouth fringed with sharp white teeth and repeated the performance.

At close range the effect was so unnerving that Megan stepped back. Miss Mandeville snatched the animal from the child.

"Bad cat!" she exclaimed. "Where were you? I told you

you were not to go out. Now you have roused the entire house. Wretched kitty!''

"Kitty?" Megan repeated incredulously.

The animal squirmed in Miss Mandeville's grasp, stretching out its neck in order to rub a furry head against her chin. Its shape was feline, but its coloring was totally unlike the tabby stripes and calico spots with which Megan was familiar. Its body was a pale fawn color, but the extremities—tail, ears, and feet—were dark seal-brown. A mask of the same shade covered its muzzle, shading up over the eyes, which were of a startling sapphire blue.

"I have never seen a cat like that," she exclaimed. Momentarily forgetting its grief, the cat returned her stare with one of insolent boredom. Its whiskered face was as round as an apple.

"I don't suppose you have," said Miss Mandeville. "There cannot be more than two or three of them in England. It is Siamese. A childhood friend of mine, who is captain of a vessel in the East Indian trade, brought it back to me. He knows my penchant for unusual pets."

"We had a monkey," the child volunteered. "But it died." Her mouth drooped.

"Perhaps he will bring you another," Megan said, hoping sincerely that he would not.

"Do you like monkeys, Miss O'Neill?"

"You can investigate one another's interests and hobbies tomorrow," Miss Mandeville said with a smile. "I am sorry you should have been disturbed, Miss O'Neill. The miscreant is now in custody; you can return to your bed."

"But what ails the poor creature?" Megan asked. "It seems to be in great pain."

"Oh, no," the child said eagerly. "She wants to have babies. That is why she cries. But Aunt Jane won't let her."

At the sight of Megan's face Miss Mandeville let out a peal of unrestrained laughter. "I hope we have not shocked you, Miss O'Neill. We are farming people here, and accept natural functions naturally."

"Oh, no," Megan mumbled.

"All cats cry when they are in season," Miss Mandeville went on cheerfully. "Though I must admit this foreign creature expresses herself more piercingly than any local breed."

"It sounded like a lost soul," Megan said with a shiver.

"Or the family bane, warning of approaching doom? The difficulty is that I don't want to breed her now. She had one litter of kittens last year, and to my great disappointment not one of them had her coloring; they were the usual mixture of black and white and striped. I am curious to see what would result if she were mated with another of the same breed, but my efforts to find a male have been unavailing. I am hoping Willie will fetch me one on his next voyage."

Her eyes bright, her voice brisk, she seemed as wide awake as if it were morning, not the middle of the night; and Megan, who was not vitally interested in the coloration of cats, began to think she would go on in the same vein indefinitely. The child yawned, and Miss Mandeville broke off her lecture and ordered them both to bed.

Chapter
Three

URING THE following weeks everything that happened increased Megan's appreciation of the good fortune that had brought her to Grayhaven. She gave thanks for it every night when she knelt by her bed before retiring, and only prayed that it be allowed to continue. She had not been so happy since her father died; and even before that, her deep affection for him had been shadowed by the uncertainty of their way of life and her fears for his honor. Here she felt sheltered and safe and loved.

The little girl, Caroline, was as endearing as her aunt had claimed. Loved and therefore loving, she expected kindness from everyone she met. There were, to be sure, normal demonstrations of temper and misbehavior. She could not keep a frock clean for more than an hour; if she was not stealing away from lessons to play in the stableyard or the barns, she was in the kitchen begging bread and jam from the infatuated cook, or painting her apron with watercolor to see if it would not look prettier so. But these were small sins, and when the repentant sinner flung sticky arms around Megan's knees and cooed, "I do love you, Miss Megan," that softhearted young woman had a hard time enforcing even the mild discipline Miss Mandeville insisted upon.

With Lizzie she was on the best of terms. The housekeeper had taken a fancy to the pathetic bedraggled creature who had fallen into her arms, and Megan sensed Lizzie would have felt the same way about one of the stray cats or injured birds Lina was constantly bringing to her for treatment.

The physical comforts she enjoyed were pleasant, too. When, on the day after her arrival, she had asked Miss Mandeville where she was to be lodged, the latter had raised a surprised eyebrow. "Is the room not to your taste? It is next to Lina's, so I thought it convenient. But if you lack anything . . ."

In the other families Megan had known, children were relegated to a distant part of the house, along with the persons who cared for them. However, Miss Mandeville did not believe in exiling children from human society, as if they were wild beasts or savages. Besides, as she frankly admitted, she liked the company; it was a big, rambling house, and without Lina she would have been entirely alone in the west wing.

Miss Mandeville had firm convictions about a good many things. She was the center of that peculiar household, and the source of its unusual structure.

Megan's guess about Jane Mandeville's age had been close to the truth. She was only twenty. Her brisk manner and her capability, in a number of areas, made her seem older. She was interested in everything and skilled at almost every task she undertook, but she had not a speck of feminine vanity. Admittedly she was not pretty, or even "handsome"—that kindly euphemism applied to any young lady of elevated social standing—but she had a quality that made her appear more attractive than women with well-formed features and figures. Languid boredom never dulled her eyes or drew her face into lines of weariness. She found life a source of unending amusement, and her enjoyment made the lives of those around her more worth living.

All the same, she was undoubtedly eccentric. The shock Megan had felt the night Miss Mandeville spoke so openly about "breeding" and "mating" was repeated a dozen times in succeeding days. Jane thought nothing of kilting up her skirts and climbing a tree to get a handful of cherries for Lina, and on one occasion Megan watched in horror as she plunged through a group of staring onlookers to snatch a kitten from under the hooves of the big bull. Though her clothing was of fine material, it was almost as plain as the drab gowns a governess was supposed to wear, and her hair, disdaining curls and waves, was pulled into a knot or bundled any which way into a net. Her small, capable hands were too brown and calloused to be pretty; but she had dainty little feet with arches so high water could flow under them—the traditional sign of three hundred years of noble ancestry. They were her only beauty and her only aristocratic feature. Her round, snub-nosed face and wide mouth were as common as brown bread.

Of all the lady's peculiarities none struck Megan so forcibly as the one she learned about the morning after her arrival. Miss Mandeville had joined her and Lina in the breakfast room, but had risen after a hasty bite or two, remarking that it was time she was off to work.

"I had hoped to spend a few hours with you today, but there is trouble with one of the looms at the mill. If I don't see to it, those foolish men will stand around all day scratching their heads and debating the matter."

"The mill?" Megan repeated.

"Mandeville's Best Woollens and Worsteds. I don't suppose you have heard of it; we are a small concern and prefer to stay that way. Till this evening, then, Miss O'Neill—Lina."

Lina's giggle made Megan realize she was gaping in an unbecoming manner, but she was unable to control her amazement. Mandeville's Best Woollens! And she had taken Edmund Mandeville for a gentleman.

The distinction between the gentry, who lived on rents from great estates, and the new middle class, whose wealth came from mines and manufacturing, was perfectly clear in the minds of the parties concerned. The two classes might meet in the line of business, but they did not care to mix socially. The absurd fluttering produced at a middle-class dinner by the presence of even a minor sprig of the nobility and the insupportable triumph of the hostess who had succeeded in gaining such a prize had been caricatured, but not greatly exaggerated, by contemporary writers. Education, good manners, wealth had nothing to do with it; one drop of decadent blue blood made its possessor superior in the eyes of everyone except, perhaps, God—and the aristocratic snob was convinced that He reserved the highest clouds in Paradise for the nobility.

When Megan had first met her prospective employer, in the offices of Miss Jordan's Superior Agency, everything about him had spoken of noble birth—his graceful figure, his fine clothing, his lazy, soft voice. The pallor of recent illness made his waving brown hair appear darker, and the military mustache and long sideburns set off features of aristocratic symmetry, as finely chiseled as his sister's were blunt and commonplace.

Megan dismissed this disloyal thought. Miss Mandeville was a true lady, even if she did look like a housemaid. But what on earth did she have to do with the mill? The only women who went to such places were the unfortunates who operated the machines—women of the poorest class, forced to work because their husbands were unable or unwilling to support their families.

Lina was still staring. Her eyes were as big and blue and curious as those of the Siamese cat.

Ta-chin was the only member of the household Megan did not care for. She was fond of cats generally, and still mourned the loss of Miss Prissy, a beloved white Persian who had been left with a landlady in Paris when her father had been forced to make one of his hasty exits from a city full of gentlemen who were anxious to interview him about his debts. But Ta-chin was not an ordinary cat. She made no secret of her utter indifference to Megan, and her hoarse comments sounded unnervingly like speech in some unknown tongue. The conventional theory that dogs are more inclined than cats to devote their love to a single person is far from accurate; most dogs are genial, undiscriminating idiots, slobberingly grateful for attention from any passerby. Ta-chin was truly a one-person cat. Her infatuation with Jane was almost abject; she would squat for hours at that small lady's feet, staring at her adoringly. She tolerated the servants and Lina, and was, in fact, more patient with hugs and squeezes than one might have expected, but she looked upon lesser persons with a cool curiosity that held a certain hint of criticism. Lina's eyes had the same look now.

Megan frowned at her. "Eat your breakfast," she said sharply.

Lina's lower lip went out in an alarming manner, but she did as she was told. Immediately Megan felt guilty. She could not imagine why she had been so brusque. It would be a mistake to turn the child against her. Her position depended to a great extent on Lina's fondness.

"Porridge is not my favorite breakfast either," she confided, in a conspiratorial whisper. "But we must eat every bite or Lizzie will scold us."

Lina was easily coaxed. They made a game of it, taking alternate bites, and finished the despised porridge in record time.

Megan's curiosity about Jane and the mill was not so easily dispelled. Ordinarily she did not like to encourage servants to gossip, but—she told herself—Lizzie was not an ordinary servant, and the situation was certainly out of the ordinary.

Lizzie was delighted to explain. "Why, miss, she's at the mill all day and every day, since her poor papa died—and even before, when he was too sick to tend to business. I don't know how they would get on without her. You wouldn't believe the things she does, all those papers full of writing and figures—that's the worst, all those numbers—but she reads them pretty as you please and tells the men what they should do."

"And they take orders from her?" Megan asked.

"Well, but you see, she's Master John's child. There was nobody like him—the kindest master in the county. He took her with him to the mill when she was a tiny little thing. She was the pet of the place; the men laughed at her first-off, but it warn't long before they found she could add a column of figures faster than any on 'em, and she knew how all the nasty machines worked. . . ."

Megan was sorry she had asked. The old woman rambled on and on, boasting of Miss Mandeville's accomplishments. She actually seemed proud to see her mistress doing a man's work.

As Megan was to learn, the old nurse had not exaggerated by much. Miss Mandeville was more modest, but her explanation made it clear that she ran Mandeville's Fine Woollens and Worsteds.

"There was no one else to do it," she explained. "Edmund was away, first at school and then at university; when the Crimean affair began, he was wild to go, and Father did not feel he could stand in the way. It is a family business, you see. My grandfather founded it, and the workers like to feel that the family is still involved. I do very little, I assure you, beyond settling disputes and making sure all is working smoothly."

"I did not mean to criticize—"

"I assure you, I did not mean to apologize! There is not a machine in the mill I could not repair if I had to." Her eyes sparkled with amusement as she observed Megan's surprise. "No doubt you think me peculiar, Miss O'Neill, but you must take me as I am. I am too old and set in my ways to change."

28

"I think you are the kindest person I have ever known," Megan said sincerely.

"Then you must have met with only very unkind people. No"—she extended an impulsive hand—"that was a stupid thing to say. I know your life has not been easy. Would you like to come to the mill with me one day and see for yourself what goes on there?"

It was several days before the visit could take place. Megan did not press it; she had read the published reports of the commissions sent out to investigate conditions in mines and factories, and the descriptions of weary child workers falling asleep after twelve hours at the looms had haunted her for days. The mines, to be sure, were even worse, but an outraged nation, learning of small children crawling on all fours through fetid tunnels dragging coal carts, had forced the passage of legislation correcting some of these evils. Still, Megan was not looking forward to seeing the mill children, and when Miss Mandeville finally proposed that she and Lina accompany her next day, she voiced shocked protest.

"I will come, thank you. But the child—"

"It will not be her first visit. Good heavens, Miss O'Neill, what are you expecting to see? I think you are in for a surprise."

Though the mill was due south of the house, on the other side of the hill, there was no through road, so they took the long way around, through the small village of St. Arca Underhill. The big barracklike buildings, with their tall chimneys spouting smoke, had nothing attractive about them, but when the carriage drove into the stone-paved yard, Megan was impressed at the air of cheerful, purposeful industry. The men who turned from their work to touch their caps or their forelocks were all stout and healthy in appearance, and all greeted the diminutive figure of their lady-manager with grins or waves. Jane led the way into the countinghouse through an outer office where several clerks sat perched on their high stools, and she greeted each man by name before proceeding to her own office. Once inside, she whipped off her bonnet and tossed it onto a chair, with a look of great satisfaction. She seemed almost to sniff the air as if it were filled with perfumed odors—which was certainly not the case.

It was a curious little room, quite unlike Megan's vague notions of what such establishments should be. Papers and account books were everywhere, and a table was littered with samples of the fabrics manufactured in the mill—tangled webs of scarlet and Lincoln-green thread, swatches of vivid plaids and stripes, and every solid color from black to pale cream. But there were several incongruous features—green plants on the windowsill, a few comfortable chairs, and a table near them holding a plain silver tea set, like the sort of arrangement that might be found in a lady's sitting room.

Lina went at once to the windowsill, announcing with a comically knowledgeable air, "The flowers are very thirsty, Aunt Jane. Shall I give them water?"

"Yes, please. You know where to find it."

The child picked up a small watering can and hurried out. Miss Mandeville waved a hospitable hand toward the overstuffed chairs. Seating herself behind her desk, she seemed to gain a foot in height.

"I had a chair specially made," she explained. "It was easier to have the chair raised than the desk lowered; and I believe it puts one at a disadvantage to be so much smaller than the workmen and buyers who face one across it."

Megan was much struck by the cleverness of this idea. "And this cozy little corner, like a lady's parlor?"

"That is another of my sly schemes," said Miss Mandeville, trying in vain to look devious. "It disarms some of the gentlemen in a way you would scarcely believe. After a nice chat and a cup of tea, they are unable to complain when I present them with their bill."

A succession of workmen and clerks followed one another

into the room, each with a report or a problem of some kind. Megan listened in growing amazement. She could not imagine how one small head, however clever, could keep track of the multitudinous details brought to its attention.

From time to time Jane tossed her an explanation. "We maintain an infirmary in connection with the mill. We do our best to avoid injury, but some accidents are inevitable. Which reminds me that I meant to ask. . . . Ah, here he is now. Good morning, Sam. You are late today."

"I had to have repairs made on the throstle. I told you yesterday the flyers wasn't right."

The speaker was young and rather short in stature, and so broad of chest and shoulder that his height appeared to be less than it actually was. When he removed his cap a tuft of black hair sprang up at the back of his head. He put up his hand to flatten it, in a gesture as habitual as it was ineffective, glancing rather self-consciously at Megan as he did so. His features, rounded and rather coarse, reminded her of someone, but she could not think who.

"If it happens again, we must consider replacing the throstle," Miss Mandeville said. "There is a new model. . . ."

The ensuing conversation was unintelligible to Megan, so she turned her attention to Lina, who had finished tending the plants and was foraging among a heap of papers on a side table, looking for a blank sheet on which to draw a picture. Miss Mandeville appeared to be paying no attention, but before long she said suddenly, "Sam, have you time to show Miss O'Neill around the mill? (Miss O'Neill —Mr. Sam Freeman, one of our foremen.) And take Lina with you, please, Sam, she is wrecking havoc with my papers. Bring them back—preferably without stains—in an hour."

With a shriek of joy Lina flung herself at Sam. "I want to see the big pots of paint!"

He stooped to pick her up and, with a smile that transformed his rough features amazingly, said, "Do you then, my honey? I make no promise about stains, Miss Jane; this one is like a magnet to attract the dye, even though I hold her safe away from the vats."

"I know," Miss Mandeville agreed, with a sigh. "The last time her frock looked like a cleaning rag, every color of the rainbow. Do your best; a man can do no more."

Shifting the child to his shoulder, where she clung like a little monkey, Sam opened the door and stood back to let Megan pass through. He didn't seem to relish the role of guide, or appreciate her company; after the first quick glance, he had not even looked directly at her.

As they passed through the various stages of the processes that turned the rough bales of wool into finished cloth, Sam's comments were brusque to the point of rudeness. Admittedly, the noise of the machines, particularly in the huge high-ceilinged room that contained the power looms, made it difficult to hear even a shouted explanation. Megan did not ask for elaboration, she only nodded and tried to look intelligent. In fact, she had not the slightest interest in the process and only the dimmest hope of ever understanding it. However, she noticed that almost all the workers were adults. Some of the women at the looms were very young, in their early teens, perhaps, but there were none of the pallid, pathetic children she had dreaded seeing.

Much more to her taste was the infirmary, where the brief tour ended. Megan's admiring exclamation at the sight of the neat little room seemed to please Sam; he smiled with unselfconscious pride.

"It's the finest in the county—indeed, in the country, save, perhaps, for the one at Mr. Owen's mill in Lancashire. He's a fine man, Mr. Owen; he and Miss Jane exchange ideas, and he visited us here a few years back."

"Robert Owen, the Socialist?" Megan asked. One of her employers had mentioned the name in terms of impassioned anger that had made it stick in her mind.

Sam scowled. "If a Socialist is a man who cares for the welfare of his fellow man, then Mr. Owen is a Socialist. And so am I."

Megan decided to abandon the subject. She preferred Sam's pleasant smile to his frown.

She was introduced to the nurse, a bustling matron with an accent so thick Megan could hardly understand a word she said. But her gestures were self-explanatory, and Megan had no difficulty expressing the expected congratulations. There were only four beds, and the other accommodations were of Spartan simplicity; but the wide windows, which now stood open to the summer breeze, were double glazed, and the presence of a vent for a stovepipe suggested that sufferers who occupied the place during the winter months could expect the most modern comforts.

The time had passed more quickly than Megan realized. When they returned to the office, they found Miss Mandeville gloved and bonneted, ready to leave. At the sight of Lina she exclaimed, "Dreadful child! What did you do, sit down in a puddle of dye?"

Such appeared to be the case. The back of Lina's frilly skirt was purple from the waist down. Involuntarily Megan glanced at Sam and saw on his face the same look of amused guilt she felt on her own. Miss Mandeville cut his apologies short.

"Never mind, she will have to ride home in her shift, like Lady Godiva. That is a local tale, you know, Miss O'Neill; we are proud of the lady's charitable impulse and resent the liberties sensational writers have taken with her costume. Have you ever ridden horseback naked? I did not suppose you had. I assure you that even a saint would find it uncomfortable."

As she spoke, her nimble fingers divested Lina of the paint-stained frock and lifted her into the carriage. Lina broke into a fit of giggles and insisted on standing up so that everyone could see her unconventional costume. Miss

Mandeville did not protest, but directed Megan to keep a firm hold on the rear of the small pantelets.

Turning for a last look, Megan saw that Sam was standing in the yard watching them. Finally that elusive sense of familiarity crystallized.

"He looks like you," she exclaimed, and then clapped her hand to her mouth, wishing she had not spoken.

"Not surprising," said Miss Mandeville calmly. "My grandmother was the sister of his grandfather. You'll see the Freeman features all over the neighborhood. They have lived in the parish for centuries. Sadly, however, the line seems to be dying out. Sam's kin have died or emigrated; he is the last to bear the name."

"He seems quite a superior person," Megan said.

Miss Mandeville's eyebrows rose. "Superior to what? His father was Papa's right-hand man and helper, though he could neither read nor write. Sam has taken steps to improve himself in the skills worldly people consider important; he is literate, he reads extensively, and he is perfectly well acquainted with the use of a knife and fork. More important in my opinion is the fact that he is his father's son, with all Mr. Freeman's honesty and intelligence."

"Oh, to be sure," Megan murmured.

Miss Mandeville did not pursue the subject. The remainder of the ride home was spent in trying to keep Lina from falling out of the carriage, which she seemed bent on doing.

The days settled into a pleasant routine. Megan's teaching duties were not onerous. Lina was intelligent enough, but she could not sit still for five minutes without wriggling or tapping her feet. As the balmy weather continued, teacher and pupil spent a great deal of time out of doors, exploring the grounds. The child was more receptive to instruction when she was allowed to move about, and Megan took advantage of their walks to introduce French vocabulary, which Lina picked up with surprising facility.

In the evening, after Lina had been handed over to the nursemaid, Megan sat with Miss Mandeville in the latter's pleasant little parlor, next to her bedroom. There was nothing extraordinary in this—a governess was expected to perform the duties of a companion when her employers required it—but gradually the two girls, so close in age, drifted into something akin to friendship. After a time Miss Mandeville suggested they use each other's first names.

"We must be formal in company, I suppose," she said with a shrug. "But I am a firm believer in following my own inclinations instead of the stupid dictates of propriety, and I am always thinking of you as 'Megan' now."

The evenings were quiet ones—Jane never went out and seemed to have few callers—but Megan enjoyed them. Like Lina, Jane could not sit with idle hands, and when she was not working on some garment for the child, who wore them out at an astonishing rate, she was doing Berlin wool work or sketching. One skill she lacked was music; her admiration for Megan's playing and singing was unbounded, and almost every evening ended with a little recital.

Rapidly as the friendship developed, it was almost a month after Megan's arrival before Jane confided her worry about Edmund.

"I have written to him every day, but have received only two brief notes in reply," she said, frowning at the unoffending fire screen she was embroidering. "I expected him long before this; I pray he is not worse." •

The same fear had occurred to Megan, but she said reassuringly, "Surely his friends would communicate with you if they had any concern for his health."

"No doubt you wonder why I don't go to London and see for myself," Jane said. She had a disconcerting habit of making accurate guesses of that sort, as if she could read other people's minds. "I don't because Edmund asked me not to leave Grayhaven. He says his mind is more at ease if he knows I am looking after things here."

"Perhaps he doesn't want you fussing over him," Megan said with a smile. "Men hate that."

"Not Edmund. He adores being coddled. Or at least he did

when he was young." Jane's hands, holding the needle with its trail of scarlet wool, dropped into her lap. Her eyes took on a far-off look. "Sometimes, when he had no other boys to play with, he would let me play Soldiers and Radicals with him. You may guess, Megan, who was the Radical! When the gallant soldier was wounded, the radical became the nurse instead. I tore up my petticoats to make bandages and stole quantities of sweets and preserves to tempt his appetite. . . . How I was scolded! But I was used to that; my petticoat was often in tatters, for I was a sad tomboy."

The bright vision of childhood faded. Jane's smile was tinged with sadness. "I missed him desperately when he went off to school, and I have seen so little of him since. . . . This last year was the worst; every newspaper I read was filled with horrors. But you know of the awful suffering in the trenches before Sevastopol. I visualized Edmund freezing on those bleak heights in winter, wounded and abandoned—and the hospitals were worse than the trenches. It is still going on; and I feel guilty, Megan, when I thank God for Edmund's miraculous survival, when so many are still suffering and dying."

Her voice broke. Touched by this rare demonstration of sensibility, Megan put her hand over the fingers that had given up all pretense of working.

"It will soon be over, everyone says so. And conditions have improved; you know of Miss Nightingale and the wonderful things she has done with the hospitals."

"Yes, God bless her. She makes me proud to be a woman. Well, but this is a depressing conversation. Shall we have some music? Play something very loud and very cheerful, please."

When she knelt beside her comfortable bed that night, Megan prayed for the suffering men in the Crimea. Her plea that she be allowed to remain in the house that was daily becoming more dear to her was tacked on to the end of the petition instead of constituting its main thesis.

ii

HER UNSELFISH piety was rewarded, as is so often the case, by a day of extreme personal discomfort. She awoke to the sound of rain and the sight of dreary gray skies. A tightness at the back of her throat warned her of the beginning of a cold, and as the day wore on, all the other horrid symptoms of that affliction made their appearance. Deprived of outdoor exercise by the weather, Lina was maddeningly naughty. When she finished the day's misadventures by burning her hand on the fender, after being warned a dozen times to stay away from the fire, Megan snapped at her instead of expressing sympathy. Lina howled, Megan blew her nose, and the cat spat at both of them before leaving the room in search of more civilized companionship.

Having looked forward all day to the evening meeting with Jane, Megan was discouraged to find her friend in equally gloomy spirits. Soon after they settled down with their sewing, the maid entered to announce a visitor, the mention of whose name sent Jane into a rage.

"Belts? Mr. Belts? How dare he call at such an hour, without an invitation? I am not at home, Bessy."

"He says it is important, miss."

"I will be at the mill tomorrow if he wishes to see me. Why are you standing there, Bessy? Didn't you hear me clearly?"

The maid scuttled out, and Jane began to embroider furiously, jabbing her needle in and out of the canvas with a vigor that suggested she would have preferred a living target. Apparently Mr. Belts accepted his dismissal, for no further message was delivered. After a time Jane's temper cooled. She stopped attacking the canvas and apologized.

"You must think me very rude."

"Why, no. It is certainly a strange hour to call."

"But typical of George Belts. He continues to cherish the unfounded delusion that I am delighted to see him whenever he chooses to honor me with his presence."

"Oh?" There was inquiry in Megan's voice. She did not venture to express the question she wanted to ask, but it was not hard to fathom; and after a moment Jane began to laugh, falling into such a fit of merriment that her feet flew up in the air and the chair came perilously close to tipping over.

"You are so well bred, Megan," she chuckled, wiping her eyes. "Why don't you ask straight out? You are dying to know whether George Belts is a suitor, and whether I am playing coy in order to increase his ardor."

"Oh, Jane, I assure you—"

"Well, of course you are. It is the common habit of fashionable young ladies to act that way. But you ought to know me well enough by now to understand that I am not a fashionable young lady. And if you had seen Belts, you would wonder why I don't pour boiling water on his head from the window instead of just turning him away from the door."

"Is he very unattractive?" Megan asked interestedly.

"Oh, yes, very. He is rather too thin than too fat; his hair is not *much* gray for a man of sixty; he has very hairy hands with long grasping fingers. But the crowning unattractiveness is that he doesn't care a fig for me. He wants the mill."

"You do yourself an injustice, Jane," Megan protested. "Any man of taste would find you—"

"He is not a man of taste. He owns several clothing factories in Yorkshire, and he is looking for a source of cheap cloth."

"Dear me." Megan was disconcerted by this cynical appraisal.

"He never actually had the effrontery to propose," Jane continued. "But he was working up to it; I could see it coming on. So, rather than waste his time and mine, I told him I despised him and that I would rather burn the mill to the ground than see him have any share in it."

The soft, complacent voice in which she expressed these sentiments brought a reluctant smile to Megan's face.

"I wonder he would show his face here again, after that."

"Oh, he is impossible to insult. I wonder why he should reappear just now, though. Curse George Belts; I am tired of thinking and talking about the miserable creature. And you, poor girl, look terrible; your poor little nose is as red as a rose. I am sure you don't feel like singing tonight. Perhaps you had better go straight to bed, and I will have Lizzie rub you with goose grease."

Megan was not eager to enjoy this treat. She offered to play, but found it difficult on account of having to stop every few bars to blow her nose. After half an hour she said good night, hoping that Jane had forgotten the goose grease, but feeling fairly sure she had not. And indeed Lizzie was close on her heels, her round red face radiating delight at the prospect of a patient to be tended. After a hot drink and a vigorous rub with the aforesaid medicament—which smelled almost as bad as Megan had feared it would—she was put into a flannel nightgown that had been toasting in front of the fire till it was red-hot. Lizzie then piled four blankets on top of her, forbade her to remove a single one of them, and left.

Megan did not so much fall asleep as swoon with heat prostration. It might have been this discomfort or the inconvenience of the cold in the head that caused her to dream that night, for the first time since she had come to Grayhaven.

It was the old familiar dream she had had many times before, from childhood on. The theme was always the same, though the locale and characters differed. She was hurrying to catch a ship or a train or a coach that left at a precise time. The destination was seldom clear, but it was a place she wanted desperately to reach, and she knew she would never get there unless she caught that particular vehicle. One after another, a dozen trifling errands detained her. The obstacles were as varied as her dreaming mind could invent, but all had the same effect—delay—and for some reason she was helpless to pass by or over them, even though she was tormented by painful anxiety about the time and a growing conviction that she would be too late.

The dream always ended before she found out whether or not she had succeeded in reaching her conveyance. When her anxiety rose to fever pitch, she woke up. So it happened on this occasion; she lay lapped in steaming heat and could not decide whether the moisture on her cheek was perspiration or tears.

Whatever its cause, the dream was not a portent of evil. The next day they heard good news. Edmund was coming home.

Chapter
Four

H E CAME riding down the hill on a summer afternoon, his dark hair windblown and dappled with sunlight. It was just as Megan's most romantic musings had pictured—the spirited horse pawing the drive, the handsome rider smiling down at the members of the household, who had rushed out to greet him. Her heart popped out of her breast and fell with a thud onto the gravel.

He had been a long time coming. The letter announcing his departure from London had been followed, not by Edmund himself, but by a succession of bundles and boxes and parcels. The servants speculated endlessly as to their contents, and Lina kept creeping into the room where they were placed to pick at the knots and pry at the nails. She was sure some of the parcels contained presents for her. Jane admitted this might be so, but insisted on waiting till "Uncle Edmund" came home.

The house and gardens were as fine as Lizzie could make them. She had driven the servants till even that good-natured crew began to grumble, and one little house-maid had hysterics when criticized for leaving dust on the springs of Edmund's bed. Not that his room had been ne-glected; Lizzie had "turned it out" once a week, dripping tears on the furniture and floor when the war news was particularly bad. But when she heard Edmund was on his way home, it required four housemaids working for four days to clean it properly.

Even Jane lost her cool composure and rushed from the mill to the kitchen to the garden. The books must be in perfect order to show Edmund; the damask rose he had once admired must be coaxed to bloom; she would make his favorite food with her own hands—there was one rich plum cake she alone could concoct. Lina flew around the house like a miniature cyclone, and Megan was too excited to make more than a pretense at lessons.

Edmund's delay gave them time to accomplish all these things, even the Herculean amount of cleaning Lizzie con-sidered necessary. On the day of his arrival, half the house-hold was looking out the windows, on one pretense or an-other; and when the cry, "There he is!" went up, they dropped whatever they were doing and ran to the door.

Just as it was in the old days, Megan thought, as she watched Edmund dismount—the adoring tenantry crowd-ing around to greet the young lord. He had a kind word for everyone and a hearty hug for Lizzie. Then he turned to Jane.

She had hung back a little. Lina clung to her skirts and stared openmouthed at the tall figure advancing toward her. For a moment brother and sister gazed at one another in silence. The top of Jane's smooth brown head did not even reach Edmund's shoulder; her face was turned up, as if tilted by the weight of the heavy bun at the back of her neck. Their faces were grave, and Megan's sympathetic imagina-tion told her why; they were thinking of the man who should have been the first to greet the wanderer. Edmund's father had died soon after he left for the Crimea.

Then Jane put out her arms and Edmund lifted her off her feet in the exuberance of his greeting.

"You have shrunk," he exclaimed. "I told you it would happen, if you persisted in walking in the rain. . . . Jane, Jane, how good it is to be home!"

"I am half an inch taller than I was when you went away," Jane protested. "It is barely possible that you are the one who has grown. But here is someone who has grown even more—comparatively speaking!"

She lifted Lina in her arms. The child had been dressed in her best white muslin, frilled and ruffled and embroidered with flowers and butterflies by Aunt Jane's clever fingers. Golden ringlets clustered around her flushed face, and her eyes were as blue as cornflowers. The finger on which she was nervously sucking did not improve the total picture, but all in all she was a child of whom any adoptive father could be proud.

Edmund held out his arms. His eyes were filled with tears.

Lina shrank away. "Why is he crying?" she asked. "Why is the man crying?"

"Because he is happy," Jane said, and laughed at the foolishness of it.

Disconcerted by Lina's cool reception, Edmund resorted to bribery. "I am your guardian, Caroline, and I have come home to stay. There are some pretty presents for you in the parcels I sent home. Come with me and we will open them."

An angelic smile spread over Lina's face. She toppled forward into his waiting arms.

"You see, I have learned the way to a woman's heart," said Edmund to his sister.

"For shame! You were not so cynical once. But stay—you have not greeted Miss O'Neill. You owe her special courtesy now, to compensate for your earlier neglect."

Then, for the first time, his eyes met Megan's.

She had taken great pains with her appearance, mindful of the emotional subtleties of the occasion. Her gown must not be too elaborate, but it should not strike a depressing note either. She had chosen an old frock with full sleeves and a modest lace collar. The pale blue deepened the blue of her eyes and set off her fair complexion. Her golden hair had been brushed till it shone, and twisted into a loose coronet that allowed countless little curls and tendrils to brush her forehead. She thought she looked very well, and the admiration on Edmund's face confirmed this impression.

"Miss O'Neill will forgive us, I know; her face beams with sympathetic pleasure in this reunion. As for my earlier crime, I will accept whatever penance she decrees. Perhaps one of those fascinating parcels contains an offering that will help win a pardon for me."

Megan was saved the necessity of a reply by Lina, who was bouncing up and down and demanding her presents. With the child in his arms and his sister pressed close to his side, Edmund entered his home, leaving Megan to follow.

She felt as if the sun had gone behind a cloud. Edmund's manners were charming, but his casual assumption that a present would excuse his forgetfulness reduced her to the same level as his three-year-old ward. Wistfully Megan's eyes followed the little group ahead of her, so close, so lovingly entwined. She felt like a beggar-woman shivering in the cold as she gazed into the window of a warmly lit house, filled with comforts she would never have.

ii

MEGAN'S MOURNFUL mood did not last long. The others were careful to include her in the celebrations that followed, and Edmund's gift showed such exquisite taste, such consciousness of what would suit her that she could not help but be flattered. The dainty filigree necklace and matching earrings, set with brilliant blue stones, were not the sort of gift a young lady is supposed to accept from a gentleman, but Megan brushed this critical thought aside. Jane seemed to see nothing wrong in it, and if Jane's finicky conscience was at ease, who was she to object?

Edmund had bought lavishly. The parcels did not stop coming; every day brought a new consignment, from an expensive French doll for Lina to fashionable ornaments for the drawing room. Once or twice Jane's forehead wrinkled when some costly trinket emerged from its packing case, but she said nothing.

The daily schedule had changed drastically, as was to be expected. Dinner was now served at a fashionably late hour, and after the first evening, when Lina had been allowed to help celebrate her guardian's homecoming, Megan had not dined with her employers. Brother and sister had much to talk about; sometimes, passing along the hall after an exhausting session with Lina, Megan would hear laughing voices from the drawing room near the foot of the stairs. Once she lingered, enraptured at the sound of a sweet tenor voice singing one of the fashionable sentimental ballads. The expert trills and chords accompanying the singer informed her that Edmund was accompanying himself. Jane's musical talents were extremely limited.

One evening, a week after Edmund's arrival, Megan and Lina were invited to join the others after dinner. Edmund was obviously pleased by the child's pretty looks and affectionate manner; he was particularly amused by the little French phrases she chirped out with the imitative facility of a parrot. When they entered the drawing room, she broke away from Megan and ran to Edmund, crying, *"Bonsoir, cher oncle. Comment-allez-vous?"*

"Très bon, ma petite. But," Edmund added with a laugh, lifting her onto his knee, "I don't think such awful respect is really necessary; may she not *tutoyer* her uncle by courtesy, Miss O'Neill?"

"Oh, I know about that," Lina said. "I say *'tu'* to Ta-chin, and sometimes to Aunt Jane, if she is in a very good mood."

After a solemn discussion of this important matter Lina retired to the window seat and the companionship of her new doll, whose elaborate French wardrobe was already showing signs of wear, having been changed so often and so impatiently. Megan's head was bent over her embroidery. She dared not look at Edmund too long, for fear her face would betray feelings she had no right to have.

After a brief silence, broken only by Lina's admonitions to her doll, Edmund said pensively, "This dear old shabby room. What memories it holds!"

"Don't let Lizzie hear you call it shabby," Jane said. "She drove the servants to the brink of revolution cleaning for you."

"You have both done a splendid job," Edmund said warmly. "I am not unaware of the labor and sacrifice you have carried too long on your small shoulders, Jane. I am here to relieve you of that burden, and my first task shall be to give this dear old house the thorough refurbishing it deserves."

"It suits me just as it is," Jane said quietly.

"You are a dear, old-fashioned little thing, Jane. If you had your way, nothing would ever change. I know you have little taste for fashion and elegance; I am counting on Miss O'Neill's advice in such matters, for she has seen many fine homes."

Megan pricked her finger. Exultation filled her heart at the seduction of the picture that rose before her inward eye: she and Edmund consulting like husband and wife over homely details of furniture and draperies!

"I cannot claim to be an expert," she said modestly. "But of course, Mr. Mandeville, if I can help in any way. . . ."

"I am sure you can. I was impressed, in our first conversation, by your knowledge of antiquities. A venerable old manor house like this one should interest you, and your recollections of your family seat in Ireland may assist in the restorations I plan."

"I was only a child when I was last in Ireland," Megan said. But she said it very softly.

"You terrify me, Edmund, with your talk of restorations," Jane exclaimed. "Will you tear the house down around my ears?"

"My dear girl, I shan't begin anything major for quite some time; it is necessary to plan such things carefully. But the house must be spruced up; I cannot invite guests while it is in its present condition. The new drawing-room furniture I ordered should arrive this week. In the meantime, I will decide what is needed for the guest bedrooms."

Jane started to speak, then glanced at Megan and pressed her lips tightly together. The anguished glance with which she swept the room was that of a mother bewailing a change in her favorite child.

Megan sympathized, but she quite agreed with Edmund's appraisal. The damask draperies had once been vivid crimson; they were now faded to a soft rose, pleasing to the eye but otherwise unsuitable; and she could well believe that every piece of furniture in the room had been bought with the house at the time of its sale to Edmund's grandfather. The slender lines and simple wooden frames of sofas and chairs appeared austere and cold compared with the luxuriant carving of modern furniture.

She did not voice this opinion, however; in fact, her position was somewhat awkward, for it was clear that brother and sister were in total opposition on the question of refurnishing. Megan's presence restrained Jane from expressing her true feelings. And Megan wondered, suddenly, whether Edmund had made use of her and the child to avoid what might otherwise have developed into a serious difference of opinion. It was not a flattering thought.

"We will see what can be done tomorrow, then," said Edmund. "What do you say to some music, Miss O'Neill?"

Their voices blended in the most ravishing manner. Megan was in seventh heaven. Edmund's attention was fixed on her, his eyes constantly studied her lips in order to anticipate the words of the duet; now and then, when he leaned forward to turn the pages of her music, his arm brushed her shoulder. Even Jane's face relaxed into a smile as she listened.

iii

WHATEVER THE nature of Edmund's wound (a matter which Megan had never inquired into, for reasons of delicacy), the long period of convalescence had restored him to perfect health. He threw himself into his plans for the house with zestful energy.

Plump sofas and armchairs, their bulging red velvet seats framed in writhing rosewood, replaced the old furniture, which was borne ignominiously away to the attic. The centuries-old boxwood hedges were trimmed into shapes nature never intended them to have, despite the head gardener's anguished insistence that it was the wrong time of year for that activity. Edmund had taken a fancy to have a formal garden, in the Italian style, and a profusion of simpering nymphs and inadequately draped goddesses took up residence on marble pedestals.

The furniture of the bedchambers was next to go. Jane barricaded her doorway with her own small person and threatened violence if a single object in her quarters was touched. Edmund gave in, laughing.

His room was in the same wing, but on a different corridor, on which the principal guest bedrooms were also located. On one of these latter he bestowed his most anxious attention, and one day Megan was called upon to offer her advice.

She took a fancy to the room, despite its quaint, outmoded decor. It was a corner room, with an oriel window, whose ceiling, like that of the chamber itself, was covered with delicately molded plaster reliefs of twining vines and flowers. Had she been left to her own devices, she would have chosen the softest and most delicate fabrics, in such shades as apricot and azure, but Edmund seemed bent on grandeur instead of charm. The bedroom suite he had selected was one of the most elegant Megan had ever seen—an adaptation of the fashionable Renaissance style, it was carved and gilded over every inch of its surface, and the washstand top was of dark-green Italian marble, veined in gold. She was able to make several useful suggestions, however—an abundance of lamps, for example, and rose-tinted shades for the lights on the dressing table.

Jane made no secret of her disapproval of these innovations, but her objections were usually voiced in a good-humored grumble, and Edmund could always cajole her out of her moods. On one occasion Megan overheard a snatch of conversation that explained one part of Jane's reservations. She caught only a few words; one of them was "expense." Edmund's reply was more distinct. "My dear girl, stop fussing. I have several schemes in mind to make us rich. No, I won't tell you about them now; you will learn in due course."

Resisting the temptation to linger, Megan walked on and did not hear Jane's reply.

At last Edmund conceded that the house was ready to receive visitors. "I mean to do a great deal more," he declared. "But renovations will mean a matter of months and years rather than weeks, and I cannot wait so long before returning the hospitality I received in London, or in making the connections I wish to strengthen in future. What do you say, Jane, to a party of eight—five gentlemen and three ladies—early next week?"

They were in the garden, admiring the statues, which had been put in place that same afternoon. Jane was not averse to the idea of guests; she had often expressed her appreciation of the care Edmund had received from his London friends, and said she hoped to meet them soon. But when she asked who was to be in the party, Edmund said that would be a surprise. He smiled, as if teasing her; but when she persisted, he said in a serious voice, "Is it not enough, Jane, that they are people I choose to ask? I thought you would be pleased to serve as my hostess."

He looked genuinely hurt. Jane promptly apologized, and they went back to the house arm in arm.

iv

"Fool." MEGAN addressed her reflection in the mirror. "Stupid, blind, unthinking fool!"

In the intensity of her emotion her hairbrush slipped, administering a sharp rap on her temple. Insignificant as it was, the blow was the last thing needed to release the tears she had been trying to hold back. Dropping the brush, she covered her eyes with her hands and abandoned herself to a passion of weeping.

Why had she failed to realize that the very activities that had given her such happiness over the past weeks must inevitably result in the end of all happiness? Increasingly bewitched by Edmund, she had refused to contemplate the future as she reveled in the present.

The expectation of guests in the house had reduced her to her true position, a lowly, subservient role that only the kindness of Jane and Edmund had allowed her to forget. There would be no more intimate consultations on redecorating or discussions of how such matters were managed at "your family seat in Ireland"; no more quiet family evenings in the drawing room, laughing over Lina's French, singing with him, listening to him read aloud, looking at him—being with him. Megan wiped her eyes with her fingers and pushed her chair away from the mirror. Why bother? No one cared how she looked. No one who mattered would see her.

She kept Lina outside most of the morning, hoping fresh air and exercise would tire her—and hoping, also, that she might catch a glimpse of the guests when they arrived. Five of the group did come just before luncheon—three gentlemen, two of them accompanied by their wives. All were young, and the ladies were splendidly dressed. Concealed behind the rhododendron, Lina and Megan watched them get out of the carriage that had been sent to meet the morning train from London. Megan stared as greedily as the little girl. She could not help contrasting this arrival with her own, and she wondered how it would feel to drive up in a handsome carriage, wearing rose taffeta and a bonnet trimmed with pink silk roses.

The most important of the guests were not among this group. The Astleys were Edmund's particular friends; it was at their London home that he had recuperated from his injuries. Lord Henry had also been wounded, though not so severely. They had met on the ship that brought them home and had struck up a friendship that had strengthened during the weeks in London. The Astleys' country estate was in the neighboring county, but not far distant. Edmund had come from there on the final stage of his homeward journey.

Lina was not inclined to take a nap after luncheon. Excitement had rendered her quite unmanageable; she wanted to go downstairs and be with Uncle Edmund, see the ladies and their pretty clothes, show the gentlemen how well she spoke French. The fact that Megan sympathized wholeheartedly with Lina's frustration did not make it any easier to deal with. Finally she gave in.

"You cannot go downstairs; but if you will be very quiet and not make a sound, we will sit at my window and watch for the other guests. We will have a fine view, all the way down the drive and to the top of the hill."

Lina consented to accept this compromise, which was more than she had expected, and the two settled on the window seat, Megan with her sewing and Lina with her doll. The hours wore on without the event they awaited, and finally Lina fell asleep, her flushed cheek resting on the doll's stuffed body. Megan was tempted to follow suit; she was half dozing, her head against the window frame, when she heard the sound of horses' hooves.

Rubbing sleepy eyes, she leaned forward. She was surprised to see, not the carriage she had expected, but two riders on horseback. At first they were only distant shapes, without definition. Then the horses broke into a gallop. They came flying down the drive side by side and stopped, gravel spurting up under their hooves, with the precision of a trained circus act.

Edmund had said that Lord Henry was approximately his age. This man looked older, his face prematurely lined and sallow. His features were not unhandsome; the smile he exchanged with his companion showed even white teeth and lifted the lines around his mouth into a semblance of good humor.

After one quick look at Lord Henry, Megan's full attention focused on the lady; and as she stared, a hard, aching lump formed inside her and swelled until it filled her entire body.

Her hair glowed like polished mahogany in the mellow sunlight of late afternoon. Her tall, shapely form looked magnificent in riding dress—which, Megan thought spitefully, was probably why she had chosen to ride instead of sitting sedately in the carriage which now appeared, carrying the luggage. Her gown was a rich golden brown, with a hat of the same shade, turned up dashingly on one side and pinned with emerald plumes. Her smile had the same reckless curve and showed the same white flashing teeth as the smile of the gentleman at her side. The family resemblance was unmistakable.

"I should have known," Megan thought. "But I didn't want to know."

Lord Henry and Lady Georgina Astley—not husband and wife, but brother and sister. Edmund had always spoken of them by their first names—prefaced, naturally, by their titles—and that in itself should have proclaimed the truth. Children of peers of the higher ranks held the courtesy titles of Lord and Lady. But Lord Henry's wife would be Lady Henry, not Lady Georgina. Lady Georgina would retain her title even if she married a commoner. Mr. Edmund and Lady Georgina Mandeville. . . .

This was the woman Edmund wanted to marry. Megan knew it the moment she laid eyes on her, with the unreasoning certainty of jealousy.

Her dashing arrival apparently unobserved, the lady's green eyes narrowed. Before the frown could materialize, the front door opened and Edmund came running out.

"There you are at last! We have been expecting you the entire day."

Lord Henry raised his whip in a careless greeting. Lady Georgina, upon whom Edmund's eyes were fixed, responded, "It was too fine a day to sit stupidly in a jouncing carriage. And then, after all, to have our splendid performance ignored! For shame, Edmund; you ought to have been at the door watching for us."

Her voice was her least attractive feature, at once strident and slurred. She drawled the words—Megan thought—in an affected manner. But Edmund appeared to find words and voice delightful.

"I did see you, from the drawing-room window. It was wonderful! You have been practicing."

"Of course." Lady Georgina slid down into the arms Edmund had raised to assist her. "I am dying of thirst," she added. "What sort of host are you, Edmund, to keep me standing here?"

She was almost as tall as Edmund. His hands resting lightly on her waist to steady her, Edmund gave her a look of such glowing possessive pride that Megan involuntarily closed her eyes.

She heard the three enter the house, followed by the bustle of servants dealing with the horses and the luggage. Edmund's face burned against the darkness like a candle flame looked at too long—like the image of the Virgin at St. Pierre des Roches, where her father had once "taken a holiday" to escape his creditors. A small, rather ugly village in Brittany, St. Pierre was the goal of hundreds of pilgrims yearly because of its miracle-working statue. Its paint reverently renewed, glittering with gems presented by grateful petitioners, the image shone in the glow of the candles around its feet as if illumined from within. How often had she knelt on the hard wooden floor, half mesmerized by the dusky dimness and the droning litany, and stared unwinkingly at the golden crown and blue cloak, the plump, fatuously smiling face and jewel-studded gown. She had found that if she stared long enough before closing her aching eyes, she could recall a miniature image of the statue. And if, before the bright shape faded, she could say three Hail Marys and an Our Father, the Holy Mother would grant her prayer.

It was one of those childish fancies that had never been rudely shattered because it had never been mentioned to anyone, based on some now-forgotten coincidental success —a pair of new slippers with silver bows, or even cherry tart for supper. Megan had not thought of the Virgin of St. Pierre des Roches for years; and if she had remembered her innocent fantasy, she would have laughed at it. She did not remember. She did not know why her lips began the graceful words of praise and stopped moving before the first phrase was finished. She only knew she had never wanted anything so much as she wanted Edmund Mandeville.

As she sat in self-imposed darkness, a strange feeling began to creep along her veins, as if some alien substance were replacing the normal flow of blood. It spread slowly through her body, moving from her extremities inward toward her heart, warming, strengthening, stiffening every fiber.

"No," she said aloud—though there was no one else in the room except the sleeping child. "No. I won't give him up. She shan't have him. Not without a fight."

"Miss Megan?"

Megan opened her eyes. Lina was awake. Curled up

among the cushions, the child was watching her with wide, frightened eyes.

"I'm afraid you missed the guests," Megan said. "Did you have a good sleep?"

"You were talking to someone," the child whispered. "Who were you talking to, Miss Megan?"

"Why, no one," Megan said with a smile. "Don't you see? You and I are the only ones here."

Chapter Five

HE MESSAGE came while Megan and Lina were sharing their simple evening meal. They were to go downstairs after dinner, to join the ladies in the drawing room. Megan had been half expecting it. Edmund was a fond guardian; he would want to show his pretty ward to the guests—especially one of them.

Megan left Lina to the ministrations of the nursemaid and went to make her own toilette. She chose a gown she owed to Jane's thoughtfulness. There had been a run of a new fabric at the mill, a blend of wool and silk that was the result of several years' experimentation. Jane had had several dresses made of it; she wanted to tests its durability and usefulness. Light as the finest cashmere, with a soft sheen, it draped beautifully over the crinolines and layers of petticoats then in style. The color Jane had chosen for Megan was the soft blue that became her best. The design was simple, in no way comparable to the evening frocks the ladies would be wearing, but at least it was new. Megan's wardrobe held nothing that could compete with Lady Georgina's elaborate gowns; she could only hope not to appear shabby.

In fact, there was no way in which she could compete with her rival. She was like a savage going into battle against cavalry and modern weapons—like one of the remote ancestors of whom her father had told her, ragged, bare-legged men in saffron tunics, fighting armored English knights. No matter. Like them, she would go down fighting.

Excitement gave her cheeks a becoming rosy flush. She clasped the necklace Edmund had given her around her neck and with a steady hand put the earrings in place.

She returned to Lina's room to find the place in chaos. Every frock the child owned was strewn on the bed or the floor, and Lina was sitting in the middle of the hearth rug howling with rage, while Rose, the nurserymaid, stared helplessly at her.

"She says she's got nothing to wear," Rose reported. And then, because she was a good-natured girl, and genuinely fond of her little charge, she began to laugh. "Look at them frocks, miss. A regular snowstorm of 'em."

"Never mind, I'll take care of it," Megan said. "Lina, you will get your face all red and swollen crying like that; and then what will the company think of you?"

Lina stopped in mid-shriek. Megan picked up one of the least rumpled dresses and shook it out. "Put away the rest," she directed Rose.

She managed to keep Lina distracted until the summons came. Then she took the child's hand and they started downstairs.

From behind the closed doors of the dining room she heard the murmur of conversation, broken now and then by loud masculine laughter. One voice boomed out over all the rest, and Megan caught a few words that sent the blood flooding into her face. Gentlemen did tell stories of that sort over their port, but she had never expected to hear such language at Grayhaven.

Hurrying past the door, she crossed the hall to the drawing room. Here the conversation was dominated by Lady Georgina's drawling voice. She broke off in the middle of a story about a misadventure on the hunting field—not hers —and fixed the newcomers with a curious stare.

"So this is the child. Quite a striking resemblance to her —er—guardian."

The malicious suggestion came as no surprise to Megan; she had already begun to suspect that Edmund might be Lina's father. It was very wrong of him, of course. But gentlemen had those inclinations, especially when they were young and high-spirited. The girl had probably led him on. And how good, how noble of him, to give the poor nameless little creature a home and an affectionate family.

Such things happened—but to refer to them was tasteless in the extreme. Megan frowned at Lady Georgina, who was happily oblivious of her disapproval. Jane said coldly, "Her papa was a distant cousin, your ladyship."

Her tone was so harsh, so unlike her normal speaking voice, that Megan looked at her in surprise. Jane wore her usual dove-gray; this gown, made of the new fabric, set off her neat little figure but made her look like a prim maiden aunt. Her face was anything but demure. Her cheeks were red as poppies, her mouth a tight slit. She was obviously furious about something, and Megan doubted that even Lady Georgina's rude remark could inspire such a passion of anger.

Jane's eyes softened as they met Megan's. In a milder voice she performed the introductions. Mrs. Morton and Lady Denbigh nodded with the distant affability Megan's position deserved, but Lady Georgina did not so much as look at her. She continued to stare at Lina, and the child retreated behind Megan's skirts, her finger in her mouth.

Megan took a chair near Jane, lifting the little girl onto her lap. Neither of the other ladies would have spoken so openly nor stared so rudely, but the glances they exchanged, and their little smiles, were just as meaningful. Protectively

Megan held the child close. They were still in that position when the gentlemen came in; Edmund smiled at them, as if he appreciated the pretty picture they made.

"See, here is Uncle Edmund," Megan murmured. "Show him how you have missed him all day."

Edmund had become the child's new idol; with the fickleness of youth she had demoted her former favorites. Tumbling off Megan's lap in a whirl of ruffles, she ran to Edmund, who picked her up and tossed her into the air.

One of the men was unfamiliar to Megan. She concluded he must have arrived late in the day, after she and Lina had left the window. Tall and bony, with sparse gray hair and a long, lined face, he came into the room with the shambling gait of a large monkey, and his hands, thickly covered with coarse graying hair, intensified the simian look. Megan did not doubt this was the teller of vulgar after-dinner stories, and his appearance matched so well with a description Jane had once given her that she suspected his identity even before Edmund's introduction confirmed it. George Belts—Jane's despised suitor, who wanted the mill. No wonder Jane was in a rage!

Edmund carried Lina to Lady Georgina and put her on the latter's knee, where she perched like a small ruffled bird on a cold branch. Lady Georgina's expression was one of poorly veiled repulsion. Lina's finger crept back into her mouth.

The gentlemen found chairs, except for Lord Henry, who remained standing by the door, fingering his whiskers as he stared at Megan. She had seen such bold looks before; they often signified trouble to come. Feeling confident that in this house she need not fear insult, she met Lord Henry's look with one as direct, frowning slightly. His brows lifted and he snapped his fingers, so that all the others turned to look at him.

"O'Neill," he exclaimed. "Kevin O'Neill's girl."

"You forget yourself, Lord Henry." Jane's cool voice was the first to break the silence.

"No harm intended, Miss Mandeville, I assure you. I

thought she looked familiar, and just now it all came together. I knew your father well, Miss O'Neill. In fact, I seem to recall dandling you on my knee when you were a tiny thing."

"O'Neill?" Mrs. Morton repeated the name, her voice greedily curious.

"Connacht's youngest. Best fellow in the world." Lord Henry took the chair beside Megan and added, in a lower tone, "I was sorry to hear of his death, Miss O'Neill. Please accept my sincere, if belated, condolences."

Megan decided she had misjudged Lord Henry. His sister might be a rude snob, but he had lovely manners. The disclosure of her parentage had unquestionably raised her status; she could tell from the subtle way the expressions of the others had changed. Only Jane appeared unmoved.

"Miss O'Neill seems not to remember the acquaintance," she said.

"Oh, it was years ago," Lord Henry said pleasantly. "I will not admit how many years; but you see what an old dog I am, Miss Mandeville. Edmund denies it, he refuses to give me the respect owed to age and experience."

Edmund made a joking reply and the conversation became general. Megan, hands folded demurely, spoke only when directly addressed. Things were going well. Lord Henry's recognition was a bonus she had not expected—proof that some force was fighting on her side? Well, she was not so superstitious as that; but it would do no harm to say an extra rosary that night.

Lina had forsaken Lady Georgina, to the latter's undisguised relief. She had gotten over her shyness and was chattering to the other ladies in a blend of French and English. Edmund and Lady Georgina had their heads together; it was hard for Megan to make out what they were saying, but once, in a lull in the general conversation, she heard Lady Georgina say, "No, that will not do at all; it would be simpler to tear down the entire wing and rebuild." So they were talking about Edmund's plans for the house. Jane heard, too, and shot a resentful glance at the speaker.

Jane's angry color had subsided as she talked with Lord Henry. She ignored Belts as thoroughly as possible; his initial overtures having been rejected, he had joined the other gentlemen and, against all the dictates of polite behavior, they were talking business. There was no question about the subject of the conversation, for Belts's resounding voice could be heard all over the room. His comments were as boring as they were unsuitable to the occasion, concerned as they were with his own cleverness in cutting costs and raising production. Finally he paused for breath and one of the other men was able to insert a comment—something about labor regulations.

"Man, don't talk to me about the domned government," Belts cried. "Great hectoring nowts, trying to tell a mon how to run his business. But I know how to deal wi' 'em; ay, I'se sent mony a fule inspector packing with a flea in his ear and a few banknotes in his pocket."

Jane's lip curled as she listened. Observing that he had lost her attention, Lord Henry took advantage of another break in Belts's tirade to say lazily, "I believe your mill was one of those cited in the last report of the Commission on Child Labor, was it not, Mr. Belts?"

The question did not embarrass Belts, as it was meant to do. "Ay, it was," he replied with a coarse laugh. "And much good it did the interfering scoundrels. To be sure, I had to dress the place up a bit when the inspectors came, but it didn't cost too dear, and once they'd gone we was back to our old ways."

The rest of the company had fallen silent. Lady Georgina raised a hand to her lips, to cover a smile or a yawn.

"We are boring the ladies, Belts," Edmund said with an uneasy laugh. "We agreed to leave business at the table."

"Mr. Belts has no other topic of conversation," said Jane. "Perhaps he has some diverting tales to tell about the children who work from dawn till dark in his establishment, and how much he pays the floggers who whip them when they drowse over the looms."

The two ladies on the couch gasped in unison. They seemed more shocked by Jane's reference to such cruelties than by Belts's commission of them. The icy hatred in Jane's voice made a slight dent in Belts's armor of complacency; with what he obviously believed to be a conciliatory manner, he exclaimed, "Now, Miss Jane, ye dasn't believe all the rubbishy tales ye hear. Them childern is in my debt and they know it. Mostly they's the sole support of t' family. They'd starve without the wages I pay 'em, no doubt o' that."

Lord Henry made another valiant attempt to rescue the conversation. "Mr. Belts, I am as bored as the ladies. Perhaps one of them would favor us with a little music, to sweeten the evening."

Belts was not so easily distracted. He suffered from the delusion common to all boors, that his viewpoint was the only right one and that repetition in a loud-enough voice would eventually convince his hearers.

"Ay, ay, music is well enough, but Miss Jane mun get over her fancies. Just look at how she's run your mill, Mandeville; she's a contriving lass, for a female, but females has no place in business. That mill suld be fetching five times the brass. Happen it'll be different when I take it on."

Edmund sprang to his feet. Jane followed suit, more slowly. Her face was as gray as her dress. The others looked on in bewilderment. The attitudes of brother and sister, betraying guilty consternation on one side and horrified shock on the other, indicated that something appalling had occurred, but no one fully comprehended why Belts's statement had produced such a reaction. Megan understood better than the others. Her heart went out to Jane.

For the first time Jane addressed Belts directly.

"Say that again."

"This is not the time or the place," Edmund exclaimed. "Belts, you assured me—"

"What's the odds, 'twill come out soon enough," Belts said blandly. "Don't worry your head, Miss Jane; I'm giving a good price, enough to buy all the pretties and fripperies a lass's heart desires."

Jane flinched as if she had been struck a blow in the face. She looked so ghastly that Megan hastened to her side. Jane pushed her helping hand away.

"You shall not have it," she said. "I won't give it up. Not without a fight." Her head high, she walked out of the room.

Belts chuckled. "She's a sperrited little thing, an't she? I like a lass who stands up to me."

The awkward silence was broken by Lord Henry. "Curse it, Belts, I refuse to allow you to ruin the entire evening. Not another word out of you. Edmund—to the instrument, sir, at once! Georgina, you sing loudly enough to drown out even Mr. Belts. Or perhaps Miss O'Neill will favor us."

Edmund stood staring with a hangdog expression at the door through which his sister had exited. Megan almost disliked him at that moment.

"I think, if Mr. Mandeville agrees, that I should take Lina upstairs," she said quietly. "It is past her bedtime by a great deal."

Edmund started. "Oh—yes. Thank you, Miss O'Neill."

He picked up the child and handed her over. For a moment, while Lina's body shielded him from other eyes, Megan saw his true feelings, and her anger evaporated. He was genuinely sorry. It wasn't his fault that Belts behaved like a boor.

ii

As soon as she had delivered Lina to Rose, Megan went to Jane's door and knocked. There was no verbal reply, but after a long interval the door opened.

She had expected to find Jane prostrate, in a flood of

tears, responsive to sympathetic murmurs and pats on the shoulder. The stony, controlled face that confronted her left her at a loss for words.

After a moment Jane said, "You had better come in. I owe you an apology for making a scene."

It was typical of Jane that she should apologize, instead of trying to justify her behavior. Megan followed her into the room and closed the door.

"You owe me nothing of the sort. And I'm sure the other ladies understand—"

"No, they don't. They think me ill-mannered and odd. I don't give a curse what they think anyway. They are empty-headed fashion plates, and their husbands are just as stupid. Where did Edmund find such friends? What does he see in them?"

Megan was spared the necessity of replying. Jane went on, with growing passion, "I could put up with them. But George Belts! How could Edmund do it? I don't wonder he refused to tell me the names of his guests."

"He thought you would refuse to receive Mr. Belts?" Megan asked.

Jane began pacing up and down the room, her hands clasped behind her, as was her habit when agitated or deep in thought. "He knows how I feel about Belts. I was quite explicit. I suppose he took it for granted that I would behave like a lady when I found myself faced with a *fait accompli*. Well, he found out, didn't he?"

"Perhaps Mr. Mandeville does not fully comprehend how distasteful the admiration of such a man can be to a woman of sensibility. If you explained—"

"You aren't a fool, Megan; please don't talk like one. You know why I am upset."

"I know, but I don't really understand," Megan admitted. "Of course you are proud of your management of the mill; you have every right to be. But I should think it would be a relief to you to give up the responsibilities you have shouldered for so long. After you marry, which you surely will do one day—"

"I will confine my activities to breeding and embroidery, as a woman should?"

A trifle shocked, Megan nodded. Jane's rapid pace slowed. She looked thoughtful.

"Do you know, I never thought of that eventuality. Strange, isn't it, when marriage is the sole ambition of most proper young ladies?

"But that isn't the point. Selling the mill would be bad enough; it is a family concern, and my father hoped it would remain so. But selling to a man like Belts! You heard him—can't you see what would happen to the place if he owned it?"

"He does not sound like the most ethical of employers," Megan said cautiously.

"He doesn't know the meaning of the word. Megan, there is not a worker in our mill that I don't know by name. I played with many of them when we were children. I have been in their homes. Handing them over to the tender mercies of George Belts would be like selling my children to Arab slavers."

Privately Megan thought Jane was dramatizing the situation just a little. She knew about the abuses Jane feared; they were shocking, certainly, but surely by now the worst had been corrected. And people must work for a living. No one knew better than she that life was hard, except for a favored few.

Realizing that her pragmatic views would not be well received, she contented herself with gazing sympathetically at Jane and shaking her head in silent commiseration.

Jane walked more slowly. The exercise seemed to calm her; presently she said in a less passionate voice, "Thank you for listening to me rave, Megan. It has done me good and I am grateful—all the more so because you really don't understand why I feel the way I do. You had better go to bed now. Find a nice, calming book and read yourself to sleep."

Obediently Megan went to the door. Her hand was on the knob when Jane said suddenly, "It is her fault. Curse the woman! He would never have had the idea of selling if she had not put it into his mind."

Megan did not turn, or reply. Jane was not speaking to her; she was thinking aloud, scarcely aware that there was another person present.

"I know their sort," Jane muttered. "She and her profligate brother—having squandered their fortune, they have fixed on Edmund to supply them with another. She would not be content with a steady, respectable income, not she. . . . And I know the kind of persuasion she employs. 'Trade is so degrading! A gentleman should have nothing to do with countinghouses and dirty machines. . . .' I won't allow it. I must do something. But what? What can I do to prevent an alliance that will destroy everything I hold dear?"

The answer was on the tip of Megan's tongue, but she knew better than to speak. Turning the knob, she slipped quietly out of the room.

Once in her own chamber, she flung herself into a chair by the fire and tried to collect her thoughts. What an evening it had been—one surprise following another. Had Edmund told Jane of his intention to marry Lady Georgina? Was there a formal engagement?

Megan thought not. Anyone who loved Edmund could read his hopes and intentions in his manner. Jane was a shrewd little person, though; Megan did not doubt that her evaluation of the situation was accurate. If Lady Georgina refused to consider Edmund's proposal unless he consented to sell the mill, then she, Megan, was completely on Jane's side in opposing the sale. Not that there was anything she could do about it—except make it plain that there was one woman who did not consider trade, or anything else, demeaning to Edmund Mandeville.

She jumped to her feet and paced up and down, as rapidly as Jane had paced, becoming more and more agitated as she tried to think how she could turn this new development to her advantage. Finally she was forced to conclude that she was too tired to think logically and too excited to sleep. I will take Jane's advice, she thought, and find a nice soothing book. No Gothic horrors tonight—a book of sermons, perhaps, or one of the duller Roman philosophers.

The library was out of bounds that evening, but Jane's sitting room contained several bookcases, and she had been invited to make herself free with the contents. Surely Jane would be asleep by now.

Lest she disturb that slumber, she took a candle instead of a lamp and moved on tiptoe. As she had expected, the sitting room was dark. No sound was to be heard from the adjoining room. Megan put the candle on a table and began to scan the shelves.

She had left the sitting-room door open, since the guest rooms and Edmund's bedchamber were not on that corridor. When she heard the sound of footsteps in the corridor she was so startled she almost dropped the book she was holding. She knew the steps, as she knew every other feature of the man who made them. Her hand darted out and flattened the candle flame.

Edmund stopped in front of Jane's door. He stood there so long that Megan began to think he had decided not to disturb his sister's rest, but finally he knocked softly. Almost at once the door was opened. Jane was not only awake, she must have been expecting him.

If words were exchanged, they were in tones so low that Megan was unable to hear them. Without thinking, without stopping to consider what she was doing, she tiptoed across the sitting room and pressed her ear to the door connecting the two rooms.

She had never done such a thing before. As recently as that morning, she would have dismissed the very idea with scorn and loathing. Now she felt only irritation at hearing an indistinguishable mumble of speech. The ancient builders had known their trade and had not skimped on material.

Megan did not hesitate. With the skill of someone who had long practiced the art of eavesdropping, she twisted the knob, prepared to stop if the slightest creak resulted. She need not have worried. The speakers were too intent on their discussion to notice lesser sounds. As she eased the door ajar, Jane's voice burst out.

"Enclosure! First the mill, and now this—you must be mad."

"Every other landowner in the county did it years ago. Morton told me tonight—his father's income quadrupled after he enclosed his property."

"And the tenants he evicted are in the workhouse. You know how Father felt about enclosure—"

"Father is dead!" The brutality of the words startled all of them, including Edmund. He went on in a more subdued voice, "I loved him, you know that, but he was old-fashioned, behind the times. And so are you, Jane. It's not your fault; how could you be anything else, rusticating in this old house, working like a common millhand, and without decent society. Why, Jane—dear Jane—it is your welfare I am considering. I want the best for you—a season in London, the best society—"

"Such as George Belts?"

"Belts is a boor," Edmund said contemptuously. "I endure his offensive manners because I mean to make use of him, but once—"

"*He* is using *you*, Edmund. No, don't interrupt; if the mill were not a valuable property, he would not want it. Have you thought of that?"

Edmund had no answer to this, and Megan hoped Jane had made an impression. Jane thought she had; in a softer, pleading voice, she pressed her point. "You could run the mill as well as he, Edmund; you have ten times his intelligence. Why should he profit from it?"

"It is not the income itself," Edmund began.

"What, then?"

"I see no point in answering. The very fact that you can

ask such a question indicates you have no proper under-standing of a gentleman's—"

"I knew it—I knew it! She is responsible for this. She and her brother have corrupted your thinking. Edmund, she is not worthy of you; she is a selfish, worldly, immoral—"

"How dare you speak of Lady Georgina in those terms? I have asked her to be my wife."

The unseen listener lost control of her breathing when she heard that, but her gasp was drowned out by Jane's cry of protest. It would be hard to say which of the two was more stricken; but before either could react, Edmund added, "She has not yet accepted me, but I feel sure she will when I can offer her the hand of a gentleman instead of that of a mill owner."

Jane's reply to this was an outburst of impassioned rheto-ric that surpassed anything of the sort Megan had ever heard. She quoted every authority she could think of, from the Old Testament prophets to her deceased father, and some of the expressions she used made Megan's eyes widen. She grimaced to herself. Wrong, Jane, she thought. That's not the way to gain your ends; you must not call a man's beloved a whited sepulcher and a painted harlot. But poor Jane was so unworldly; she had never learned the methods women used to cut down a rival—the cool praise, the sweet compliment that concealed a poisoned dart.

Edmund did not attempt to interrupt the torrent of words. No doubt he realized it would be futile to try. Finally Jane exhausted her store of biblical epithets and found a keener weapon.

"I cannot stop you from enclosing the property," she ad-mitted in a voice rough with weary anger. "The house and estate are yours. But the mill is not. Father left half of it to me."

"Impossible," Edmund exclaimed. "The law does not allow—"

"The law is what men make it," Jane retorted bitterly. "And Mr. Trumbull was in full accord with Father—both wanted to make sure I would not be robbed of my rights even by marriage. Does Mr. Belts know that, I wonder? Perhaps you had better tell him. He'll take himself off fast enough then, and leave me in peace. Half the mill is mine, Edmund, and I will not sell. If you think you can overturn Father's will—try! I will fight you every step of the way. I will employ every underhanded method I can think of. I will stop at nothing."

Megan pressed her cheek harder against the crack in the door. She heard nothing except hard breathing. Would Edmund strike his sister? No, not Edmund—but most men would have felt justified, after such an attack. Instead, she heard something that sounded strangely like a sob. Unable to bear the suspense, she applied her eye instead of her ear to the crack.

Edmund was leaning against the wardrobe, his hands over his eyes, and his back to her. After a moment Jane appeared. She had not been crying. Her eyes were quite dry. Her hair had come loose from its net and hung in wild disorder down her back.

"Edmund," she began.

"You have hurt me deeply, Jane."

His voice betrayed the struggle he was making to control his tears. Jane was not unmoved. Her lips trembled, and she twisted her hands together.

"Oh, Edmund, what has happened to you? I don't know you any longer."

"I am not the same," Edmund said thickly. "The boy who went to battle in his crimson tunic and gold braid died on the dusty heights of Sevastopol—or perhaps it was in the hold of the ship that brought him home. Half-dead with fever himself, he heard the death rattle in the throats of men who lay all around him. They died by the hundreds, Jane, and I might have been one of them. Life is too short, too precious. . . . There are so many things I want to savor and enjoy. . . . But why talk about it? You don't understand."

"I will try to understand," Jane whispered. "Only meet

me halfway, Edmund. I will do everything in my power to help you find the happiness you deserve."

"Everything except the mill," Edmund said bitterly.

"Everything except what is dishonorable, Edmund."

Her voice was gentle but firm. Wrapping both arms around her brother, she held him close, her head resting on his shoulder.

At first Edmund remained rigid and unresponsive. At last he turned and took Jane into an affectionate embrace. His tearstained cheeks shone in the lamplight. Megan ached to burst in and comfort him with the submissive tenderness Jane had withheld. However, she decided she had better creep away. Now that the storm was over, the participants might notice that the door was ajar, or Jane might come looking for a book after Edmund left her.

Megan went straight to bed. No need of a book now; she was worn out by the tumultuous emotions she had vicariously shared. She had learned a great deal. Edmund was still free. He might not admit it, even to himself, but the insult implicit in Lady Georgina's refusal must rankle.

Most important, Megan had discovered that her position was not as weak as she had supposed. Lady Georgina had no fortune; so they were equals in wealth, in beauty, and in birth. And Megan O'Neill had important qualities her rival lacked—tenderness, understanding, uncritical adoration. She also had an ally. Edmund might be angry with his sister at the moment, but her opinion must carry weight with him.

As Megan drifted off to sleep, it occurred to her that for the first time in years she had neglected to say her prayers. She dispatched a drowsy, wordless thanks to the unseen Powers who were working to help her; what she failed to realize was that, for once, she had not given those Powers a name.

Chapter
Six

T was not to be expected that Jane or Edmund would take Megan aside and tell her how their argument had ended. Some deductions were possible, however. George Belts took his departure next morning in an extremely disgruntled frame of mind. No one in the house was left in doubt of his feelings, for he was still shouting them aloud when he climbed into his carriage.

"You're making a bad mistake, Mandeville, and you'll find it out soon enough. Oh, aye, you'll come t'me hat in hand, begod, and you'll not find me so generous next time."

So Jane had won on the question of the mill. Withdrawing from her window, from which she had enjoyed the spectacle of Belts's discomfiture, Megan hugged herself in delight.

The next step was up to her, and she achieved it the same day. It was essential that she join the guests in the drawing room every evening in order to observe how the relationship of Edmund and Lady Georgina was progressing. Eavesdropping must be reserved for occasions when there was no other way of finding out what she needed to know. It was a dangerous game; if she were caught in the act, she would probably lose her position. Besides, it wasn't easy to keep from betraying knowledge she was not supposed to have.

During the afternoon she managed to waylay Edmund and insinuate her suggestion. "In case you feel like music this evening, Mr. Mandeville, I would be happy to offer my services."

She spoke with the most charming modesty, and Edmund responded as she hoped he would, thanking her warmly. She knew she had Lord Henry to thank for this, in part; the granddaughter of Lord Connacht was welcome in company where Miss O'Neill the governess could not go.

The evening was more successful than she had hoped, though the first few moments were somewhat uncomfortable. She was not disturbed by Lady Georgina's stare, or refusal to greet her; but the warm smile and outstretched hand with which Jane attempted to compensate for her guest's rudeness made Megan blush with shame, remembering her eavesdropping the night before. Jane took the blush for embarrassment and redoubled her kindly efforts. Megan took comfort in the knowledge that she was not really betraying her friend; on the contrary, she was working with and for Jane, if Jane only knew.

When the gentlemen joined the ladies, the family lawyer, Mr. Trumbull, was with them. Edmund had lost no time in beginning his plans. Not the mill—Belts would not have left in a rage if Edmund still meant to sell it. So it must be the enclosure of the property about which he had consulted the lawyer.

Megan did not have a very clear idea of what this process involved. It had something to do with the unfenced common land, field and pasture, the use of which was determined by age-old custom rather than legal title. Parliamentary commissioners reassigned the land and, in some cases, arranged for monetary compensation for those who lost grazing or farming rights in the process. The results were increased production and greater efficiency for some, and utter penury for others, who had eked out a precarious but adequate living by grazing a few animals and raising a few vegetables on their share of the common land.

Megan concluded that Mr. Trumbull's judgment had favored Edmund. Edmund looked pleased, Jane morose under her company manners. Later, she and the lawyer fell into conversation, and though they spoke quietly, Megan thought Mr. Trumbull was trying to convince Jane of something. He did most of the talking, while she kept shaking her head.

She found this interesting but not vitally important. It did not affect her plans one way or the other. She turned her attention to Lady Georgina.

During the course of the evening she managed to provoke that lady into several rude remarks—not a difficult task—to which she responded with the most exquisite courtesy. She made sure Edmund heard the remarks and the responses, and was delighted to see him frown faintly. Close observation of the pair convinced her that Edmund was not in love. She knew the manifestations of that disease too well to be mistaken.

A minor diversion was caused by Ta-chin, who managed to slip into the room unseen and bided her time under a sofa until she considered it safe to come out. Edmund did not like animals in the house, and he was not particularly fond of Ta-chin, who refused to give him the adoring admiration he was accustomed to. That evening the cat ignored him and made a beeline for Mr. Trumbull, who was evidently a favorite. By the time Edmund noticed her she was curled up on the old lawyer's bony knee, purring hoarsely as he scratched her under the chin. Edmund's offer to have the nuisance removed was refused with a smile.

"Ta-chin and I are old friends, Edmund; you know I am fond of animals, particularly cats."

"Nasty, creeping creatures," Lady Georgina said loudly. "I cannot abide them."

Ta-chin pretended not to hear this comment; instead she waited to take her revenge, with a cunning calculation that supported Lady Georgina's appraisal of her species. Slipping quietly from the lawyer's lap, she disappeared from sight for so long an interval that everyone forgot she was there. Her reappearance was as startling as a conjurer's trick; she seemed to materialize on Lady Georgina's satin skirt, her tail lashing and all her claws fully extended.

Lady Georgina shrieked and swore, Edmund leaped to the rescue, and Jane's face underwent a series of frightful contortions as she tried to keep from laughing. Ta-chin waited until Edmund's hand had actually brushed her fur before she sailed off into space. Jane finally succeeded in enticing her out from under the table, where she had sought refuge, and carried her off in disgrace. However, Megan suspected there would be a bowl of cream for her in the kitchen. Two bowls, in fact; Megan would contribute one herself.

The evening ended with music, and Megan had the satisfaction of joining voices with Edmund in a duet that was applauded by all—almost all. It had been a triumph, but she was not naive enough to believe she had won a decisive victory. Edmund might not love Lady Georgina, but neither did he love Megan O'Neill. She needed another weapon, and at the moment she could not think how to find it.

ii

AFTER THE guests left, Megan found life rather dull. They had not been enjoyable company, but they had stimulated her, and their departure had not meant a return to the affectionate family relationships she had previously enjoyed. Edmund was busy, consulting with the lawyer and spending long hours at the mill, whose management he had assumed. Jane wandered aimlessly around the house, looking like a tragic Muse, or sulked in her room. Lina behaved like an imp.

One morning, after the child had rudely refused to repeat a single one of the French phrases she was supposed to be learning, Megan had a flash of insight. No wonder Lina was behaving badly; she had always been the darling pet of the entire household, and now she had been abandoned by her Aunt Jane and her newfound "uncle." Nor, Megan thought guiltily, had her governess been particularly attentive.

"I know," she said. "Let us take a little holiday. Just the two of us. I think we deserve it, don't you?"

"*I* do," Lina said.

"But you'll let me come with you, won't you?"

"Where?" Lina asked suspiciously.

"To the village. We might find some bits of lace or ribbon to refurbish Mademoiselle Mimi's wardrobe. She is very hard on her frocks, I must say."

Lina gurgled with amusement. "She is bad. I told her not to slide down the banister in her best frock, but she would do it. Let's go now. I will ride Robbie."

Megan was tempted to agree. Thanks to her father, who had been an excellent horseman, she had learned to ride at an early age, and took pride in her skill. Edmund had never seen her mounted; it was just possible that they might encounter him. But she reluctantly abandoned the idea. Lina's fat pony was too slow and lazy to go far, and Lina still had a deplorable tendency to roll gently out of the saddle whenever Robbie stopped or started or changed gait.

"We will take the pony cart," she said firmly. "We may have parcels to carry."

iii

IT WAS a pleasant drive, along a narrow road lined with trees whose branches were entangled with ivy and wild roses. One of Jane's first acts had been to give Megan her first quarter's wages in advance, so she had money in her pocket and every intention of squandering some of it.

Not that the village had much to offer in the way of shops. It had expanded to some degree since the coming of the railway. Thanks to the influence of John Mandeville, who disliked progress in general, and the bellowing, belching iron engines in particular, the line passed as far from his park gates as the terrain allowed, a good half mile beyond what was then the boundary of the village. Enterprising merchants had built out to join it, and this extension, referred to as New Town, had already developed the ugly stigmata of an industrial region—rows of grimy tenements, cheap shops and warehouses. Jane refused to enter the area, and Megan had not seen it since the night of her arrival.

The saint whose name survived in that of St. Arca Underhill was so obscure that she was not to be found in any of the conventional lists, even the, at that time, suspiciously overcrowded Roman Catholic calendar. Formerly the church had borne the same name. It had survived the reforming zeal of bluff King Hal, erstwhile Defender of the Faith, because, whatever Arca might have been, she was most assuredly not a papal protégée, and also because the parish priest of that period was prompt to obey the royal edict. He had never believed in a celibate clergy anyhow, and was pleased to find out he had been right all along.

The church ran into difficulty during the Civil War. Like most of Warwickshire, the village went for the Parliament, and the then lord of the manor seized the opportunity to rededicate the church. He had always had doubts about Saint Arca. She sounded like some sort of heathen. His action was met with grumbling resentment from his conservative tenants, and by the usual curses from the village witch. When he was killed at Naseby, everybody nodded with glum satisfaction and said it just went to show you.

St. Arca was mentioned in Domesday Book, but its actual age was unknown. A former vicar maintained that there had been a village on the spot in prehistoric times, and that the main road was originally of Roman construction. No one paid much attention to this theory because no one really cared.

When it reached the bottom of the hill, the quiet lane became a street, Bowerman Lane, and passed through another new section before reaching the village proper. John Mandeville had built the neat little houses for his mill workers. They were almost identical in size and design, with John's monogram over each door, but the differing tastes of the owners gave them individuality, particularly in the gardens. The main street seemed unusually quiet that day; there was no one to be seen, except a fat tabby sleeping in a bed of marigolds.

Megan slowed the horse to a walk as they entered the old section of St. Arca. She loved this part of the drive; the houses along the street were like an open-air museum of English history, from the intricate timbering of the Tudor period to the formal red brick balance of the Georgian. In the bright summer weather the gardens blazed with color—tall blue spikes of delphinium, scarlet poppies, and roses of every shade from snowy white to deep crimson.

The shop Jane usually patronized was near the Market Square, where Bowerman Lane met the road running north to the mill. Several hundred yards beyond stood the church, an ugly stone structure with which a generous but tasteless patron had replaced an earlier edifice destroyed by fire. A crowd had gathered before the church porch. Half the village seemed to be there.

Her curiosity aroused, Megan let the horse go on instead of stopping at the shop.

"Yes, I know," she said, as Lina indignantly pointed out

her error. "We'll go back; I only want to see what is happening."

The crowd began to disperse as she pulled up on the side of the road. Some of the women nodded and said "Good morning," but none stopped to volunteer information. Shading her eyes with her hand, Megan made out a white square on the church door. A notice of some kind, presumably—and one of great interest to the villagers.

Then she remembered having heard Edmund say something about posting his notice of intention to enclose. It was a law or custom, she could not recall which. Perhaps that was his notice. If so, he had been very prompt to take action.

The preliminary steps had indeed proceeded more rapidly than was customary. Edmund was efficient when he wanted something badly enough, and in this case he had had the wholehearted cooperation of the family lawyer. Mr. Trumbull sympathized with Jane's feelings, for he was fond of her, but he considered the enclosure long overdue.

Having found out what she wanted to know, Megan was about to leave when a man broke away from the group clustered around the church and walked toward the carriage. Lina stopped whining about the delay and cried eagerly, "It's Sam. Sam, here I am!"

Megan had seen Sam Freeman several times since her tour of the mill, but she had never exchanged more than a few words with him. Now he came straight to the pony cart, his hat in his hand and his dark plume of hair blowing in the warm breeze. Lina began to explore the pockets of his jacket, and Megan said with a smile, "Good morning. Are you playing truant this fine day?"

"Nay, Miss O'Neill, not I," Sam answered, with the blend of formal grammar and rustic accent that gave his speech an archaic, almost courtly, sound. " 'Twas said the notice would go up today. I wished to see it for myself and read it to the folk who lack that learning."

"And how are they taking it?"

"They'll wait and see. That's always their way."

"I suppose you do not approve," Megan said carelessly. She had not given much thought to what Sam's opinion might be; except when he was actually in her presence, she did not think of him at all. But knowing him to be a protégé of Jane's, she took it for granted he would share her views.

Sam glanced at Lina, who let out a squeal of joy when she found a bright-green boiled sweet in his pocket. It was quite dusty, and Megan wondered whether she ought not take it away from the child. She didn't want to insult the giver. . . . Before she could decide, Lina popped the sweet into her mouth.

The distraction had made her forget her question, but Sam had every intention of answering it; he was simply giving his reply careful consideration.

"Nay, why should you think that?" he asked. "There could be good or bad in it, depending on how it's done."

"So, like the others, you will wait and see."

Sam grinned. "I will. It's not so bad a rule."

He seemed in no hurry to end the conversation, but Lina's repeated demands that they proceed finally gave Megan an excuse to get away. As they turned she saw that Sam had gone back to the church and was standing, hands in his pockets, staring at the notice.

Really, she thought with an inner smile, for all his superior education he was as bovine and slow-thinking as the other villagers. With his heavy shoulders hunched and his head lowered he reminded her of the big bull on the manor farm. Except when he smiled, his face had the same heavy sullenness. He was a kindhearted animal, though; Lina had counted on finding a sweet in his pocket, so he must carry a supply for any child he chanced to meet.

With this she promptly dismissed Sam from her mind. He would have been chagrined to know how briefly he had occupied it.

Chapter
Seven

ONCE THE notice of enclosure had been posted, Edmund could do nothing more until the government commissioners arrived. He was therefore free to turn his attention toward a subject he found much more interesting—his plans to refurbish the house. He was no more relieved to be done with boring business details than was Megan; she had been boiling with frustration for days because he was absent so much. You cannot show a man how attractive, amiable, and desirable you are if he is not there.

Edmund had already consulted her about some of his plans and had indicated he meant to go on doing so, but she was taking no chances. It wasn't difficult to find an opportunity to mention her interest in architecture and drop a learned quotation or two from the authorities she had been feverishly reading. When the grand tour of the manor began, she was one of the party.

Initially Jane and Edmund were a trifle stiff with one another. They had had a violent argument the night before, after Edmund had mentioned he had hired a new manager for the mill. The man replaced had been a friend and crony of Jane's father; she had taken on as if Edmund had sent the old fellow to the workhouse instead of allowing him to retire to a well-earned rest.

Megan had not been forced to resort to eavesdropping to find this out. Some of the servants had overheard the argument, and Megan had received the information and the description of Jane's "carrying on" from Lizzie. She had been cultivating Lizzie's friendship assiduously; the innocent old woman was flattered at the attention and glad to have someone of her own station with whom to gossip. Somewhat to Megan's surprise, Lizzie took Edmund's part.

"The old man is past the work," she explained, as the two conferred over cups of strong tea in the housekeeper's room. "He must be all of seventy; high time he left it to a younger man. Why, poor Miss Jane was always having to look over his books, he was so forgetful. Master Edmund can't be bothered with such stuff."

The tour had not gone on long before Jane's resentment melted in the warmth of Edmund's charm. He was hard to resist when he put himself out—thought one biased participant—and that morning he was in excellent spirits, laughing and teasing and recalling incidents from childhood. Every room had its memories. The wide oak banister of the central staircase was the one they had greased with butter stolen from the larder, so they could slide faster. The great Chinese vase in the drawing room was where one of the stable cats had had her litter. . . .

"And when Lizzie heard the kittens squeaking, she ran out of the room swearing the ghost was after her," Jane added with a laugh.

"Then the manor is haunted?" Megan asked. "Do tell me, Mr. Mandeville; I adore tales of mystery and terror. Father used to curdle my blood with recollections of the Connacht banshee."

"My dear Miss O'Neill, you needn't suppose that because

this house lacks some amenities, it is deficient in all respects. If anything, we have a superfluity of specters. There are almost too many to be convincing; it is as if every person who ever lived in the house conjured up his own ghost."

An odd little thrill ran through Megan's limbs. Edmund saw her shiver and exclaimed, "But I didn't mean to curdle your blood, Miss O'Neill; forgive me."

"It is nothing. What do the local people say?—'A goose walked over my grave.' I told you, Mr. Mandeville, I love bloodcurdling tales."

"Then I will tell you some of Grayhaven's ghost stories, on a more suitable occasion; a winter night is best, when the wind howls in the bare branches and the firelight is dim."

"Enough of that nonsense," Jane said impatiently. "I have other duties, Edmund, if you do not. Let's get on with it."

"To be sure. We have spent too much time in this part of the house as it is. I have already fixed on the changes I mean to make here. What I want to do this morning is investigate the other wings, especially the parts that have been shut up."

Megan had hoped to get some idea of the general plan of the house that morning, but the farther they went, the more confused she became. Grayhaven had no real plan; it was not shaped like an *E* or an *L* or any other letter of the alphabet. Apparently each builder had simply tacked on a wing or a group of rooms wherever it was most convenient, without removing or seriously altering previously standing structures. She was surprised at the sheer size of the house. It did not look so large from outside.

Edmund had a better notion of the plan, though he was constantly saying he had not been in this room or that since he was a child. According to him, the oldest parts of the house were the medieval gatehouse and entrance and the adjoining Great Hall. Only the facade of the gatehouse remained; the inner floors had been removed in some past age and the interior converted into the central hallway of the house, with stairs leading up to connect with the side wings.

The Great Hall was still used on formal occasions, but Jane admitted she did not like dining there. "I am always expecting something nasty to drop down into my soup," she remarked, glancing up at the beamed ceiling.

Edmund jeered at this; had he not had swarms of workmen up into the beams before his guests arrived, cleaning and checking for signs of decay? Medievalism was the latest style; some of his friends were tearing down their homes in order to erect sham castles with towers and battlements in the best Gothic manner. To be sure, the room needed further attention: stained glass in the high windows, perhaps, and better lighting. But that could wait. The apartments beyond the Great Hall were the ones he wanted to inspect.

"How long has it been since anyone looked into this part of the house?" he demanded, wrestling with the massive key that seemed reluctant to perform its function.

"Not more than a year," Jane replied, resenting the slur on her housekeeping. "Lizzie turns out all the rooms annually, even those that are not used."

Edmund's reply was a skeptical grunt. He finally persuaded the key to turn. Once she saw what lay beyond the door, Megan was also inclined to doubt that Lizzie's penchant for cleanliness had extended to this region. If she were one of the maids, she would be reluctant to set foot in the dim, dusty corridor.

"Perhaps it is time for another cleaning," Jane admitted, sneezing violently in the cloud of dust disturbed by their footsteps.

"At least," Edmund said. Fastidiously he scrubbed at the nearest window with his handkerchief. He managed to lighten one of the diamond-shaped panes. A feeble ray of sunlight struggled through and fell upon a painted face that leaped out of the shadows with startling effect—the swarthy, smiling face of a man wearing a broad-brimmed hat trimmed with long plumes.

"So this is where the portraits are," Edmund said. "I wondered what had become of them."

"Father had them taken here," Jane said. "He said they were a gloomy lot, and he didn't care to be stared at by all the former owners."

"That man is the very imagine of King Charles the Second," Megan exclaimed. "Could it be a royal portrait?"

Edmund examined the edge of the heavy gold frame. "Here is the name. Rupert Leventhorpe. A former owner, as Jane said."

"It is like the museums in Florence," Megan said, as they walked on down the gallery. "Paintings covering every inch of the walls. Someday I would like to examine them in more detail."

"Not until after the place has been cleaned." Edmund's nose wrinkled fastidiously. "One can scarcely breathe, much less see, the dust is so thick. Jane, has my memory failed me? Is the chapel on this corridor?"

"At the far end."

"No doubt Father had it shut up, too," Edmund said. "It offended his religious prejudices—popish mummeries, and all that."

Jane gave Megan a quick apologetic glance, to which the latter replied with a smile and a shrug.

When in London, Megan had attended the Anglican church every Sunday. Her employers assumed that she would do so, and she never had the courage to object, though the thoughts that passed through her mind when she meekly bowed her head in prayer would have shocked the nuns who taught her the rudiments of her faith. They would have praised her for refusing to attend church and thereby risking a variety of martyrdom; but they would not have approved of bitterness and hate.

Jane's tolerance had the effect of making Megan less devout. Sometimes she forgot to wear her mother's crucifix, and she had not attempted to find a Catholic church, though she knew Jane would offer the carriage if she wanted to attend mass. This was not as surprising as it might seem, since resentment rather than piety had been mainly responsible for the former intensity of Megan's private devotions.

However, when Edmund threw open the double door leading into the chapel, her reaction was as natural as breathing. Unseen by the others, but for once unmindful of their presence, she touched her breast and brow in a gesture older than she knew.

The long-neglected room held few reminders of the faith to which it had originally been dedicated. The light was poor. The magnificent fifteenth-century stained glass was crusted with dirt, and thick foliage cut off all but a few streaks of sunlight. Megan realized that that was why she had never recognized the characteristic projecting shape of the apse; by deliberate design or by neglect it had been hidden by trees and shrubbery. The room had obviously not been used for years, but it had served as a place of worship after the Reformation; the plain wooden pews were as incongruous as a pair of heavy boots on a fashionably dressed woman. Megan's gaze moved unerringly to the single remaining symbol of the old religion, on the wall behind the altar in the place where a crucifix should have hung. She could not make out the details, but the scene was familiar —a Pietà, the grieving Mother mourning over the body of her Son.

Edmund moved around, exclaiming delightedly. "I remember that ceiling. Even as a child I was impressed by its beauty, but naturally I was too young to appreciate it fully. Look at the carving—lacework in stone."

"Like the chapel of King Henry the Seventh at Westminster Abbey," Megan said. "It must be of the same period— around fifteen hundred, Mr. Mandeville?"

She made it a question, though she knew she was right; her free hours had been spent in museums and churches, since she had not the money nor the inclination to seek other sources of entertainment.

Edmund was impressed. "Quite right, Miss O'Neill. You are a real scholar."

"I saw so much of cathedrals and castles and such in my younger days," Megan said modestly. "Papa had a taste for art, and cultivated mine. I only wish I had time to study the subject; it interests me very much."

"I envy you," Edmund said impulsively. "Father would never allow me to make a European tour. He said England was good enough for him and should be good enough for me; and besides, French cooking was abominable—he had heard they covered all their meat in peculiar-tasting gravies."

He laughed, but there was a tone of bitterness in his voice; and Jane, always sensitive to any implied slur against her father, said quickly, "He gave you a fine education, Edmund. I could envy you that, having had so little myself."

"Oh, to be sure, the dear old fellow did what he thought was best. As for Europe, I hope to remedy that lack one day, along with others. Jane, I am tempted to put this beautiful place into use again. Shall we have a resident parson, as they did in the old days, and hold services?"

"I doubt the vicar would approve," Jane said. "He is getting quite elderly and has plenty to do as it is."

"At any rate, I mean to tidy it up. Those dreadful pews must go. What a showplace it will be for visitors!"

Jane made a brusque, restless gesture, as if brushing away a fly. "Surely this is enough exploring for one day, Edmund. My throat is dry as dust, and Megan probably wants a cup of tea."

"When I have finished with this side of the west front. There is a staircase farther along this corridor, if I am not mistaken."

"Yes, it leads to. . . . Edmund! If you mean to explore the old wing, I must beg to be excused."

"I declare, you are as superstitious as the servants," Edmund said, laughing. "Are you afraid of ghosts, Jane?"

"No; only of dirt and cobwebs and rats."

"So you admit your housekeeping has been negligent. That is the oldest part of the house, Jane, except for the gatehouse; like the chapel, it probably dates from the early Tudor period. I must and will see it."

"Oh, very well," Jane said with an exaggerated sigh. "But I refuse to use that staircase; it is probably unsafe as well as dark and dusty. We had better go back to the hall; there is a doorway into the old wing on the first floor."

As they retraced their steps, Edmund said reminiscently, "One of our favorite occupations as children was to look for secret passages and hidden rooms."

"And we never found a thing," said Jane, whose temper was deteriorating.

"We didn't know how to go about it. I am convinced the place has some mysteries—a priest's hole, at the very least. After all, many of the former owners were Catholics—"

"Like everyone else in England before the Reformation."

"Jane, you are turning into a grouchy old woman," Edmund declared cheerfully. "I will not allow you to shatter my romantic fancies. I meant, of course, that after Henry the Eighth, the owners of Grayhaven remained of the old faith. They would not have been popular with the great Elizabeth; most English Catholics considered her illegitimate and Mary of Scotland the rightful queen of England."

Again Jane shot an anxious glance at Megan, and for a moment the latter feared she would warn Edmund that he might be treading on sensitive ground. Megan did not want her to do this. Edmund might not care one way or the other; his comments thus far had indicated a state of mind as tolerant as his sister's. Her Catholicism might even be an asset under certain circumstances—faintly exotic, with a hint of martyrdom nobly born. But until she had determined what was best she wanted nothing to mar the image she was endeavoring to create—that of the perfect, orthodox English lady.

"If that is so, there might be a priest's hole at Grayhaven," she exclaimed. "What a fascinating idea."

"Anything of that sort would be in the old wing," Edmund said as they mounted the stairs. "That is one of the reasons why I am anxious to reopen it."

Megan was relieved to find herself in familiar surroundings. Several corridors led off the first-floor landing; those to the right entered the eighteenth-century wing, where she and the others had their rooms. Edmund turned to the left, toward a single door under a low archway. Megan had never seen it open; as Edmund put his shoulder to the heavy panels and the door swung back with a sullen, resistant groan, she decided she did not blame Lizzie for neglecting to clean here. The narrow, winding passageways and dark rooms, with their clouded leaded casements, conveyed a sense of oppression that Jane clearly shared. With a shudder, the latter declared, "You surely don't mean to put guests in these rooms, Edmund! They are too dark and gloomy."

"A little more light would not be amiss," Edmund agreed. He crossed to the window and tugged at the heavy draperies. Dust motes danced in the light. "But I don't share your appraisal, Jane; this would be a handsome room if it had more windows. That could easily be done."

"It is a very stately chamber," Megan said diplomatically. Privately she thought she would not care to sleep in the elephantine bed, with its gloomy hangings. The furniture was black as ebony, carved with bizarre shapes.

"Exactly," Edmund exclaimed. "It must have been the room of the lord of the manor. Who knows—Queen Elizabeth may have slept in that bed."

ii

AN ARMY of workmen descended on the house. Scaffolding enveloped the walls, the sound of hammers and chisels drowned out the birds' songs, and Lizzie lamented constantly about the mess. Megan was in her glory. She was indispensable to Edmund, he consulted her about everything. She even feigned enthusiasm about his intention of opening some of the rooms in the Tudor wing, and watched approvingly as workmen began to demolish the wall in order to insert larger windows. Jane had washed her hands of the whole business. She spent long hours in her room and refused to watch or comment upon the changes.

One afternoon toward the end of August, she joined Edmund and Megan, who were in the library consulting some builders' catalogs that had recently arrived. When invited to share this activity, she shook her head.

"You will have to give up your remodeling for a day or two, Edmund. The harvest is almost in."

"So I should suppose, having observed the reapers at work," Edmund replied. "Are you suggesting I should lend them a hand?"

"In a sense. Shame, Edmund, you've forgotten."

"Forgotten what?"

"Bringing in the Maiden. You must be there; Father never missed a year."

"You can hardly blame me for forgetting," Edmund said. "The last such celebration I attended was the year before I left for school. How old was I—eight? I took it for granted that antique custom had lapsed."

"What is it?" Megan asked curiously.

"I suppose one would call it a harvest festival," Edmund said carelessly. "The locals have some peculiar games, but it is really an excuse to eat and drink and take a day from work."

"It is more than that," Jane said.

Edmund looked at her curiously, but she pressed her lips together and said nothing more. Good-naturedly he said, "Very well, I suppose I must. In fact, we will make a family holiday of it; that was always the way, if I remember. Miss O'Neill may enjoy seeing how primitive we are in this supposedly modern nineteenth century."

Miss O'Neill was not at all interested in primitive customs; the fact that Edmund had included her in the family holiday was enough to make the event one to be anticipated and enjoyed.

It was midmorning before they set out. Jane had insisted they dress in their best and had set the example by wearing a gown Edmund had given her. It had enormously full skirts and puffed lingerie sleeves of sheer batiste; it was a measure of Jane's devotion to the cause that she even wore a crinoline under it, this being a contrivance she had never consented to countenance before. The dress was extremely pretty and very fashionable; but for some reason Megan could not fathom, it looked absolutely dreadful on Jane. Her look of martyrdom as she held the matching parasol stiffly at the perpendicular didn't help.

The North Field was the last to be cut, and as the party picked their way through the gray stubble of barley, Megan saw that a single shock still remained, its shining fronds waving in the breeze. The farm workers and their families were all present, and they, too, wore their Sunday clothes, some of the older men appearing in exquisitely embroidered and smocked linen.

Either Edmund had been coached in his role, or he remembered more than he admitted of earlier occasions; he stood smiling and unperturbed when a gaggle of old women rushed at him as if intent on attack. One of them seized his arm and held it; another bound a garland woven of field flowers around his sleeve. Then they all shouted, "A forfeit, master, a forfeit!"

"The forfeit will be paid," Edmund cried. A hearty cheer arose.

"What on earth are they doing?" Megan whispered to Jane.

"The forfeit is the supper that will be served later," Jane replied in a low voice. "Along with several barrels of strong ale . . . sssh."

The other watchers drew back, and a group of men advanced to within six feet of the lone remaining barley shock.

All of them were young; some of the sunburned faces were grim and intent, a few grinned self-consciously. They each carried a sickle. At a given signal they hurled their tools at the shock. Another cheer went up when one cut cleanly through, and the shining bundle sagged sideways. Before it touched the ground, a dozen willing hands had seized it.

The sheaf was tied and twisted. One of the younger girls stepped up and placed a wreath of flowers on top of it, and a joyful chorus hailed "The Maiden." The crude image was then lifted onto a cart filled with the last of the crop, and it jounced off across the stubble accompanied by a singing, shouting crowd.

Jane and Edmund stood side by side, waving. Edmund's arm was around his sister's shoulders; they were closer, physically and emotionally, than they had been for a long time. Megan caught Lina's little petticoat just in time to keep her from running after the cart. As the child jumped and clapped her hands, Megan realized that the others felt something she did not. The brief, peculiar ceremony had not amused her; she had found it primitive and a little frightening. Was it because she was a stranger in an alien land, or because she sensed a deeper meaning in the archaic rite?

The mood passed as Edmund turned to offer her his other arm. Later that afternoon, as she stood with him and Jane greeting the harvesters arriving for the traditional feast, she felt as if it were an omen, a foreshadowing of a future day when she would stand at his side and greet other guests as his wife.

Her happy dream ended two days later, when the Astleys returned from Scotland.

Chapter
Eight

EDMUND WAS off the moment Lady Georgina's message arrived, drawn like a needle to a magnet. Megan did not even know he had gone until late afternoon, when Jane came to the nursery, where Megan was halfheartedly trying to impress the first few letters of the alphabet upon her charge.

Though she saw at once by Jane's face that something had happened, she was given no opportunity to ask; Lina rushed at Aunt Jane and proudly displayed a row of staggering *A*'s and tipsy-looking *B*'s.

"You appear to have worked very hard," Jane said seriously. "You deserve a treat. Would you like to have supper with Lizzie in her room?"

Lina clapped her hands. Lizzie told wonderful stories about brownies and elves and the People of the Hills, and when Jane was not around to supervise, she stuffed her pet with sweetmeats.

"I thought we might dine together," Jane said, turning to Megan. "Edmund is away—"

"Away!" The cry broke from her before she could stop herself.

"To Astley Park for a few days." Jane spoke quickly, as if bent on getting the worst over with.

So she knows, Megan thought, observing Jane's tactfully averted eyes. It doesn't matter. I don't care. Astley Park. I thought they had gone for the whole autumn. He never spoke of her or seemed to regret her absence. . . .

"As soon as you are ready, then." Jane rose from her chair. "You know my old-fashioned habit of dining early."

After Lina had gone to Lizzie, Megan stayed in the empty nursery, staring numbly at the open window and the green lawn beyond. The rational part of her mind told her she was overreacting. Her situation was no worse than it had been originally, when she first realized she loved Edmund and must fight a dangerous rival to win him. If anything, she had gained ground. She was part of the family now; Edmund treated her with almost as much warmth as he did Jane, and he valued her opinion more than he did his sister's. Her spirits lifted; she imagined Edmund greeting Lady Georgina —realizing as he took her hand that it was not as soft and warm as the hand he had held, too briefly, the afternoon of the harvest festival—looking into her bold green eyes and remembering other eyes, soft and blue and tender—mounting his horse and riding impetuously over the hills to throw himself at her feet and tell her. . . .

The vision burst like a bubble in the sun. Real life wasn't like that. She had made great progress, but it was not enough; something more was needed, something momentous enough to weight the scales in her favor. For the life of her—and at that moment the matter seemed almost that important—she could not think of anything. I had better try prayer, she thought, with a cynicism that would have been foreign to her nature a few weeks earlier. I won't ask for intercession—only for a suggestion.

The chiming of the mantel clock brought her back to reality and reminded her Jane was waiting. She smoothed her hair and straightened her dress. The prospect of dining with Jane roused neither anticipation nor reluctance; she measured every activity in terms of how it could serve or hurt her present obsession, and the best she could hope for from Jane was passive acceptance.

Jane had refused to let Edmund redecorate her room. It had a quaint, rather shabby charm that suited its occupant and created an atmosphere of comfortable relaxation. For the first time Megan could remember, Jane's writing desk was tidy. The books and papers were gone, and the front was closed, showing the delicate shell carving. Simple muslin curtains swayed in the evening breeze. It had been a warm day, but autumn was approaching; patches of yellow and rust showed among the green of the leaves outside.

It was not long before Megan realized Jane had something on her mind. Reticence and subterfuge were both foreign to her nature; the only thing that kept her from expressing her feelings was concern that they might give pain to others. As the lulls in the conversation lengthened and Jane's abstracted look deepened, Megan became uneasy. With the natural egotism especially common to the young, she concluded that Jane was thinking about her. Perhaps the invitation had had a purpose more specific than mere congeniality. Jane was fond of her and Jane thoroughly disliked Lady Georgina—but that did not mean Jane wanted her for a sister-in-law. Jane appeared to be as indifferent to class distinctions as a woman could be—but, as Megan had learned, those who most loudly profess liberal opinions are often the first to deny the application of those principles to their own situation. She had never hoped to enlist Jane as a witting, committed ally; she had only intended to use Jane's prejudices for her own ends. Now she realized, sickly, that Jane could be a formidable opponent. She might even persuade Edmund that Lina did not require a governess.

Jane continued to pick at her food and avoid Megan's eyes. Finally the latter could stand the suspense no longer. If Jane would not speak, she would.

"Dear Jane, you seem distracted this evening. Is something troubling you?"

Jane pushed away an untouched plate of pudding and rose to her feet. "Am I as obvious as that?" she asked, clasping her hands behind her and pacing up and down.

"Candor and honesty are admirable qualities."

"Humph." The grouchy grunt was precisely the sort of sound her peasant grandfather might have uttered. Megan could not help laughing, but her anxiety had not been relieved. She was wise enough to avoid a direct question. After all, she might be wrong. There was no sense in putting into Jane's round little head ideas that had not been there before.

"Is it something to do with the estate?" she asked. "Or the mill?"

"Everything about the estate and the mill troubles me," was the gruff reply. "But there is little I can do about either. No doubt I am unreasonable. Everyone tells me I am. If enclosure must come, and I suppose it must, better that it should be done now than at some future time, when a less conscientious owner might control it. But I didn't mean to talk about that. The truth is, I am avoiding the subject foremost in my mind. It is . . . it is somewhat delicate. Perhaps I shouldn't mention it."

Megan clasped her hands to stop their trembling. She was tempted to remain silent, in the hope that Jane's delicate conscience would prevail and the damning accusation would not be made. But desperation gave her courage. Uncertainty was worse than anything Jane might say, and she had already begun to formulate her answer. Something along the lines of, "You don't suppose, Jane, that I would have the presumption . . ."

Before she could speak, Jane burst out, "It's that woman!"

Megan felt dizzy with relief. "What woman, dear Jane?"

"Lady Georgina. I think I hate her, Megan. I never, never really hated anyone before. It is a horrid feeling."

"She is not an agreeable person," Megan said.

"She is the worst possible influence on Edmund. And he means to marry her."

"I—" Megan checked herself in the nick of time. She was not supposed to know that. It was one of the pieces of information she had acquired from eavesdropping. She must pick her way carefully, as through a treacherous swamp. There were solid clumps of earth here and there—the facts she might legitimately know—but it would be fatally easy to slip and find herself sinking into the mire.

"I did not know that," she amended her statement. "I'm sorry you dislike the idea so much."

"Oh, Megan!" Jane swung around to face her. "How can you sound so calm and hypocritical?"

"In my position it is necessary to conceal my feelings. Perhaps that is hypocrisy. For me it has been a matter of simple survival."

"I know, I know. Maintain your reticence, it is your right. But there is no reason why I should not speak my mind to you, is there?"

"I would be honored to have your confidence." Megan smiled at Jane, and the latter's anxious, guilty face cleared.

"Well, then. It isn't selfishness that makes me dislike such a marriage, Megan—at least, not entirely. I want Edmund's happiness. He does not love that woman. He is dazzled by her rank and her—oh, I don't know what it is— I find her so detestable, it is hard for me to imagine how she could attract a man. He will be miserable with her. She will tempt him to extravagance he cannot afford and to acts that will undermine his honor—and her brother will aid and abet her."

Megan had time to collect her thoughts and frame a question that would not betray her. "Perhaps she will not accept him, Jane. Surely I have heard her express her contempt for what she calls "trade," and the people who live off its profits."

"Oh, yes, that is precisely the sort of stupid, prejudiced opinion one would expect of her. In fact, she wanted Edmund to sell the mill; can you imagine?"

"How ridiculous," Megan said.

"Yes; as if Edmund could be anything but a gentleman, whatever his occupation. If she loved him, she would not care what he did for a living. She wants his fortune, preferably in a large lump sum, so she can settle her debts and those of Lord Henry. But she will have him any way she can. She has few other suitors, and they are as impoverished as she is."

"Jane! How do you know that? You didn't—"

"I did." Jane nodded defiantly, though the crimson banners of embarrassment flamed in her cheeks. "I hated to stoop so low, but I felt I must. I sent a friend—someone I trust—to London to make inquiries. It was not hard to learn the truth. The Astleys are well known to the city moneylenders."

"In your place I would have done the same."

"Would you? You are kind to say so; for if a person of your high principles would consider it, I am not so wicked as I thought."

It was Megan's turn to blush. Jane mistook it for modesty and again apologized.

"I should not have brought the matter up. It was cruel and inconsiderate of me to intrude in the slightest way . . . to introduce a subject which might cause you. . . . Oh, dear. I won't mention it again, Megan, I promise. I just had to get it out; I was boiling and stewing inside, and it was driving me wild. I will do everything I can to prevent that marriage! There, I have said it. Thank you for listening to me. I feel much better now."

She meant what she said. Megan, finding the subject greatly to her taste, tried several times to bring it up again, but Jane refused to take the bait.

When they parted, Jane stepped forward and kissed Megan on the cheek. She had never done such a thing before. It was a visible demonstration of the statement she had not felt able to voice; it was the affectionate embrace of a sister.

Chapter Nine

MEGAN SAT at her dressing table, peering into the mirror and trying to twist a recalcitrant curl into place. It kept springing out in the most exasperating manner. Suddenly she let out a gasp and leaned forward, staring in dismay at the gleaming coil between her fingers. Was it—no, it could not be!—a gray hair?

After an agonized examination she concluded, with a sigh of poignant relief, that she had been mistaken. Not that premature grayness, or wrinkles, or any other sign of decay would surprise her; she felt as if she had aged ten years in the past month.

September had passed into October; the trees flaunted garments of crimson and amber, and the nights had a clear, crisp sharpness. Still the help she prayed for had not come; the "something" she needed was as far from appearing as it had ever been. Lady Georgina was still in the picture. In fact, she was in the house at that very moment, with her brother and a party of other guests.

With a guilty glance over her shoulder, as if someone were watching, Megan plucked a few petals from the crimson roses on the table—the last of the year. She rubbed them against her cheek. Gray hairs and wrinkles might not have appeared as yet, but she was undoubtedly losing her healthy color, and her face was thinner than it had been. They were the unmistakable signs of unrequited love.

Love, at least, did not waste away from lack of nourishment. If anything, her passion had grown. She knew every feature of Edmund's face; had she possessed skill in drawing, she could have reproduced it with utter fidelity, from the way his hair curled back from its center parting to the small bluish scar beside his firm chin. His voice sent waves of dizziness through her; the slightest movement of his hands roused wild dreams of touching and caressing. She had had several encounters of that nature with importunate employers, and the memories of fumbling hands and clumsy kisses, which had once made her shudder with disgust, took on a different aspect when she thought of Edmund's hands, Edmund's lips.

Recklessly she pinched off a clump of petals and scrubbed furiously at her other cheek. There was still hope. The engagement had not been announced, and until it was—until the marriage actually took place—she would continue to fight.

But she wished she had a more fitting battleground than the dark, dirty cellars under the house.

Edmund's most recent enthusiasm had begun ten days before. Bored with his architectural renovations, which were nearing completion, and forced to wait until the arrival of the commissioners before proceeding with his plans for enclosure, he had looked for a new interest and had found it, of all places, under the house. The cellars were not as extensive as the house itself, but they formed a sizable subterranean maze, and only a small part of them was presently in use. No one had ventured into the deeper recesses since Edmund's grandfather had made his first tour of inspection as a new owner. A thorough man, but a practical one, he had decided that the foundations were sound, the dirt incredible, and the space not needed; there was no reason why anyone should go into those regions again.

Megan had of course offered to go with Edmund when he announced his intention of exploring. In fact, she had jumped at the chance, for initially Jane flatly refused to take part, and Megan felt sure some useful inspiration would come to her while she and Edmund wandered hand in hand through the gloomy depths. There might be mice. Or a bat, whose fluttering, flapping presence would be ample excuse for a fearful maiden to fling herself against someone's broad chest. At worst she could stumble, or pretend to be afraid of the dark.

To her annoyance Jane changed her mind as they were preparing to set out. It was particularly vexing, because the cellars were as dark and nasty as Megan had expected they would be. The only thing missing was the bat.

Yet there was a horrid fascination in their tour; in the light of Edmund's lamp their shadows formed a phantom entourage, sometimes rushing wildly ahead, sometimes cowering back as if they had discovered some terror along the path. The rooms they passed were filled with incredible objects, most of them rusted or rotted into shapelessness, and looking unpleasantly like troglodytes or gnomes shrinking from the light that had invaded their kingdom of darkness. The feeling of oppression that weighed on Megan was not so much fear as awe; she felt like an intruder in an ancient tomb or a sanctuary where mere humans were not allowed to go.

"I hope you know where we are, Mr. Mandeville," she said at last. "I am completely lost; if I were alone I would never find the way out, and after wandering for days I would succumb to fatigue and terror—"

"And become one of the ghosts of Grayhaven," Edmund said with a laugh. "No fear of that, Miss O'Neill." He stopped and directed his lantern at the paper he carried. "This rough sketch of the plan of the house helps me to find the corresponding regions below. If I have calculated correctly, we are now under the Great Hall, not far from the chapel."

"I want," Jane said suddenly, "to find a stair. Going *up.*"

"Why, Jane, I am surprised; I thought you were afraid of nothing. Don't worry, your big brother will protect you. Let me see." Again he consulted his plan, and nodded. "Yes, there should be a flight of stairs at the end of this passage; they lead to the ground floor of the North Tower. There appear to be a few more rooms here; we may as well look at them as we go. But watch your step—the passage seems lower here. There is a ramp, or perhaps the remains of steps."

"I don't want to go *down,*" Jane insisted. "I want to go—"

"You made your point, Jane. The descent is not great, only a few feet, and I promise you we will soon be ascending."

Megan marveled at his cheerfulness. He seemed quite unaffected by the breathless discomfort that afflicted her and Jane. She took courage from the sight of Edmund's tall, graceful frame ahead. But she wished he would not swing the lantern so casually. The shadows leaped in a maniacal dance.

He offered his hand when they reached the part of the passageway where the floor dipped down. Jane declined his assistance; needless to say, Megan did not, and even through the depression that weighted her spirits she felt the customary thrill at the touch of his warm fingers.

"This looks interesting," Edmund said, indicating a closed door on their right, at the bottom of the slope. "Old oaken planks, almost a foot wide. And the ironwork is much more elaborate than we have seen elsewhere."

"I expect it is locked," Jane said hopefully.

"I am sorry to disappoint you," Edmund replied. His hand was on the blackened iron handle, and as he applied pressure, the door swung slowly open.

At first Megan saw nothing except darkness. The limited beam of the lantern showed no walls and only the dimmest suggestion of a darker substance underfoot. It was as if he had opened a door into infinite night.

Leaning forward, Edmund held the lantern out at arm's length and moved it from side to side. There were walls after all; and with their appearance the place lost its eeriness and became only a room, much larger than the storage rooms they had seen, but equally filthy and empty of menace.

Edmund stepped forward. Something crackled under his foot, like dry twigs breaking. He stooped to get a better look, and as the light dropped to illumine the floor, a simultaneous exclamation of surprise and disgust came from Megan and Jane. The rubble-strewn dirt surface was littered with bones, some brown and brittle, some pale and delicate as a Chinese carving in ivory. Most appeared to be rodent bones—at least they were small enough for that—but before she averted her eyes Megan saw one empty-eyed skull that was only slightly smaller than her clenched fist. A cat, or a gruesomely large rat?

Edmund went on, his forward progress marked by a series of crunching sounds.

"Amazing," he said. The room seized on the final diphthong and threw it back in a diminishing musical hum. As he continued to speak, the soft ringing accompanied his voice like a ghostly orchestra.

"This is quite unlike anything we have seen. Stone inner walls—and fine masonry, too. These columns with low arches above—the space between has been filled in, rather roughly. Miss O'Neill, you are the expert; have you ever seen this sort of work?"

For once his extended hand held no charm for Megan. "I —I would rather not come closer," she murmured.

"I quite understand. I'll come closer to the door. Can you see now?"

"It does remind me of something," Megan admitted, trying to concentrate on the stonework and not on the bone-littered floor. "I believe I have seen similar construction in old churches. St. John's Chapel at the Tower of London, for instance."

"I thought so." Edmund's gleeful voice roused the echo to spectral jubilation. "It is Norman work. Just think of it— eight hundred years old!"

He continued to exclaim as he made a circuit of the room. The crackle of dry bones and the incessant humming murmur inflamed Megan's nerves. She did not want to be the one to end the visit, or show lack of interest in the discovery that had delighted Edmund so much; but she wished Jane would suggest that they leave. Jane, however, stood silent beside her, seemingly as fascinated as Edmund.

Finally Edmund consented to go. There was another door to be investigated, but to Megan's relief it would not open.

They found the stairs, and as they emerged into the comparative brightness of the upper floor, Edmund began to laugh.

"You look like two frightened little owlets thrust from the nest," he chuckled. "Your feathers are ruffled, Jane."

Megan's hands went instinctively to her hair. She hoped she did not look as rumpled and smudgy as Jane. The latter's gown, face, and hair were liberally streaked.

"Never mind," Edmund went on. "You were intrepid explorers—for the most part—and I promise your suffering was not in vain. I think that in a few days I will have something exciting to show you."

Now, a week later, Edmund's surprise was to be unveiled. With the help of several workmen he had spent three days in the cellar, but he refused to tell Jane and Megan what he was doing, or allow them to join him. Emerging on the evening of the third day, flushed with triumph and exceedingly grubby, he had sent invitations for the weekend to a number of friends. They had arrived the day before; the promised revelation was to take place this morning.

After one last critical inspection Megan decided she was ready to appear. She meant to look her best; she had few enough opportunities to be in the same company with Lady Georgina and let Edmund compare their charms. As she went down the stairs, she heard the sound of voices from the drawing room. Except for the Astleys, these guests were strangers to her; and suddenly the prospect of walking into a room filled with critical, curious faces was more difficult than she had imagined. They sounded so at ease, so sure of themselves. . . . She nerved herself to go on. You are welcome in this house and in that room, she told herself. You have every right to be there. Edmund made a point of asking you.

If only she had some inkling of what he had discovered! She had read everything she could find on the Normans, but without a definite clue she was at a loss. One thing was certain, though. Lady Georgina would be even more ignorant and far less interested.

When she walked into the drawing room, conversation stopped and every eye turned toward her. The moment of discomfort was brief; Jane hurried to her side, and Edmund greeted her with a smile before turning back to the gentleman with whom he was conversing.

Jane went around the room with her, introducing the guests. Megan paid little attention to the names, for she had immediately observed that Lady Georgina was not present. There were only two women, both middle-aged and plain. Mrs. Merrick clung possessively to the meek little man who was presented as her husband. The other lady, a Miss Willis, had a long, mournful, sheeplike face and gold-rimmed spectacles. She looked so much like her brother that they might have been identical twins; her skirts were unfashionably narrow and her jacket was mannishly tailored. In general, the company was quite unlike the first group of guests Edmund had invited—older, less elegantly dressed, and tediously respectable in appearance.

When Lady Georgina appeared, she looked like an exotic

bird in a flock of crows and starlings, though she was dressed very simply in one of the riding costumes that suited her athletic figure best. She stood in the doorway, tapping her riding crop against her boot as if bored or impatient. When Edmund saw her, he broke off his conversation and hurried to her side.

"I began to fear something had happened to you," he said.

"When I am on horseback? You know better than that. I was tempted not to return until evening. Your new acquisition is a wonder, Edmund. He goes like the wind."

"You rode Bucephalus?" Edmund exclaimed. "He is still half wild; I gave orders that no one was to ride him."

"And I countermanded your orders." She smiled, looking directly into his eyes.

Megan's hands itched to slap the beautiful, smiling face. She was beautiful—in her way—and more unmannerly than any village lout. She behaved as if she and Edmund were alone in the room; she had not even taken notice of Jane.

"I suppose we must now have your dreary surprise," Lady Georgina drawled.

"Henry is not here yet," Edmund said.

"You know he seldom rises before noon. Never mind him. Let's get it over with." With superb insolence she took his arm and led him away.

Laughing but not unwilling, Edmund called, "Follow the leader," and beckoned the others to follow.

Megan's only satisfaction was the glance she managed to exchange with Jane. The latter's snub nose was elevated, as if she smelled something unpleasant.

As they made their way through the hall to the stairs, Megan found herself with Mrs. Merrick, who drew close to her and murmured, "Isn't that Lady Georgina Astley?"

"Yes."

"What a handsome woman she is."

For once Megan spoke as directly as Jane might have done. "I think she is very rude."

Mrs. Merrick put her hand over her mouth to hide a malicious smile. "Oh, my dear, the Astleys are known for their foul tempers. Her aunt is mad, you know—quite, quite mad. They keep the old woman shut up in the attic at Astley Hall, and the tenants say she howls like a wolf on nights when the moon is full."

Megan, who was regretting her lapse, reacted to this choice bit of gossip with a frigid stare, and Mrs. Merrick hastily added, "They are one of our oldest families, of course; the title goes back to the fourteenth century. So one must make allowances, mustn't one?"

They came to the top of the stairs just in time to prevent Megan from making another regrettable reply. Seeing how narrow and steep the steps were, Mrs. Merrick demanded her husband's arm, and Megan was able to get away from her.

Megan was not so far sunk in shamelessness after all, for Mrs. Merrick's ill-natured gossip had disgusted her, much as she disliked its object. What despicable snobs people were, tolerating from "our oldest families" behavior that would have been roundly condemned in a merchant or tradesman.

The passageway was so narrow they had to go two by two, like the animals entering the ark. Megan found herself with a tall, stooped man who was talking, apparently to himself, about Aristotle. When they reached the mystery room, she stared in surprise at the transformation the past week had wrought. The room was now brightly illumined by hanging lamps. The floor had been cleared of debris to a considerable depth; it was now several inches lower than the corridor, whose floor had formerly been on the same level. Stone paving blocks were visible; out of consideration for the sweeping skirts of the ladies, they had been swept clean as a parlor floor.

The others crowded in ahead of her, gathering in a circle around Edmund. Megan stood apart. Disinterestedly her eyes wandered around the stone-vaulted ceiling and walls. Thanks to her reading and the improved light, she was able to make a better appraisal of the room's features. The flattened arches and squat pillars, now reduced to pilasters by the filling in of the formerly open spaces between them, were certainly early twelfth century.

She must have spoken the words aloud; the tall, stooped gentleman, who had been circling the group like an anxious puppy, trying to find a gap in which to insert himself, turned to her as if he saw her for the first time.

"Yes, yes, you are correct, young lady; it is Norman masonry, without a doubt. Not unique, you know. Not at all. No. I could quote you half a dozen other examples. But rare. Yes. Certainly rare and unusual. Young Edmund has something remarkable here."

Hearing his name, Edmund looked up. "There you are, Professor. The rest of you must make room. You have had your chance; let the professor see."

Everyone moved back, except for Miss and Mr. Willis. They were on all fours, peering down at the floor.

The object of their attention was a slab of metal some three feet long. It had been polished till it shone like gold, and on its surface was the incised figure of a woman wearing a long archaic gown and ornate headdress. Her hands, clasped on her breast, held something that appeared to be a cross or crucifix.

"Ha!" The professor put his hands on his knees and bent over. "My dear fellow, how splendid. It is a monumental brass, and a fine one. One of your ancestors, I suppose."

After a moment Edmund said with a self-conscious laugh, "Someone's ancestor, certainly—or ancestress, rather."

"But what is it?" Mrs. Merrick demanded. "A portrait? And what is it doing down here?"

Her husband, obviously the scholar of the family, cleared his throat as if embarrassed by his wife's ignorance. Before he could explain, Jane said quietly, "It is a tombstone. There are others, all over the floor. Stone, instead of brass."

Mrs. Merrick gazed wildly at the paving stones. "Do you mean there are people buried here? How very odd."

"Most unusual," the professor agreed. "And very old—such brasses were common in the fifteenth century. In the majority of cases, however, only the figure of the deceased is of metal, set into a stone frame."

One of the Willises—it was difficult to distinguish which was which—raised its head and bleated, "The inscription is quite interesting, Mr. Mandeville. You have read it, no doubt; do you object to my taking a copy?"

"Not at all," Edmund replied. "I must confess I have not read it. The old script is difficult, and I am no scholar."

"Then you may be interested to know," said the other Willis, "that your ancestress's name was Ethelfleda."

Lady Georgina laughed. Her voice had such a note of wildness that the others looked at her in surprise.

"No doubt the lady was of Saxon blood," the professor said in tones of mild reproach. "It is a famous name, your ladyship; the daughter of our great King Alfred was Ethelfleda, Lady of Mercia. That territory included the county in which we—"

"Spare me the lecture, sir," Lady Georgina interrupted. A slight tremor, like a chill, ran through her body, but her forehead shone with perspiration. "History bores me. This place bores me. I cannot imagine why you brought us here, Edmund. I have had enough."

She started for the door. Edmund, visibly disconcerted, took a step forward and a step back, as if uncertain whether to follow.

"Antiquarian research is not to everyone's taste," Megan said, in her gentlest voice. "Perhaps we could come another time, Mr. Mandeville—those of us who care for such things."

After this hint the others were persuaded to follow Lady Georgina. Jane was the last to leave. Her expression of faint perplexity, as her eyes moved from the rude columns to the flagstoned floor, was lost on Megan. The latter was busy congratulating herself. It could not have been better—Lady Georgina's contemptuous disinterest, her own erudition and appreciation. She had even been given the chance to make excuses for the lady's rudeness.

She had no way of knowing that the seemingly trivial incident had far greater importance. Another invisible weight had dropped onto the scales that measured her fate.

Chapter
Ten

DURING THE following weeks Megan's spirits swung back and forth like a pendulum, now hopeful, now despairing. A smile or a compliment from Edmund made her hopes soar; his absences, many of them to Astley Hall, sent her spirits plummeting. Lady Georgina came no more. She had declared she could not endure the commotion and noise of remodeling; when Edmund was finished playing with his toys, she would visit him again.

Edmund reported this comment as if he found it highly charming. Megan, who had become adept at listening at keyholes, heard Jane's acrimonious reply. "Quite a superior attitude from someone who lives in a ramshackle tumble-down house and has no servants except those who work for nothing because they are too incompetent to find another position."

"Your prejudice makes you completely unreasonable, Jane," Edmund exclaimed angrily. "I won't discuss the matter again."

Hearing the note of finality in his voice, Megan lifted her skirts and tiptoed away from the door. Jane was so lacking in guile! Her rudeness only hurt her cause; but in a way, it was a relief to hear Jane say the hateful, biting words she yearned to say herself.

Jane was at loose ends, and was not at all happy about her increased leisure. Since Edmund had taken over the mill, she had not gone near the place. Megan knew, from Lizzie, that Jane had offered to initiate Edmund into the mysteries of the business—for mysteries they must be to him, after so long an absence—and had been curtly refused. At any rate, Edmund apparently had no difficulty taking up the reins. For the first few weeks after the change of command he had been at the mill every day. Gradually his attendance had fallen off; since the installation of the new manager, he had stopped going altogether. Instead, Mr. Gorm came once a week to the manor, loaded down with ledgers and papers. Megan had seen him once and could understand why Jane found him repugnant; he reminded her of Uriah Heep in Dickens' novel, always bowing and scraping and speaking in a soft, apologetic mumble. However, she told herself, an unpleasant manner did not mean he was not good at his job.

Though Lady Georgina avoided Grayhaven, her brother became a constant visitor, dropping in on Edmund with the familiarity of an old friend. On these occasions Jane would often ask Megan to dine with them, especially when Lord Henry was the only outsider present. Megan wished she could attribute this mark of distinction to Edmund, but she knew better; Jane disliked his lordship almost as much as she did his sister, and counted on Megan to distract his attentions to herself. The latter's position was unusual, and she knew she had to thank Lord Henry for some of the courtesy with which she was treated. She would like to have resented him for his sister's sake, but she could not help being flattered by his compliments. Jane had hinted of libertine and profligate habits. With a man that usually meant. . . . Megan knew what it meant, but preferred not to use the words, even in her private thoughts. However, Lord Henry had never shown that sort of interest in her. She could not have mistaken it, since she had experienced it before—once from an employer whose persistent attempts to seduce her had finally forced her to give up her position, and again from the eldest son of another household. She had lost that position, too, when the young man's mother discovered them struggling in a back corridor and, naturally, accused Megan of leading her innocent boy astray.

One evening when Lord Henry had dropped in, they were in the drawing room waiting for dinner to be announced when a disturbance was heard in the hall. The butler, an old servant who had been with the family since the time of Edmund's father, threw open the door and began, "Excuse me, sir, but there is someone here—"

He was set aside, gently but firmly, by Sam Freeman. Seeing a stranger, he stopped short. "Beg pardon, Mr. Mandeville—I did not mean to disturb you—but there has been an accident at the mill."

Jane instantly got to her feet, her embroidery falling disregarded to the floor. "How bad?" she demanded.

"Not good. Jack Moxon—Will's youngest—four fingers crushed."

"I'll come at once."

The exchange had been so rapid that the others had not had an opportunity to speak. As Jane turned, Edmund said loudly, "Sit down, Jane. You—Sam, is it?"

"Sam Freeman . . . sir." The pause was almost imperceptible, but it did not escape Edmund. His eyes narrowed.

"What do you mean by coming here like this? Are my employees unable to deal with such matters?"

"I have always come to Miss Jane and to her father, when there was trouble," was the calm reply. "It was by their wish. I thought you would want me to continue."

"You were mistaken." The explanation had done nothing to soothe Edmund's temper; and, indeed, it was conspicuously lacking in apology or humility. "The manager, Mr. Gorm, is the person to consult."

"Please, Edmund." Jane had ignored his order to sit down. She and Sam stood side by side, facing Edmund. The resemblance Megan had noticed was even stronger now, magnified by a common attitude and expression. They might have been brother and sister, confronting a mutual enemy. Edmund could hardly fail to notice this, and Jane's speech could not have been more poorly timed.

"Please, I must go—I had better go—Father always—"

"Must I remind you again that times have changed?" Edmund's voice was quiet, but the anger the presence of outsiders forced him to suppress crimsoned his face. "Freeman —the injured man is in the infirmary, I take it? A doctor has been called?"

Sam nodded. "I am glad to hear it," Edmund said sarcastically. "Then I fail to see why you are here. Miss Mandeville is not a nurse, her presence would only be a distraction. Get back to the mill. In future, report to Mr. Gorm, and do not come here again."

"Yes, sir." Sam's face had resumed its stolid blankness. His eyes shifted. "I beg pardon for disturbing you."

There was nothing obsequious in the words, or in Sam's dignified withdrawal. In fact, Megan had the distinct impression that the apology had not been offered to Edmund. Sam had glanced briefly at her when he spoke.

Jane remained on her feet, her hands twisted together. "It must have been the reed stop," she muttered. "I meant to have it replaced. . . ."

"For the love of heaven, Jane," Edmund cried. "Such inconsiderate behavior, before a guest—"

"My dear fellow, don't apologize." Lord Henry laughed and waved a negligent hand. "It has been most diverting— a glimpse into England's past, so to speak. The old paternalistic system, when master and man were one family."

The last word might have been innocently chosen, but it

brought a deeper frown to Edmund's face. "I believe I asked you to sit down, Jane. And tell me, pray, why the fellow had the impertinence to speak of you as 'Miss Jane.' "

Jane appeared to return from a great distance. "He might as well call me 'Cousin Jane,' " she replied. "Surely you remember that Grandmother Mandeville's maiden name—"

Dinner was announced at that moment, to Megan's relief. With Lord Henry's help she managed to keep a conversation going that did not include any references to the mills or the Mandevilles' family connections. Edmund did not speak a single word to Jane. Wrapped in her own thoughts, she appeared not to notice or care.

Later Megan went to her listening post behind the door in Jane's sitting room. She suspected Edmund was still angry with his sister; and sure enough, it was not long before he came.

Lizzie had mentioned other encounters between brother and sister, but this was only the second such meeting Megan had heard with her own ears. The tempers of both had worsened since the first confrontation. Edmund did not apologize or try to explain himself. He went straight to the attack, accusing Jane of lowering herself, encouraging familiarity from people who were beneath her, having common tastes that humiliated and degraded both of them. Jane counterattacked. Cruelty, neglect, and selfishness were only a few of the crimes she charged him with. But finally she broke down under the sting of his cold, venomous words. When she started to cry, Edmund left, shutting the door emphatically behind him.

Megan stood listening to her muffled sobs for some time. Rationally she was on Edmund's side, but her heart ached for her friend. She wished she could do something to comfort Jane; but of course that was impossible.

ii

AFTER THE commissioners completed the assignment of property to be enclosed, Edmund was busy fencing and developing his new land. He had learned that he was not only the principal landowner in the parish, but almost the only one; his father had quietly bought up most of the small independent holdings during the depression years of the forties, when farmers found it impossible to make ends meet. John had acted out of kindness, allowing the former owners to stay on as tenants and giving them a far better price than they would have been able to get on the open market, but that charitable impulse had proved to be a sound financial judgment as well. Edmund's only source of annoyance was that the village, and the land it occupied, had a separate status, based on some antique charter. All in all, though, he was immensely pleased with the results, and his mood was so exuberant that Jane was unable to quarrel with him, though she tried to do so when he hired a bailiff to manage the estate, as he had hired a manager to run the mill. Her father had always walked his own land. . . .

"And worn himself out before his time," Edmund retorted good-naturedly. "Leave business to me, Jane. Buy yourself some new frocks and bonnets—and what do you say to a personal maid? Someone who could arrange your hair and teach you how to dress properly."

Jane's new frocks were plainer than ever—dull grays and browns, with demure white collars. Edmund declared she looked like a Quakeress. Megan was sure he understood the nature of Jane's rather pathetic revenge; and, as if determined to conquer her, he announced that he meant to give a ball. If she did not order an appropriate dress, he would do it himself.

At first Megan was pleased by his excellent spirits. The hostility between Jane and Edmund made life uncomfortable for everyone—especially one who had heard their bitter exchanges and could not admit that she had. As time passed, however, his happiness made her uneasy. His financial situation did not seem enough to account for it; and the announcement of the ball brought her fears into focus. Lady Georgina had condescended to attend, since the house was now habitable, by her definition. If Edmund had reason to hope for a positive answer to his next proposal of marriage, he might announce his engagement at the ball.

It was to be the grandest affair ever given at Grayhaven. Unfortunately there was no ballroom, this basic necessity having been unaccountably neglected by earlier builders; and though Edmund had plans for an additional wing that would incorporate such a feature, he was too impatient to wait the year or more such a construction would take. It was Lord Henry who suggested a solution—why not use the Great Hall? The minstrels' gallery at one end would serve for the orchestra; the library could be used as a card room for gentlemen who preferred that amusement to dancing; and the drawing room could be set up with tables for supper.

Edmund was delighted with the plan and invented further improvements. The guests would wear costumes, medieval by preference. He would open up the portrait gallery, as he called it; and the chapel—

"Why not make that the card room?" asked Jane, who had listened in stony disapproval. "The decanters of whiskey and brandy would look fine on the altar, and the pews would be convenient for those who take too much to drink."

"Perhaps not the chapel," Edmund conceded. "But it is no use your throwing cold water on the scheme, Jane; you cannot put me in a bad temper. Have you decided on your costume?"

"Boadicea," Jane replied at once. "I shall paint myself blue to fit the part."

Edmund looked at her half in alarm and half in amusement. "An ancient warrior queen would suit you. But please —no blue paint."

"Then I won't come at all," Jane said, stitching away at a new apron for Lina.

However, by coincidence or intent, Edmund had struck upon an idea that could not help but interest Jane. She was an excellent needlewoman and enjoyed inventing new patterns. Once Megan caught her poring absorbedly over a volume of engravings showing notable personages of history—in costume. But she did not succumb completely until one afternoon in early November.

Snow had fallen the previous night, and the view from the window was a study in monochrome—gray skies blending into white ground, broken only by an occasional branch, leafless and stark, rising out of the ermine covering that had buried shrubs and bushes. The bleak landscape made Jane's sitting room seem even cozier; a fire blazed on the hearth and the lamps shone brightly. Lina was playing with her doll, and Megan and Jane were sewing when Edmund burst in.

"Disaster!" he exclaimed. "My costume has just come from London, and look what the wretch has done to it."

Megan had been trying in every way possible to learn what Edmund meant to wear. She had some notion of attempting a feminine version—Katherine of Valois to his Henry the Fifth, or a medieval lady to his knight in shining armor. Now she could only think adoringly how handsome he looked.

His knee breeches and long, sleeveless coat of rose-pink satin were trimmed with gold braid. The sleeves and collar of the shirt were fine white lawn, lavishly embroidered. In his hand he carried a plumed, broad-brimmed hat; now he clapped this on, completing the picture of a seventeenth-century cavalier.

"Look," he repeated in tragic tones. "The hat is well enough, but the jerkin is far too big and the shirt is even worse; the sleeves hang down over my hands. How can I draw my sword to fight for king and country if my sleeves get in the way?"

Yet he managed it quite neatly, whisking the blade from the scabbard and flourishing it aloft. Megan applauded, and Lina rushed to him, exclaiming, "Oh, Uncle Edmund, how pretty you are."

"Thank you, my dear." Edmund patted her head. "Jane, what am I to do with this wretched jerkin, or tunic, or whatever it is called? I haven't time to make another trip to London."

"Let me see." After tweaking and tugging and mumbling to herself, Jane announced competently, "It only wants taking in at the side seams, and the shirt at the shoulder line. Better still, I might remove the cuffs of the shirt and trim off the extra length there."

"I would be eternally grateful, dear girl. I'll change and bring it to you now."

After he had gone, Lina announced that she wanted a pretty dress like Uncle Edmund's, knee breeches, sword, and all. Especially a sword.

"I will make you one, sweetheart," Jane said absently. Catching Megan's eye, she added with a smile, "Out of silver paper and cardboard. Well, Megan, I suppose we must think of what we are going to wear. Have you decided?"

Megan simulated surprise. "I had assumed I would not be going to the ball."

"You sound like Cinderella. Of course you are going."

Edmund came back with the despised garments over his arm.

"Are you sure you have time for this?" he asked. "There is no decent tailor nearer than London, or I wouldn't impose; but I don't want to interfere with the sewing of your costumes."

"We were just speaking of that," Megan said, pleased that his use of the plural noun had confirmed her invitation. She had had every intention of attending, naturally, but was glad she had not been forced to use any of the devious schemes she had concocted in order to attain this end. She added, "We cannot decide what to wear. Perhaps you have a suggestion, Mr. Mandeville."

"It will have to be something simple for me," Jane said firmly. "Something rude and primitive—a Saxon maiden, perhaps, like the lady whose tombstone you found."

"Ethelfleda?" The name came smoothly from Edmund's lips, like that of a friend often spoken. "She was not Saxon, Jane, or a peasant; the professor said the brass was fifteenth century."

"The name is Saxon. The costume of that period would be easy to make—just a simple tunic and a mantle over it."

"Nonsense. You saw the elegance of her gown and head-dress. I like the idea, though, of coming as our ancestress."

"Edmund, you know she was not."

"She might have been. On the maternal side, at least, our family has lived in this region since heaven knows when. However, Miss O'Neill would suit the role better. She has fair hair."

"And how do you know Ethelfleda was fair?" Jane asked skeptically.

"You insist she was Saxon. Danes, Angles, Saxons—they were all blond, were they not?"

"I have not the least idea," Jane replied. "But perhaps Ethelfleda's maternal ancestors were also from this region—members of the small, dark race that lived here long, long ago. Persecuted by invader after invader, they sought refuge in the deep forest and became the gnomes and brownies of legend."

"What an imagination you have, Jane," Edmund said uneasily. "Do as you like; I leave it up to you."

Jane picked up the satin waistcoat and began taking out stitches. After Edmund had gone she worked in silence for a time, then cast the garment aside.

"I have an idea," she said. "Come with me to the linen room and let us see what we have."

iii

On the afternoon of the ball Megan stood before the long mirror in Jane's bedroom while the latter made the final adjustments to her costume. Her mouth full of pins, Jane mumbled, "Turn—more to the left."

Like the earlier ones, the final fitting was taking place behind closed and locked doors. Jane intended the costume to be a surprise; not even the servants were allowed to help for fear they would give it away.

Megan did not understand the insistence on secrecy, but she would have agreed to more outrageous demands than that. Jane had outdone herself this time, declaring, truthfully, that she sewed better than the village seamstress and meant to make the costumes herself. She had worked night and day on the dress, with Megan's help.

Thinking of Edmund's pink satin cavalier, Megan had suggested a seventeenth-century lady. There was a portrait in the gallery of a woman, perhaps the wife of the swarthy gentleman who resembled Charles the Second, in a lovely gown of that period. But Jane had something else in mind, and when the linen room failed to provide what she wanted, she had made a trip to Birmingham to find it. This was a measure of Jane's devotion to her scheme; she hated Birmingham, with its grimy streets and smoking factories. In one of the shops she had found a piece of ivory brocade, and carried it home in triumph.

The dress was creamy white with silver threads, its hanging sleeves and low neckline banded with strips of white fur vandalized from a winter coat Lina had outgrown. A broad silver sash belted the gown high under Megan's breasts. The oversleeves hung loose from the elbow, almost reaching the hem; long, tight-fitting undersleeves were made of sheer white muslin, as was the filmy veil that hung from the horned headdress. This last was Jane's masterpiece; she had wrestled with wires and horsehair for hours before constructing a framework covered with white velvet that looked like the illustration in the book she had chosen to copy. Silver nets, twinkling with brilliants, held Megan's hair in twin coils on either side of her face.

Jane rose and spat pins into her hand. "It's still too long. Take it off and I'll fix the hem."

Megan turned from her rapt contemplation of the mirror. There was little vanity in her appraisal; the gleaming figure looked like a statue carved of ivory and precious metal, not like the image she was accustomed to see in her glass.

"What of your own costume, Jane?" she asked. "The guests will be arriving in a few hours, and you must be downstairs to greet them."

"My costume is finished and everything is in order. Take it off, Megan."

Edmund had left little for his sister to do. He himself had supervised the servants in the arrangement of the downstairs rooms, and the kitchen staff had been baking and brewing for days under Lizzie's critical eye. That morning a consignment of specially ordered food and drink had arrived from London, together with the waiters who were to serve it.

Megan did not know whether she dreaded the ball or looked forward to it. Her sources of information—eavesdropping, gossip with Lizzie, even a covert examination of the daily post—had failed to deliver any evidence that Edmund's wooing had been successful. Yet something told her that the coming night would mark a turning point in her life, for good or ill.

Later in the afternoon she went to the nursery to see if Lina had settled down. The child had been in wild spirits all day, darting from room to room and getting in everyone's way. No one had time to play with her; her adored Uncle

Edmund scowled and told her to go to her room, and even Lizzie, who could usually be depended upon to greet her with hugs and sweeties, sent her flying from the kitchen with a smack on the seat of her little frock. Eventually Lina had been captured by the nurserymaid and carried upstairs howling and kicking.

When Megan entered the nursery, she was not surprised to see Rose collapsed in a chair, her cap all on one side.

"Where is Lina?" she asked, waving the girl back as she started to struggle to her feet.

A voice called out, "Don't look! Wait till I'm ready."

Lina's voice came from an alcove that had been curtained off to serve as a playhouse, an animal's lair, or the cave of Ali Baba, as conditions required. Before long she emerged and struck a pose.

"Look! I am just like Uncle Edmund."

Someone—and Megan thought she knew who—had made the child a miniature cavalier's dress in pink satin similar to that used for Edmund's costume. An old riding hat of Jane's, pinned up with a feather, perched atop her golden curls, and she waved a magnificent cardboard sword, painted silver, with a hilt wrapped in gold braid.

"You look splendid, darling," Megan said.

"Aunt Jane says that if I am very good she will come upstairs later and take me down so that I can peep in at the people."

"That is kind of Aunt Jane. Are you going to be very good?"

"Oh, yes. Aren't I, Rose?"

Rose grinned and rolled her eyes, but she seemed to have the situation in hand, so Megan went back to her room to dress, wondering how Jane had found time to make the little girl's costume. She had no idea what Jane planned to wear; would she really paint herself blue and swathe herself in a tablecloth, as she had threatened? It would be like Jane! Finally she gave in to her mounting curiosity and knocked on Jane's door.

"Who is it?" a voice demanded suspiciously.

"Please let me in, Jane. I am sure you must want some help in dressing."

Jane laughed. "I don't need any help. But come in if you like."

When Megan opened the door, she understood the laugh. It wasn't as bad as she had feared; Jane's rosy cheeks were not blue. But she knew Edmund would be furious.

Jane's dress was a simple cylinder of coarse wool hanging straight from the shoulder to the floor and tied around the waist with a scrap of the same fabric. The pattern was a plaid of soft brown and saffron. On her feet she wore plaited sandals. Her hair hung down in long braids. As Megan stared, she took up a brown homespun shawl and tossed it around her shoulders.

"There," she said. "An ancient British maiden, circa six hundred A.D. Don't stare that way, Megan. It is quite authentic. I found an engraving in a book."

"I—I don't doubt that it is an accurate copy, Jane. But I am afraid Mr. Mandeville won't be pleased with it."

"Why not? He wanted me to go as an ancestress; I am confident that my ten-times great-grandmother looked just like this. It is time I was going downstairs. *À bientôt.*" Flinging one corner of the shawl over her head, with a gesture worthy of Boadicea herself, Jane swept out.

Megan hastened back to her room, not knowing whether to laugh or wring her hands. She only hoped Edmund was in a good mood and would find Jane's little joke amusing.

Her own costume was easy to put on. The close-fitting undergarment was a simple shift that laced up the front. Only the sleeves and deep flounce at the hem were meant to show, since the ivory brocade robe covered the rest of it. This garment, with its wide neckline and flowing, gored skirt, simply slipped on over the head and was fastened under the breast with the silver girdle.

Megan shook out the long sleeves and turned to look at her reflection. Unlike Jane's, her room did not have a full-length mirror; but by stepping back she could see most of her figure in the glass over her dressing table. She had already arranged her hair in the loose coils demanded by the costume. Now she covered them with the nets, pinned the latter in place, and carefully lifted the headdress from its stand.

Perching there it had a grotesque look, more like a great white moth than part of a woman's attire; but when Megan settled it on her head, and the gossamer veil floated around her shoulders, it became part of a strangely glamorous ensemble, and the figure in the mirror was transformed into a person Megan scarcely recognized. The familiar contours of her face, even the shape of the underlying bones, looked different. In a sudden panic she pressed her hands against her cheeks and was foolishly reassured by the touch of her own flesh.

The guests had already started to arrive when she came onto the landing from behind the screen that had been set up to separate the family quarters from the rest of the house. At the foot of the stairs were Edmund and Jane, and an incongruous pair they made—the elegant cavalier and the diminutive figure in homespun. Edmund's rose satin and lace made Jane's plaid shift look even worse, but Jane appeared quite composed. Smiling and nodding, she greeted the guests as they arrived; and Edmund smiled and nodded too.

Megan slipped quietly down the stairs behind them and entered the Great Hall. Fresh coats of whitewash on the ceiling emphasized the magnificent patterns of the timbered roof, with its great beams lifting from wall to wall like the ribs of a ship. The floor had been sanded and waxed till it shone like glass, the walls were hung with tapestries or draped in satin. Hundreds of candles and lamps cunningly shaped to imitate antique torches made the room bright as day. Hothouse plants in huge containers turned one corner into a charming bower, with chairs and couches for those who were not dancing. From the minstrels' gallery on the far wall came the sound of the orchestra tuning up.

The room was filling rapidly. Edmund had invited all the county families and many friends from London. There were quite a few knights in armor and ladies wearing Mary Stuart caps. The Elizabethans were also popular; Megan saw at least three women in farthingales and red wigs. The effect was dazzling—rich soft velvets and shimmering satin, the glitter of gems, the flash of lamplight on swords and silver shoe buckles—particularly after evening parties where half the participants were garbed in funereal black. But Megan was happily aware that her own costume was handsomer than any other, and that people were turning to look at her.

A touch on her arm roused her from her contemplation of the brilliant scene. When she turned, a little cry broke from her. Looming over her was the figure of a monk, all in black; his hands were hidden in his loose sleeves and his hood shadowed his face.

The monk let out a ringing laugh and threw back his hood, showing the face of Lord Henry.

"My dear Miss O'Neill, forgive me; I could not resist joining you, since we make such a striking contrast—you in white, the spirit of purity and virtue, and the Black Monk, in all his sinister menace. Purity suits you, my dear; you are very lovely tonight."

Megan saw that he had been drinking. His speech was smooth and unslurred, his movements controlled, but the unusual floridity of the compliment, and the glitter of his dark eyes, betrayed him.

"Yours is certainly an effective costume," she said.

"I chose it for that reason, and for its comfort. Look at those poor fools in armor! How they plan to trip the light fantastic in those clanking suits I cannot imagine; and before the evening is over they will feel like boiled lobsters. Speaking of dancing, Miss O'Neill, I hope you will honor me with the first waltz."

Though she would rather have danced with Edmund,

Megan was relieved of the fear of standing alone when the music began. She smiled a gracious acceptance.

"I have not seen your sister, your lordship. She is here, of course."

"Oh, yes. You mustn't ask me to describe her gown; I have no skill in such things. But I see a certain lady bearing down on us like a ship in full sail. I am sure it is you she wishes to speak to, so I will beg to be excused. I will return in time to claim you."

The lady in question was Mrs. Merrick, who greeted Megan as effusively as an old acquaintance. At first Megan was a trifle puzzled by her warmth, but she soon discerned the reason for it. Mrs. Merrick was in search of gossip.

"Is it true?" she asked in a hoarse whisper. "Is Mr. Mandeville announcing his engagement this evening?"

The shock was so great that Megan was unable to control her emotions. Mrs. Merrick mistook the sudden rigidity of her expression and hastened to reassure her. "Oh, I am such an old friend, they would not mind if you told me. Then I would be in a position to confirm or deny the rumors I constantly hear; for idle gossip, you know, is something one does not like to encourage."

"I know nothing of an engagement," Megan said.

"Oh. You would know, being such a confidante of his sister's. . . ."

"Excuse me." Megan walked away, hardly aware of where she was going. After blundering into a potted aspidistra she found a chair and sank down onto it.

A few moments of quiet allowed her to recover herself. What did Mrs. Merrick know? She was probably the originator of the rumors she had mentioned; her mean, probing little mind would always be inventing stories.

Megan managed to cling to this comforting thought until Jane and Edmund entered the room. Jane was on the arm of Sir William Gilbert, their nearest neighbor, a gruff old gentleman of sixty-odd. Edmund escorted Lady Georgina.

She wore the very dress Megan had thought of wearing —the graceful flowing skirts and wide lace collar of a cavalier's lady. The broad-brimmed hat with its white plumes had been adopted by seventeenth-century ladies from the headgear of their husbands; it suited Lady Georgina's arrogant, handsome features. Her face wore its usual half-smile; she seemed fully conscious of the honor she did Edmund and the others by deigning to appear. And Edmund shared her opinion. He strutted like a peacock. But, oh, how handsome he was! And what a pity men had given up satin and lace for dull black broadcloth.

The music began. Jane hopped off with Sir William, who displayed the energy, if not the skill, of a much younger man. Edmund swept his partner into the dance. Her eyes fixed on the latter pair, Megan saw the other dancers only as a brightly colored blur. Then the broad green leaves before her were swept aside, and a face peered in.

"So there you are," Lord Henry said. "Not shy, are you? No reason to be; you are the most beautiful woman in the room. Come, or we will miss the first waltz."

She was nineteen years old, and if modesty prevented her from accepting Lord Henry's compliment at face value, she knew she was one of the prettiest and best-dressed women present. She could not help enjoying herself, even if her heart was breaking.

Socially the evening was a success. The men begged for dances and the ladies glared jealously. What more could any young lady ask? But for Megan the affair was not complete until Edmund finally asked her to dance. His look of admiration made her heart flutter.

"You are magnificent, Miss O'Neill. I ought to have offered a prize for the finest costume; you would certainly win."

"The lady in the costume deserves a prize too," said Lord Henry. He had hardly left her side all evening, and Megan was beginning to find his proprietary air annoying. "Don't infringe on my territory, Edmund; Miss O'Neill has promised me all the waltzes."

"Then she will have to break her promise," Edmund said, offering his arm.

The warmth of his touch, around her waist and on her hand, made her forget Lord Henry and everything else except the fact that she was, at long last, in the arms of the man she loved. After they had circled the room, their steps matching perfectly, she observed that he was frowning slightly, and she asked, "Is something wrong, Mr. Mandeville?"

"No, nothing. Except . . . his lordship. I trust he has not offended you in any way."

This was an advantage she had not expected. In a flash she sorted through a variety of possible responses.

"No, sir," she murmured, lowering her eyes.

Edmund's arm tightened protectively.

"Don't be afraid of complaining to me. His lordship is my dearest friend, but you are under my protection, and any insult to you is an insult to me."

"I thank you, Mr. Mandeville, from the bottom of my heart. Rest assured I would not hesitate to seek your protection; I feel the most complete confidence in your kindness."

She tipped her head back and looked into his eyes with an expression of limpid trust, hoping to heaven that her headress would stay in place. He was visibly affected. A deep breath made the ruffles at his breast quiver.

Megan's heart sang. Her feet seemed scarcely to touch the floor. After an interval Edmund said, "I cannot get over my admiration of your costume. You are the picture of the noble lady I envisioned when we discussed the subject recently."

"Jane deserves the credit. It was her idea and her workmanship."

"So I assumed. If only she would devote the same attention to her own appearance!"

Megan's eyes followed his to where Jane stood talking animatedly to a stout lady in Grecian robes. She had wrapped the homespun shawl around her arms and looked like a little French peasant girl of the poorest class. Megan laughed and shook her head.

"Jane will never fall victim to feminine vanity. But her sweetness of character must make everyone love her. I will never forget her goodness."

She meant every word she said, but she knew her generous praise would sit well with Jane's brother. Unfortunately the music ended before she could say more, and Edmund did not ask her to dance again before the supper interval was announced.

Lord Henry had earlier claimed her for this. When he came to find her she saw he had been at the decanters in the library again. His face was flushed, and when she took his arm he pressed hers close to his side in a familiar manner.

Megan took care to seat herself in such a way that no further familiarities were possible. She was only too well acquainted with the pressure of knees and hands under the table. Lord Henry did not persist; instead he devoted himself to the wine, and when the supper was over she managed to elude him.

It was now well after midnight, and the energy of the dancers had flagged. Some of the older county families had gone home; others wandered off or lingered in the drawing room, stuffing themselves on the exotic delicacies provided by the London caterers. Megan was a little tired too. She had refused one partner and was sitting quietly in the corner when she saw Lord Henry weaving through the dancers, his eyes searching the room. He was now showing the effects of liquor and she did not want to dance or talk with him. There was no point in risking possible embarrassment unless Edmund was nearby to champion her. She slipped out of her corner and down one side of the room until she reached the door leading to the portrait gallery.

After the heat of the ballroom the corridor was delightfully cool and quiet. Many of the candles had burned out; the others, flickering in the draft from the windows, gave the painted faces on the wall an eerie illusion of life. Eyes seemed to wink, lips smiled or scowled. Outside the darkness was complete, except for the pale glow of snow on the ground. As she stood taking deep breaths of the cool air, she saw a few white flakes flutter down.

Benches and antique chests had been placed along the wall, but no one occupied them now. Megan was about to sit down when the door behind her rattled, as if an unsteady hand were attempting to open it. Not wishing to encounter Lord Henry in such a deserted place, she stepped into one of the small rooms leading out of the gallery. There were three of them, hardly more than alcoves, and barely large enough to contain a few chairs and a low table or two. Edmund had arranged them nicely, with plants and hangings. They offered few hiding places. Hearing heavy, uneven footsteps approaching, Megan lifted one of the hangings and stood behind it.

The footsteps paused at the door, and after a moment the voice she had expected to hear said loudly, "So there you are. I have been looking for you."

Before her heart could skip more than a beat, the sound of an answering voice told her that this time she was not the object of Lord Henry's search.

"You had much better stay away," Lady Georgina drawled. "He will not propose with you standing by."

"Damn. Then he hasn't spoken yet? I told you, Georgie—"

"Lower your voice, Henry."

"Why the devil should I? You were a fool to refuse him the first time—"

"You are drunk," said his sister coolly. "Curse it, Henry, you'll spoil everything. If you must talk—and I see you must —let us at least find a private spot. No, not there, it is not private enough. This way."

Megan knew she must follow. Never again would she have such an opportunity to hear an unguarded, candid conversation between these two. She tiptoed to the door and peered out. The passageway was empty in both directions, and the chapel doors stood wide open. Holding her skirts to keep them from rustling, she stole quietly along the passage and looked around the door. The Astleys were standing near the altar, talking in low, vehement tones.

The only possible hiding place was behind the door—not the one on this side, she would be visible to anyone coming from the ballroom. Again she glanced into the chapel. Lord Henry had collapsed into a front pew and his sister was bending over him. Megan darted across the opening and took up a position behind the other leaf of the door.

The first words she heard made her thrill with indignation.

"For God's sake, don't fall into a drunken stupor here," Lady Georgina exclaimed. "Edmund's delicate pride would be mightily offended if he found you drunk and snoring in his precious chapel. I thought you were after that little chit of a governess. Though it would be better if you waited till Edmund and I are married."

"Can't wait," Lord Henry grumbled. "Waited a long time already. No harm in it, Georgie, she's ready and willing."

"Then go and find her."

"Not yet. First—make sure of Edmund."

"That is my task. I can finish it tonight if you will keep out of my way."

"You've got to manage it, Georgie. We can't hold off creditors much longer. Damned insulting duns. . . ."

"I have him in the palm of my hand. I need only close my fingers."

"Poor Georgie. A fine thing for a woman like you—you deserve a prince or a duke."

"Edmund will do well enough. I can endure his low connections for the sake of his money. And there are other compensations. . . ."

Lord Henry laughed and made a suggestion that brought the blood rushing to Megan's cheeks. She clenched her fists. If only Edmund could hear this!

When the door at the end of the passage opened and she saw the rose satin costume, she knew that for once her prayers had been answered. Her nails dug into her palms. Just a little longer, Holy Mother—make him walk softly, make them go on talking.

Edmund was normally light on his feet. Tonight he seemed particularly anxious not to be heard. He advanced slowly, peering into the alcoves as he passed them. He was some distance from the chapel when he heard the voices; as he came nearer, Megan shrank back, fearing he might catch a flash of white through the crack.

Lady Georgina was trying to convince her brother to go, but Lord Henry had passed into the lachrymose, sentimental stage of drunkenness, and continued to lament his sister's sacrifice. Hence the first audible words to reach Edmund's ears were, "Poor, dear Georgie. Marrying a low-bred boor to save your wretched brother. He will never forget you, darling girl."

Edmund stopped as if struck in the face. If he had entertained any doubts as to Lord Henry's meaning, Lady Georgina's reply removed them.

"I have my own duns to think of. Marriage is the only way out, and thanks to our somewhat questionable past, Edmund is the only man fool enough to offer for me. Stay here and sleep it off, then; I am going to—"

Edmund had moved forward, each step slow and wavering. Lady Georgina's speech broke off in a gasp when she saw him; but she made a valiant attempt to undo the damage.

"Ah, Edmund. Have you come looking for me?"

"I was looking for you," Edmund said.

"And I for you, dear Edmund. But poor Henry is not himself; I found him and brought him here to rest, wishing to spare you—"

"You wish to spare me? It is too late, Georgina. I heard what you called me."

"Edmund, what can you possibly mean?" Her wheedling

tone rang false, but she might have persuaded him, he was so anxious to believe in her, if it had not been for Lord Henry.

"Oh, why the devil pretend, Georgie? Edmund . . . Edmund's man of the world. Knows a fair trade when he sees it. Business proposition, marriage. Old honorable name, title —money. Fair enough."

"Get out." Edmund's voice was barely recognizable. "Both of you. Get out of my house."

He had advanced far enough into the room so that Megan could no longer see him. It was not difficult to follow the ensuing action, however.

"Now, old chap, keep calm." Belated awareness of his error sobered Lord Henry somewhat. The pew creaked as he got to his feet. "Just a joke, that's all. Heard you coming, and thought we'd play a little joke."

The sound of a ringing slap, a shriek from Lady Georgina, and a muffled oath from Lord Henry were followed by a moment of tense silence.

"You'll pay for that, Mandeville," Lord Henry said thickly. "By God, you'll pay."

"I have paid, and dearly," Edmund replied. "Must I call the servants to put you out?"

There was no audible reply. Megan could well imagine the burning looks and sneers that were being exchanged. Then Lady Georgina came into her field of vision, closely followed by Lord Henry. They paused for a moment; exchanged a silent glance; Lord Henry offered his arm; and the pair walked, with some dignity, along the gallery and out of sight.

It was several minutes before Edmund followed them. His face was ashen except for two spots of hectic color high on his cheeks, and he swayed like a man who had received a mortal wound. Slowly he reached for the chapel door and started to close it.

Megan had only seconds in which to think what to do. Edmund was in a state of shock, barely aware of what he was doing, but he could hardly miss seeing her when he closed the door behind which she was standing. Bad enough to be caught in the humiliating pose of a sneak and eavesdropper; but if Edmund knew she had overheard his humiliation, he would never want to see her again. She flung herself to the floor and closed her eyes.

It was a risk, a terrible risk; she dared not open her eyes even the slightest slit. But she heard Edmund's exclamation and felt his hand first on her shoulder, then on her cheek. She did not stir when he slipped his arm under her and lifted her so that she was supported by his bent knee. After he had repeated her name several times, in tones of growing concern, she let her eyelashes flutter.

"Thank heaven," he exclaimed. "I feared. . . . What has happened?"

"Where am I?" Megan murmured. Then her eyes widened, and she shrank away from him. "Unhand me, you villain—I will appeal to Mr. Mandeville, he will not allow. . . . Oh! It is you, Mr. Mandeville! Thank God! He pursued me, he caught me here, when I tried to hide from him, he. . . . I remember nothing more."

Sobbing, she turned her face into Edmund's shoulder.

The tears were genuine. She was suffering from intense nervous strain. But one part of her consciousness waited, coolly, to judge how the performance had affected Edmund.

"Did you see Lady Georgina?" he asked.

"I remember nothing from the moment that fiend overpowered me till I opened my eyes to see your face."

"So you have been their victim too," Edmund muttered.

Megan decided to pretend she had not heard this. She sobbed more violently. Edmund's arm pressed her close. "There is nothing to fear now," he said gently.

There was no calculation—at least, not much—in Megan's heart when her arms stole timidly up to embrace him. She had dreamed of this moment for so long. Edmund's quickened breathing assured her he was not immune to the appeal of her yielding body and tearstained face. His vanity having been wounded by one woman, he found solace in the adoration of another. Their lips met in a long, passionate kiss.

After that it was a foregone conclusion. Edmund raised her to her feet.

"Will you marry me, Megan?"

Chapter
Eleven

JANE WAS delighted. At least Jane said she was, and Jane never lied. Megan decided she must have imagined the fleeting expression—not so much a frown as the shadow of one—that passed over Jane's face when she learned Megan was to be her sister.

Jane was the only one to be told. Megan found Edmund's reasons for waiting quite reasonable. It was necessary for her to be better known in the neighborhood, her parentage and position announced. He did not want the slightest hint of patronage to mar her acceptance as his wife. He had worked it all out with a painstaking concern that touched Megan deeply. Even her wardrobe—she must begin dressing in a manner suited to her new station. As the elegance of her attire increased, so would the respect with which she would be treated, as Jane's friend and equal—an old family connection, happily renewed.

Megan would have agreed if he had proposed introducing her as a descendant of the lost Dauphin, and rightful Queen of France. She drifted through the days in a fog of happiness; the bleak winter days seemed bright with sunlight.

The sun finally did shine one day, after a week of sleet and rain, and she decided to take some needed exercise by walking to the village. She wanted to run and dance and shout her exultation to the skies; and she did let out a shout or two once she passed the park gates. Then she settled down to a brisk walk, swinging her arms and smiling idiotically at everyone she met.

The village was not as pretty as she remembered. Closely curtained windows and closed doors had an air of rejecting strangers; the once bright little gardens were barren stretches of earth and dried weeds. The section of houses where the mill workers lived might have been wholly uninhabited. A meager wisp of smoke from an occasional chimney was the only sign of life, and there was a new look of indifference or neglect—a broken gate here, a window stuffed with rags instead of glass, a dangling shutter.

Like the rest of the village, the shop was empty. Megan had learned to share Jane's fondness for the place, which was at once haberdasher, milliner, draper, and half a dozen other establishments. Some of the merchandise had not been disturbed in twenty years. New acquisitions were simply piled on top of the old, and a customer who had time to rummage in the heaps of odds and ends might come upon unexpected treasures.

Mrs. Miggs, the proprietor, was a widow and a foreigner —that is to say, she had come from Somerset thirty years before to marry Mr. Miggs, and the villagers still regarded her as an outsider. She was a cheerful soul, shaped like a cottage loaf and possessing a mind as pleasantly disorganized as her stock. Perched on a high stool behind the front counter, where a row of large glass jars held the bright-colored sweets Lina favored, she sat knitting all day long, shouting suggestions and questions at her customers without ever leaving her seat. When Megan entered that morning, to the musical jingle of the bell over the shop door, she looked up from the bright blue scarf she was knitting, but her greeting lacked its usual heartiness.

Megan wondered what ailed her, but did not ask; Mrs. Miggs's troubles were her own affair. She began turning over the untidy piles of merchandise. It was like a treasure hunt. She found a paper of old-fashioned boot buttons, half of them missing, and a saltware mug with busts of the Queen and Prince Albert—a memento of the royal wedding, fifteen years before.

Seeing a shimmer of blue among a coil of bootlaces, thread, and knitting worsted on a nearby table, she started to untangle it, and found a pretty bit of ribbon, suitable for Lina's doll. All at once an object in the corner, which she had taken for a heap of old clothes, stirred and mumbled. Megan started, pricking her finger on a darning needle entwined in the yarn. Looking again, she found herself under the intent scrutiny of a pair of malevolent black eyes, presumably part of a face almost hidden by shawls and scarves.

"Good morning to you," she said. "I did not see you before."

A wrinkled, blue-veined hand emerged from the wrappings and clawed at the folds of fabric, disclosing the face of an old woman—or possibly an old man—the beady little eyes and shrunken face had lost all distinctions of gender. An orifice appeared under the bony nose and a shrill voice squeaked out a comment. Megan could make nothing of it; the mouth appeared to be quite toothless. She nodded and smiled, though the tone had been far from affable, and then hurried back to the counter with her ribbon.

"I am afraid I disturbed your—your friend," she said in a whisper. "I did not see her . . . him?"

Mrs. Miggs sighed deeply. " 'Tis Mr. Miggs's old mother. Her do have her liddle house, but never won't stay there in winter, her comes to me and. . . . Noo, miss," for Megan had turned, intending to render the courtesies her ignorance of the bundle's identity had prevented her from making before.

" 'Tain't no manner of use to speak; her hears none o' what you zay—"

A peremptory, high-pitched grumble gave the lie to this comment. Mrs. Miggs's face sagged into lines of deep depression. "There, you zee—her do hear what her wants to hear! That's tuppence, miss, and thankee for your trade."

"It is good of you to care for your mother-in-law," Megan said, proffering the coins.

"Her'll drive me to my grave, miss, that her will," said Mrs. Miggs in tones of gloomy conviction. "Eighty-odd years old, but her'll see me coffined. The customers won't come when she's by, they be that frightened of the old witch —oh, yes, that's how they call her. And she do bless for the bleeding, I'll zay that. . . ."

"I assure you, you won't lose my trade," Megan said, trying to conceal her amusement. "I'm not afraid of witches. Nor is Miss Mandeville."

"Her do favor Miss Mandeville. The dear Lord knows why; her do favor no one else." The old woman squealed out a comment, and Mrs. Miggs shouted angrily, "Bide quiet, Mam, unmannerly you be, speaking zo about the young lady."

"What did she say?"

"I'll not repeat it. Her's an ignorant old body. Don't you be a-listening to she."

"Please don't worry about it. I will hope, on your account, that we have an early spring. Good day, Mrs. Miggs—" She raised her voice and added, "Good day, Granny."

A low growl was the only response to this courtesy.

When Megan left the shop, the sun had gone behind heavy clouds and a cold wind tugged at her bonnet. She regreted her decision to walk; her new black pelisse, trimmed with beaver, was quite warm, but the return journey, uphill and in the face of the wind, would not be pleasant.

As she started up the street, she saw a familiar form

approaching. His brisk stride and cheerful whistle made the gray skies a little less dismal. Catching sight of her, he came to meet her, cap in hand.

" 'Tis not a fit day for you to be out," he said; but his smile robbed the words of their sternness.

"Good morning, Mr. Freeman," Megan said.

"It looks like rain," Sam said. "I'll walk with you a ways —if you've no objection, that is. I'm going that way."

"I would be glad of your company." Megan did not point out that he had been going in the opposite direction.

They walked in silence for a time. Sam was deep in thought, and Megan saw no point in wasting conversational elegancies on a man who was not accustomed to that exercise. When they reached the workers' town, she could not help exclaiming, "How dreary it looks, and how ill-kept. One would think they could at least keep the houses painted and make necessary repairs."

"Paint costs money," was the sharp reply. "The old squire kept the place up proper. His son chooses to buy gewgaws for the great house instead of roofs for his tenants."

"You must not speak of Mr. Mandeville that way," Megan said coldly.

Instead of being offended, Sam smiled at her. "Your loyalty does you credit, miss."

They had left the village and were on the road leading up to the park gates before he spoke again.

"I've educated myself, you know. Been to school the past six years."

Megan was secretly amused. Rich or poor, gentleman or peasant, men were much alike. All of them cherished the delusion that a woman was certain to be fascinated by their accomplishments and ambitions.

"I would have thought you were too busy at the mill to find time for school," she said.

"It's at night I go. Mr. Knightly, at Northgate, holds classes at his house. He's a learned man, Mr. Knightly."

Megan was impressed. Northgate, a neighboring village,

was almost five miles away. It required some dedication to cover the distance several times a week, after a long day at work.

"You go on foot?" she asked.

"Mostly." He added gruffly, "I'm learning Latin. Mr. Knightly said last month I was ready for it. Do you know Latin, miss?"

"I have studied it. But I suppose you think women should not trouble their heads with that sort of thing."

"Why not? Women have brains, just like men. And you can't judge brains by their size; look at Miss Jane, she's got more sense in that little head of hers than—"

He broke off with a sheepish glance at Megan. She decided to overlook what would obviously have been another slighting remark about Edmund if Sam had not stopped himself.

"You are to be commended for improving yourself," she said pleasantly.

"I won't be a foreman all my life. I've got plans." Sam plodded on for a few more paces, his lips moving and his brow furrowed. Suddenly he burst out, "My mother would like it if you would take Sunday dinner with us."

The invitation was so unexpected that Megan forgot to watch where she was going. She stumbled over a rut, and Sam caught her by the arm. He continued to hold it as they stood facing one another; and his embarrassed look confirmed the suspicion that had taken root in her mind. She was not well acquainted with rural customs, but she thought she knew what this invitation implied.

"I'm sorry," she said. "I fear that is impossible."

Once over the first hurdle, Sam faced the others like a man. "I love you," he said. "I don't have much to offer now, except that; but I'd work for you, there's nothing I wouldn't do to make you happy. I don't expect you to care for me, not yet. All I want is a chance to make you care."

Megan tried to feel angry and offended. Sam had no way of knowing she was already promised to another man; but the difference in their stations was great enough to give her legitimate cause to resent his offer. Yet the simple dignity of his speech made it impossible for her to be indignant. She tried to soften her refusal.

"I am flattered and touched, Mr. Freeman, truly I am. But I am engaged to someone else."

He had not expected an immediate acceptance, but he had not anticipated a final blow to his hopes. The healthy color drained from his face, leaving it as gray and rigid as stone.

"I'd not want you to break a promise," he said slowly. "If it's a promise from the heart, and not some outworn word, from childhood maybe, that you've no mind to now. . . ."

The situation had become very uncomfortable. With some notion of ending it quickly and cleanly, leaving no room for forlorn hopes, Megan said, "I am to marry Mr. Mandeville. So you see—"

"Him!" The word exploded like an epithet. "Him, with his pride and his vanity? Oh, my little dear, he hasn't the wit to see your worth; he thinks to deceive you and shame you. . . ." And he caught the astonished girl into a close embrace, pressing her head against his heart.

Megan's initial protest was muffled in the folds of his rough jacket. Her attempts to push him away were totally ineffectual; she might as well have been pressing against a stone wall. Finally she managed to turn her head enough to make her voice heard.

"How dare you! Let me go this instant."

Sam obeyed so promptly that she lost her balance and would have fallen if he had not taken her by the shoulders.

"I know it's hard for you," he began.

"It's a lie," Megan shouted. "I love him and he loves me —and we are going to be married—and— Look here. Look at this, if you don't believe me."

She tugged at the gold chain around her neck and succeeded in drawing from under her bodice the ring it held. She had worn it next to her heart night and day since

Edmund gave it to her. The sapphire sent out a sullen blue spark, as if echoing her angry defiance.

The ring, or her rage—or both—convinced Sam. Instead of letting her go, his fingers tightened till she winced with pain.

"So it's true. You'd marry a villain like that—a man without kindness or caring. Oh, but he's a gentleman, isn't he? It's jewels and fine clothes and warm living you want—what do you care that they are paid for with blood? 'Twill be a fitting match—pride and vanity with greed and selfishness!"

He pulled her roughly to him and kissed her on the mouth.

His lips were hard and chapped. The painful grip of his hands was no embrace, but an angry assault. He let her go as suddenly as he had taken her. She stumbled back, one hand nursing her bruised lips, the other groping for support. It found a bare branch, whose thorny surface scratched her palm through her thin kid glove.

"Wait," Sam said hoarsely. "I never meant— Let me tell you—"

When he put out his hand she fled, staggering and stumbling, expecting at every moment to be seized and held. When she reached the top of the hill she had to stop; her stays were too tight, and every breath stabbed like a knife. Looking apprehensively back, she saw he was nowhere in sight. He had retreated, like the coward and bully he was.

Her bonnet had come off and was hanging down behind, held only by its strings. She bundled her hair into its net and put the bonnet back on; then walked slowly toward the gate, her hand pressed to her aching side.

Edmund would rave when he heard. He would see to it that Sam lost his job at the mill; he might even want to charge him with assault. Megan made a wry face. No, she would not tell Edmund. She didn't want to speak of it to anyone, or think of it again. The incident had been disgusting and degrading. The very thought of it made her feel contaminated.

But she couldn't help thinking about it. Again and again the memory returned, so vividly that she seemed to feel again the burning pressure of his lips on hers and the bruising strength of his arms.

Jane was the first to notice her abstraction. "Why, Megan, did I see you shiver just now? Come nearer the fire. You look quite pale this evening."

"I trust you have not taken cold," Edmund said. "You ought not have walked so far today. After this, take the carriage."

"I have not taken cold; I am only a little tired," Megan answered.

A short time later, when Jane left the room on some errand or other, Megan went to Edmund and sat down on a hassock at his feet. "I am out of sorts tonight," she murmured. "Can you guess why?"

"If I knew, I would take steps to make it right," Edmund said, caressing her curls.

Megan switched to French. Things sounded so much more elegant in that language. "I love you so much, Edmund. I want to belong to you, completely. How much longer must we wait?"

They were married three weeks later, in the village church, with half the county in attendance and the conventional crowd of loyal tenants outside. One face was conspicuously absent; but Megan had not expected he would attend.

Book Two
JANE

Chapter
One

JANE PUT down her pen and pressed her fingers against her aching eyes. Her head ached, too. That was what happened if you were foolish enough to pour over columns of crabbed figures by lamplight.

If only she had more time! But the account books must be back in the countinghouse before morning. She would not have been able to get them if she had not forgotten to give Edmund her extra set of keys.

She was almost certain Mr. Gorm, the new manager, was embezzling money. However, her examination of the books had failed to uncover definite evidence. Gorm's accounting system was unfamiliar to her—but then, she thought humbly, she had never learned the proper way, only the old-fashioned methods that had satisfied her father.

She had protested when Edmund mentioned that he had decided to replace Bert Osborne. Bert had been with the firm since her father's time. She could not imagine the place without his tall, stooped figure bent over the desk in the outer office. Admittedly he had become a little absent-minded in recent years, but if she kept a watchful eye out for neglected entries, there was no problem. Honesty and dedication were rare qualities, as Edmund would one day learn.

She had tried in vain to follow Gorm's system of balancing expenditure against income; also the figures for the past quarter seemed to be missing. Yet the mill must be making money, Edmund spent it lavishly enough. He was generous, too, always asking her if she wanted an increase in her household allowance. Remembering the days when she had known to the penny precisely how much she had to spend and where it came from, she sighed and reached for the pen.

It was useless. She had neither the time nor the skill to understand the accounts, and even if she had, they represented only a fraction of the information she needed. Edmund's personal accounts, the estate records, breakdowns of wages and salaries—there was no way she could get her hands on these, and without them she was helpless. The last item was the one that worried her most. She had a nagging sense of something badly wrong, though the total paid out for wages in the last year was the highest she could remember.

She had deliberately stayed away from the mill since Edmund took over its management. It had been a mistake, her offer of working with him until he learned the business; she might have known it would offend his masculine pride. But she had maintained a covert contact through Sam, and some of the things he told her worried her a great deal. Of course one had to make allowances for Sam's prejudices; he had become a fiery radical of late, and although she had a certain sympathy with that position herself, she had been shocked by some of the quotations he hurled at her. She feared Mr. Knightly had been recommending dangerous books to his star pupil. That man Engels, for instance. . . . And where had Sam gotten his ideas about trade unions? They were no longer illegal, but some employers would instantly discharge a man who tried to organize his fellow workers.

Now even that tenuous contact was gone. Sam had left the neighborhood several months earlier, without so much as a word of good-bye. He was working in Birmingham, so the report ran. His departure increased Jane's feeling of isolation and helpless ignorance; desperation had finally forced her to the degrading expedient of stealing—there was no other word for it—the account books.

Winter scratched at the window with sleety fingers. It would be a nasty ride in such weather, over the hills and into the teeth of the wind that rattled the barren boughs like dry bones. She knew she had better get it over with, but instead of rising she slumped lower in her chair. The bitter unseasonable cold was a physical reflection of the desolation that blighted her spirits. It was hard to believe that April was already here.

One year ago, almost to the day, she had climbed the hill and watched the black rainbow arch over Grayhaven. "A purely natural phenomenon, scientists say. . . ." But the dark glamour of the sight had affected her strangely, and she had felt a shock of superstitious terror when the slender girl's figure had materialized out of the night. The People of the Hills could bring good luck or the reverse. Some said they were the spirits of the heathen dead, who had lived before the birth of the Saviour; not good enough for Heaven or wicked enough for Hell, they lingered on, shrinking and fading. More often than not the wishes they granted had a way of twisting and turning on the recipient, just as Megan's coming had signaled the end of peace and happiness at Grayhaven.

Jane pushed the unkind thought away. She truly loved her sister-in-law, and scornfully discounted the malicious whispers about penniless girls who captured wealthy men. Megan adored her husband—sometimes to excess, Jane feared. She had been delighted when Edmund announced his intention of marrying the girl for whom she had come to feel the affection of a sister. Not only did it remove the danger of the Astleys, but it proved Edmund had not been corrupted by pride. He chose to marry for love.

But even there. . . . Only yesterday Megan had come to her room in floods of tears, having just discovered that her hopes of becoming a mother had been shattered again. Administering the sisterly pats and hugs appropriate to such distress, Jane had said soothingly, "But, my darling girl, it is early days yet. You have plenty of time."

"Do you really think so?"

Jane suppressed a smile. "I am a mere spinster, of course, and should not have opinions on such matters; but I really do think so."

"I know I am being silly." Megan wiped her eyes. She had the knack of crying without the usual disfigurements of swollen eyes and red nose. Tears only made her blue eyes look bigger and softer, and her wet lashes, stuck together in starry points, appeared to be an inch long. "You are such a comfort, Jane. Only—Edmund wants a son, so much."

Jane could not deny it. He had begun speaking of his plans for the as yet nonexistent child immediately after his marriage, with a solemn gravity that had given his sister considerable amusement. It was all part of Edmund's harmless snobbery, this wish for a son and heir to carry on his name.

She did not mention this to Megan, but consoled and teased her back into her usual sunny spirits. Now, in the dull solitude of pre-dawn darkness, even that unimportant incident seemed a portent of trouble to come. The wind had dropped to a steady moan that sounded like Megan's desolate weeping.

With an effort, Jane forced herself to move. She had little enough time as it was; the mill opened at six. And she was talking herself into a fit of depression, sitting here and imagining trouble where none existed.

She put the account books into an oilcloth bag that would protect them from a betraying trace of damp. Edmund would have exclaimed in horror if he had seen her; she wore a pair of his old trousers, shortened and retailored by her own hands. Riding astride was much easier; besides, the costume reduced the chance that she might be recognized. When she had tucked her hair up under a cap like the one the millhands wore, she looked like a little boy.

The trickiest part of the adventure was getting out of the house unseen. However, she was now the only one on this corridor. Edmund and his bride occupied his old room, and Lina had been relegated, greatly against her wishes, to the former nurseries. Edmund did not share his sister's views on the training of the young.

Jane took the precaution of covering her trousers with a long cloak before she crept out of her room. To think that she had come to this in the space of a single year—stealing like a thief, disguised and apprehensive of discovery, through the halls of her own home.

ii

THE FOLLOWING week spring burst through the bonds of winter like a freed prisoner. Some of Edmund's new plants, unsuited to Midland winters, had succumbed to the cold, but the common country blossoms were undaunted by weather. Snowdrop and crocus and primrose duly made their annual appearance, and Jane decided life was not as dreary as she had thought.

Though still suffering from the remains of a severe cold, she decided to celebrate the season by making a trip to the village. The inclement weather had kept them all housebound for weeks, and when Lina begged to go along, Jane could not refuse. Edmund had not seen fit to find a new governess, nor had Jane suggested it; she still thought Lina too young for formal education. But the child missed Megan's attention. Not that Megan was unkind—quite the contrary. Of late, however, she had rather avoided Lina, as if the sight of the child reminded her of something she did not want to think about.

On their return, Jane delivered Lina to the nursery and went in search of Edmund. She found him in what had become his favorite retreat—the library. Here he spent several hours a day writing or poring over books whose titles she had never bothered to examine. Usually Jane respected his desire for quiet and privacy, but on this occasion she burst into the room without knocking.

"I have just now returned from St. Arca," she announced.

"How interesting." Edmund closed his book. "Naturally I would not expect you to keep such momentous news to yourself."

Jane hated it when he spoke in that drawling, sarcastic voice. He did not use it often, but it never failed to annoy her, and now it acted like salt on an inflamed wound.

"The town has changed in a way I would not have believed possible in such a short time. The new warehouses and dreadful little houses near the railroad station—sprung up overnight, like mushrooms and no more substantial—"

"You seem to be accusing me of driving the nails and laying the bricks with my own hands. I have no control over what happens in the village."

"You own property there. And the mill workers' section is your responsibility entirely. I have never seen it so neglected. Everywhere I went I heard of leaking roofs, broken windows—"

"So you have been encouraging my tenants to whine to you. Thank you for your loyalty, Jane."

The cold anger in his voice, the level unsmiling hostility in his look, struck Jane like a blow. It was not the first time his remarks had affected her that way, however, and she tried to recapture the righteous indignation his accusation of disloyalty had shaken.

"I did not criticize you to them, Edmund, I only listened."

"You encourage them by listening. I had not meant to say

this, Jane; forgive and forget is my rule, and I thought it would serve no purpose to reproach you—but you have done me a great disservice in your handling of the mill and the estate. Oh, I freely admit it was not entirely your fault, Father was equally guilty; but the precedents you established between you by giving way to the unreasonable demands of every ne'er-do-well and malcontent have made things very difficult. It is high time the workers learned a little manly fortitude and independence. Let them make their own repairs. The houses were built for them, at a nominal rent—"

"Which you have recently raised."

"And if you had had the courtesy to ask why I did so, instead of ranting like a termagant, I might have tried to explain the need for the act. Under the circumstances I decline to do so." He opened his book and began reading.

There was enough justification in his criticism to weaken Jane's resolve. Wretchedly she acknowledged her error. By losing her temper she had only injured the people she meant to help. Edmund might have responded to pleas and flattery; the damage was done now, and any further speech would only make matters worse.

Nor would this be a good time to ask for an increase in her household allowance. She would have to wait a day or two, so the connection was not so obvious. She walked slowly out of the room, her head bowed and her steps lagging, the picture of submission; but her mind was already busy at work trying to think how she could remedy the ills she had seen, without angering Edmund even more.

iii

WITH THE small means at her disposal, Jane managed to make some of the necessary repairs, though not as many as she would have liked. If Edmund noticed, he made no comment;

but she supposed he was unaware of the changes, since he seldom went to the village. She was glad he did not ask her about them, for she might have been forced to admit that her efforts had resulted, not in thanks for what had been done, but in sullen resentment for what had not. Somehow a wall had grown up between village and great house, and through no choice of her own she was on the wrong side of the wall.

Relations between her and Edmund were back to normal, on the surface, at least. To do him justice, he was always pleasant and affectionate—unless she did something to annoy him. In an effort to return his goodwill, she inquired about his reading, and was told he had determined to improve his understanding of history and the fine arts. This somewhat unexpected interest puzzled her at first; then she realized Edmund was trying to find an avocation that conformed to his notions of the proper occupation for a gentleman. A leisurely, dilettante's pursuit of knowledge was quite acceptable, provided the information acquired had absolutely no practical value.

The peace treaty between Russia and the Allies had been signed at the end of March, but official celebrations were delayed until May 29, which was declared a national holiday. Bonfires, rockets, and fireworks blazed out across the land, but Edmund irritably refused to attend the festivities in the village, where the bonfire had been abuilding for weeks.

"Peace should be welcomed with prayer, not pagan ceremonies. Mr. Higgins will think us barbarians."

The gentleman referred to was the new vicar, who was dining with them that evening. He had replaced Mr. Jones, who had died in January. Among the applicants for the living, Edmund had discovered Mr. Higgins, who was a former schoolmate—at least they had been at the university at the same time. Jane rather doubted they had been close friends, for Edmund's interests at that time had not been academic. She liked Mr. Higgins; he was the only one of

Edmund's new friends who combined the manners of a gentleman with the inquiring mind of a student. His diminutive stature and jerky, quick movements, together with his protruding front teeth, reminded her of a squirrel, and he had the exuberant curiosity of that small animal. He approved of Jane, too, perhaps because she was one of the few women of his acquaintance who were noticeably shorter than he.

Observing a trace of wistful regret on the vicar's face when Edmund vetoed the bonfire, she said teasingly, "I think Mr. Higgins likes fires. I know I do; there is a little of the pagan in all of us, isn't there, Mr. Higgins?"

"Er—well—I suppose that is true." Mr. Higgins could never quite make out when she was joking. "At least in the sense that our modern holidays, even those of the Church, may incorporate features that go back to prehistoric times."

"But bonfires are a universal expression of rejoicing," Megan said. "I remember as a child dancing around a great fire in the castle courtyard. It was a yearly event, and we children had not the slightest notion of its significance, if any; we simply enjoyed the dancing flames and the air of celebration."

"Aha!" Mr. Higgins sat up alertly. "You speak of your family seat in Ireland, Mrs. Mandeville? You are privileged to have seen a dying custom, long since disappeared except in remote regions of Scotland, Wales, and your native Hibernia. I would wager the date was the first of May, was it not?"

"It was sometime in spring," Megan replied. "I can't remember the precise date."

"Near enough, near enough." Mr. Higgins actually bounced with excitement. "Yes, you saw the Beltane fire. The word surely derives from Baal, the name of the ancient Phoenician god so frequently mentioned in Holy Scripture. There is a similar ceremony in Perthshire, where my brother-in-law resides; it is the lingering remnant of an ancient sacrifice, when the ashes of the immolated victim were scattered on the fields to ensure good crops. But forgive me, ladies—I see by your looks of astonishment that I have offended your delicacy by referring to such brutish customs. I am apt to be carried away by my enthusiasm; it is a fault I must learn to curb."

"You credit us with more delicacy than we deserve," Jane said with a smile. "My sister-in-law is better educated than I, but even I know of the cruelties of ancient religions. We must be thankful that the Christian faith has introduced kindlier customs."

"Yes, certainly," Mr. Higgins agreed; but he looked so depressed at the thought Megan could not help laughing.

"Cheer up, Mr. Higgins, I am sure you can find a number of horrid pagan ceremonies, even in this modern country. Tell him about the harvest festival, Edmund."

Mr. Higgins pricked up his ears interestedly as Edmund good-naturedly complied.

"Fascinating!" he exclaimed. "I look forward to observing it for myself. Like the Beltane fire, the ceremony of the Corn Maiden or Corn Mother has almost died out. Curious that it should survive here, so close to factories and railroads."

"You haven't heard the whole of it," Edmund said. "I am one of the chief actors, and if I may say so, I play my part very prettily. Next year I shall put on a good show for you, since I know what to expect. Though Jane coached me in advance, the sight of those fierce beldames rushing at me was much more terrifying than I had expected, and the grip of their bony old hands was surprisingly rough. I was secretly relieved when they only tied a garland of flowers around my arm, instead of beating me with their sticks."

He told the story in his best style, with gestures and exaggerated looks of alarm, but Mr. Higgins did not join in the laughter.

"Your alarm was justified," he said seriously. "That rude shock of corn you described is a degenerate descendant of a fertility goddess once worshiped in this area. And two thousand years ago, my dear Edmund, the ladies would not have bound a garland around your arm. They would have cut your throat so that your blood would ensure the next harvest."

Edmund burst out laughing. Jane, with a more sensitive understanding of the little vicar's feelings, exclaimed in mock horror, and Megan added, "How dreadful, Mr. Higgins."

"Oh, my unfortunate enthusiasm!" Mr. Higgins smote himself heavily on the brow. "I would not for the world have distressed you ladies."

Megan assured him she was not deeply stricken, and the incident was forgotten—or would have been, had not Mr. Higgins continued to berate himself whenever he thought of it. Jane grew quite fond of him, and accepted with calm amusement the infatuated glances he began to bestow on her. She knew he would never have the courage to ask for her hand; he was a younger son, with no means except his stipend, and he was wise enough to sense he would not be welcomed by Edmund as a brother-in-law.

Mr. Higgins became a frequent caller, and it was he who carried the distressing news of the catastrophe that came upon them in midsummer. He came to the house asking for Edmund, who was engaged in one of his infrequent meetings with his bailiff, so Jane invited the vicar to join her and Megan in the drawing room until Edmund was free. Instead he remained standing in the hall, his normally cheerful face so grave that she immediately asked what was wrong.

"I don't know that I ought to mention the matter to you ladies," he explained solemnly.

"I assure you, I am only too well acquainted with sad cases of illegitimacy and crime. They occur here as well as in the city."

"I wish that were all."

Jane longed to take him by the shoulders and shake him.

Nothing irritated her so much as being treated like a child —or a woman. Fortunately Edmund came along just then, and Mr. Higgins concluded Jane was strong enough to bear the bad news.

"There is cholera in the New Town. One of the children works in the mill; so I thought I ought to warn you, Edmund, that there may be other cases among your workers."

Cholera was a tragic commonplace in the cities, but thus far St. Arca had remained remarkably free of the dread disease, escaping even the terrible epidemic of 1848. The saint had thereby acquired some reputation as a patron of good health, for the villagers would have laughed at the suggestion that the stream from which most of them derived their water could have anything to do with the matter.

Jane knew better. It required far less common sense than she possessed to make the connection between overcrowded, insanitary living conditions and the recurrence of epidemics such as cholera and typhoid. Only the year before she had read a pamphlet by a London physician named Snow—published at his own expense, since none of the medical journals would accept it—which proved beyond a doubt that an outbreak of cholera in a particular section of Soho had been caused by a single contaminated well. That the first case here should be in New Town, with its refuse-strewn streets and foul dwellings, confirmed the assumption. Surely the immediate improvement of these conditions was the only way of preventing future epidemics—even, perhaps, of controlling the present outbreak. If she could convince Edmund and the other property owners of this. . . . But there was little chance of that, when the brilliant medical deductions of Dr. Snow had failed to convert even his own colleagues.

Preoccupied with these thoughts, she failed to note the significance of one word Mr. Higgins had mentioned. When it dawned on her, she broke rudely into the conversation.

"Did you say one of the children works in the mill? How old is it?"

Mr. Higgins looked surprised, but he answered readily, "Nine or ten, I suppose. As an old bachelor I am not skilled at judging—"

"Be quiet, Jane," Edmund said curtly. "Higgins, am I to understand that you visited that infected house before coming here?"

"I was called, so of course I went," Higgins answered. For once there was no apology in his voice or manner, only astonishment that the question should have been asked. Jane almost loved him in that moment, but poor Mr. Higgins was never to know the degree of her regard. He went on, "Of course, I changed my clothing and bathed before coming. I felt I had to talk with you at once; this is a serious matter, and we must act."

"I suppose so. Well, come into the library. No, Jane—" for she had instinctively started to follow. "I will talk with you and Megan later."

As they walked away, Jane noticed that Edmund kept as far away from the vicar as he possibly could. She went to the drawing room, and since she saw no reason to conceal a fact that must soon be generally known, she told Megan about the cholera. They were discussing it when Edmund came in.

"Isn't Mr. Higgins joining us?" Jane asked. She would have liked to show the vicar some sign of favor; heaven knows she had teased him often enough.

"He has already gone, and he will not be coming again."

"Why, Edmund?"

"No one from the village is to be admitted, nor goods of any kind. Whatever we need will be brought from Warwick or Birmingham. The servants who wish to be with their families must go now and not return. None of us will leave the grounds until I decide it is safe to do so. I speak particularly to you, Jane. I know your romantic notions, and I will not have you trotting off with baskets of medicine to nurse the sick."

"I had no such notions, I assure you," Jane said angrily.

"But we can't shut ourselves off from the entire world. With sensible precautions—"

"I warn you, Jane. If you violate my orders, if you go to the village or the tenants' houses, I will not admit you back into the manor. I will not take the slightest risk of bringing infection here. It is my duty as a husband, and as a father of children—though I admit those prospects seem never likely to be realized."

Megan's head jerked as if he had struck her. Jane was too appalled to reply at first.

"Very well, Edmund," she said, after a moment. "I will do whatever you say."

"I expect no less, Jane. Higgins seems to have the matter well in hand. I have promised him any financial assistance he requires—within reason, of course. I hope you will admit I can do no more."

"It seems so," Jane said.

"I am glad you approve." Turning to Megan with an affectionate smile, he went on, "You see, my dear, there is nothing to worry about. You won't mind a few weeks of quiet retirement; we will entertain ourselves quite pleasantly, I assure you."

Jane made her excuses and got away as quickly as she could. How could Edmund speak so fondly to his wife after administering that cruel and unwarranted rebuff? It was as if he had no recollection of saying the words—as if some stranger had taken possession of his physical body and used his vocal cords.

She fled to her room and threw herself down on the sofa. It was not the first time she had sought that refuge; the faded chintz had been pummeled by her fists and spotted by her tears, and even kicked, upon occasion. As she lay there, the familiar scent and feel of the fabric calmed her and she was able to think more clearly. There was no excuse for Edmund's unkind words, but perhaps there was some reason for the state of mind that had prompted them. He was panic-stricken, frantic with fear. His actions made that plain, however calm and logical he might appear. So much for her plan of persuading him to investigate the New Town water supply and clean up the filthy sewers. Reason and common sense could not reach a mind solely concerned with personal survival. But why was he so terrified? Had his new responsibilities destroyed his former careless confidence?

Then the answer came to her and she wondered why it had taken her so long to understand.

Disease had killed more men in the Crimea than the blades and bullets of the enemy. The army hospitals had been pestholes of disease, with a mortality rate of 42 percent until Miss Nightingale took charge. In the overcrowded wards and corridors the men had been packed like herrings, so close they were actually touching. Edmund must have seen cholera—may have watched in helpless horror while men at his very side passed through the ghastly stages of the disease—the vomiting and diarrhea, the agonizing muscular cramps and the final collapse. She had read a description and had found it horrifying; how much worse to see the reality, not at a safe distance, but within inches of one's eyes.

Feeling a little better, Jane sat up and brushed the hair from her face. She must be more understanding. She had no right to judge those who had suffered while she remained safe and sheltered at home.

Relieved, to some degree, of one source of distress, she suddenly remembered another. Children. A child of nine or ten working in the mill. Not only was that a violation of her father's principles, it was against the law.

This time the flare of indignation was briefer, perhaps because she was exhausted by emotion. Or perhaps, she thought, as she dropped back into the embrace of the old sofa, I am finally learning to control my quick temper. . . . There was no sense confronting Edmund with her accusation in his present mood. Besides, she did not know the facts. Her father had paid little attention to labor laws, since conditions in his factory were always far better than those demanded. Jane tried to remember what he had said about the last Act, that regulated the hours of employment in the textile mills. Something about children under nine—but had the Act prohibited younger children from working, or had it only limited their hours of work? She could find out—but why bother? For every complaint she made to Edmund, he would have an answer—logical, sarcastic, and irrefutable.

Chapter
Two

T HAT SUMMER was as hot as the winter had been savagely cold, as if nature were attempting to strike an average for the year. The older inhabitants, mopping streaming brows, declared they had never known such weather. At least Jane assumed they did, for she had no contact with anyone outside the house. Her ignorance of what was happening was the hardest part of the ordeal. Edmund was her only source of news—where he derived his, she did not know—and his reports were terse and infrequent. So many new cases, so many recoveries, so many deaths. . . . Sometimes Jane was tempted to run away, like a workhouse child, with a bundle under her arm and her trinkets done up in a kerchief. Common sense always intervened; her sacrifice would not help the sufferers, and she could not abandon Lina and Megan.

She was worried about Megan. The girl's increasing pallor and listlessness might be attributable to the heat and the tension, but Jane suspected there was another reason. Edmund was no help; he spent more and more time alone, sometimes reading, sometimes dabbling in his latest hobby, painting. He had taken drawing lessons in his youth but had never displayed any special talent, so Jane was not surprised when his rendering of "Grayhaven Manor from the Hilltop" made that stately residence appear to have been struck by a small earthquake. Her lack of appreciation had been obvious; since then Edmund had not shown her his paintings. Nor had he included his wife in his private diversions. As Megan's pretty looks faded, he seemed almost to avoid her.

Jane got into the habit of walking to the end of the park every day and looking out through the gates, which were now closed and chained, by Edmund's orders. As she stood there with her face pressed against the bars, she felt like a condemned prisoner—or, more appropriately, the unwilling resident of a superior sort of asylum for the insane.

One afternoon she stood looking out, as she had done so often. She had forgotten to put on a bonnet or hat, and the sun beat down on her bare head. The air was thick and heavy as oil, without the slightest hint of a breeze. A pale haze dimmed the sunlight without lessening its heat. If only it would rain, she thought wistfully. A good violent thunderstorm would clear the air.

At first she doubted the evidence of her own eyes when a form appeared on the road, among the green gloom of the overhanging trees. Passing from shadow to sunlight and back into dappled shade, it gradually advanced; and, catching sight of her wistful face peering out through the bars, it raised a black shovel hat and waved it in greeting.

"Mr. Higgins!" Jane cried. "Is it really you?"

He stopped a careful ten feet away and, taking a handkerchief from his pocket, wiped his perspiring face.

"You have no idea how glad I am to see you," Jane said eagerly. "How glad you are safe and well! I have been worried about you. You look pale, and very tired . . . but I don't know why I am babbling like this, instead of letting you talk. Tell me everything. Tell me what is going on."

Impulsively Mr. Higgins started forward, beaming till his teeth seemed to protrude at right angles to his face; but he caught himself before he had taken more than a few steps. Perspiring even more profusely, and trying not to, he did not attempt to reply until she had stopped speaking.

"You cannot be more pleased to see me than I am to see you, Miss Mandeville. And may I tell you how much I appreciate your kind expression of interest in my welfare! It is more than I had any right to expect, and I can only—"

Jane had thought of him, with genuine interest and concern. Now that she saw him unscathed, she began to lose patience with him.

"Tell me what is happening," she interrupted.

"Happening. Oh. I am delighted to be the bearer of good news, Miss Mandeville. We have had no new cases for over forty-eight hours. I think we may hope that the worst is over."

"Thank God," Jane exclaimed.

"Believe me, I do. Yet the suffering has been great—very great. It is strange; the rest of the country seems to have been unaffected. His ways are indeed a mystery. . . ."

He turned his handkerchief in his hands, as if looking for a dry spot. Jane said reluctantly, "I must not keep you standing in the heat, Mr. Higgins. I hope we can welcome you at the house before long, and then you can tell us more."

"That is a pleasure I have long looked forward to. And I must not keep you; you ought not to have come out without a head covering, Miss Mandeville. I will just leave my letter here in the usual place. Perhaps you had better step back. Edmund has not yet removed his restrictions, and although some of them are in my opinion excessive, I am in complete sympathy with his refusal to risk the slightest danger to those he loves."

He would not come forward until she had backed away.

She watched incredulously as he placed a folded paper in a crevice in the gatepost.

"Is that how you communicate with Edmund?"

"Yes. I believe," Mr. Higgins said with a faint smile, "that the missive is removed with firetongs and fumigated before he opens it. However, I am in complete sympathy with his refusal to—"

"It does seem excessive," Jane said, having heard this opinion already. "And inconsiderate. You have enough to do, I am sure, without this additional task."

"It is a positive pleasure, I assure you. I have often stood here looking at the house and thinking of you—of all of you—but, if I may be so bold, of you in particular, Miss Mandeville. . . ."

"I had better go," Jane said. "Until Edmund relaxes his rules—"

"Yes, yes, you are quite right. Let's hope my exile will not last much longer."

He stood looking after her until she was out of his sight. Jane smiled to herself and shook her head ruefully. She should not have greeted him so warmly. But she did not regret the encounter; the news was the best she had heard for a long time. Even the heat seemed less oppressive.

The hoped-for storm did not come. When they met for dinner, Megan said fretfully, "It is too hot to eat," and pushed her untouched plate away.

Edmund, who was eating his mutton with as much appetite as always, did not reply. Jane felt sure that by this time he had read Mr. Higgins' latest communication, yet he had not said a word about it. Finally she could contain herself no longer.

"Have you had any word from the village, Edmund?"

Edmund took another bite, chewed it carefully, swallowed, and said, "Yes. Higgins believes the worst is over."

"That is wonderful news!" The color flooded into Megan's pale cheeks. "Why didn't you tell us, Edmund?"

"I would have done so in time."

"Then we can go out," Jane said.

"If no more cases occur, another week should see the end of our isolation."

"A week!"

"Jane, I beg you will not glower at me in that mutinous fashion. You are very selfish to think only of yourself, in the face of the suffering others have experienced. I have had losses too, you know. Half the millhands were out at one time. Production has fallen by some twenty percent."

ii

WITH FREEDOM almost in sight, Jane found herself more bored than ever, and a few days later, when she discovered Edmund preparing for a journey, it was more than she could bear.

"Why can't I go with you?" she demanded.

"Jane, how childish you sound. I am going on business—to Birmingham, if you must know. I mean to avoid the village altogether, and I expect you to do the same." He laughed and tweaked her hair—a brotherly gesture he had not made in weeks. "Give me a smile instead of pouting and I will bring you a pretty present."

He laughed again when, instead of smiling, she made a rude face at him, but she was learning discretion; she waited until he had closed the door before muttering, "It's all very well for you to be cheerful. You can do what you like. Even Birmingham would look good to me!"

"He is not going to Birmingham."

She had thought herself alone; the voice startled her, so that she whirled around. Peering out of the shadows at the back of the hall was the pale face of her sister-in-law.

"He is not going on business," Megan continued.

"Where, then?"

Megan turned and walked away without answering. The

glimmer of her light summer dress faded into the darkness under the stairs.

Jane watched her, uncertain as to whether to follow and demand an explanation, or leave well enough alone. Edmund had referred so often and so bitingly to her blundering ways, her bluntness and lack of tact, that she had lost confidence in her ability to help others. She felt especially awkward about Megan. They had grown apart since the marriage. Jane regretted this, but felt it was only natural. Megan's primary loyalty must be to her husband. She didn't want to involve Megan in the arguments that so often divided her and Edmund; but perhaps she had gone too far in the other direction.

In an effort to recapture some of their former intimacy, she suggested they have an early dinner together in her sitting room. Megan seemed brighter and more alert at first. Glancing around the room, she said with a smile, "What happy memories this recalls! You were very good to me then, Jane."

However, she said nothing of a personal nature, and gradually Jane sensed something forced and unnatural about her vivacity and bright, rapid speech. Yet she was in no hurry to leave, despite her increasingly frequent glances at the clock. It was almost midnight when she rose, apologizing for keeping Jane so late.

"It's too hot to sleep," Jane said. "Don't hurry away."

"Oh, I shall sleep." Megan produced an unconvincing yawn. "I am very tired. I am sure I will sleep soundly tonight."

After she had gone, Jane sat thinking over her last words in an effort to understand the strange intensity with which they had been uttered. "I shall sleep; I will sleep soundly tonight. . . ." A possible meaning came to her; and she started up, putting out her hands as if to push the idea away. The strain of the past weeks had turned her brain, or she would never have thought of such a dreadful thing.

She got ready for bed, hoping sleep would cure her of her

sick fancy; but in the darkness the monstrous thought grew stronger, swelling like some obscene fungus. Megan had no reason to take her own life and every reason to live; but lack of reason was the essence of insanity. What did she know of Megan's family background or her private fears?

Jane knew she was being morbid, but she couldn't stop herself. After squirming and tossing for what seemed like hours, she gave up trying to sleep. She would look in on Megan. She would feel like a fool in the morning, but anything was better than lying awake imagining senseless horrors.

The night was hot and breathless. She didn't bother with a gown or slippers, but went straight to the door. Surefooted in the dark, for she knew every inch of the way, she moved along the corridor and was about to step onto the landing when she heard a sound that made her draw back into the shadows. It came from the other corridor, where Megan's room was located.

After a moment or two a faint light appeared. Normally Jane was not superstitious, but she had worked herself into such a fit of the vapors that she half expected to see one of Grayhaven's ghastlier apparitions—Rob Romer, executed for treason by the Virgin Queen, carrying his head under his arm, or the White Lady, wringing shadowy hands and weeping tears of blood. Before she had time to become really frightened, the candle and the person who held it passed into her field of vision and on down the stairs. It was Megan, fully dressed in a dark, slim gown, her hair neatly coiled around her head.

Relief, astonishment, and renewed alarm passed rapidly through Jane's mind as she heard the rattle of bolts and chains and the sound of the front door opening. The house was miserably hot; it was possible that Megan had also been unable to sleep. All the same. . . . Jane ran back to her room. It took only a moment to slip into a loose gown and a pair of low-heeled shoes. Retracing her steps, she went down the stairs and let herself out.

The waning moon gave less light than she would have liked. It was several minutes before she could be sure that no living form moved on the front lawn or the graveled drive. Megan must have gone to the garden; though why, if that was her destination, she should have chosen to go out the front door, Jane could not imagine.

Megan had not gone to the garden. When Jane reached the end of the west range, she saw her sister-in-law moving quickly toward the stone wall that bordered the south side of the park. The hillside was relatively steep at that point; at the foot of the slope, beyond the wall, flowed the stream that had once supplied the moat, in the days when Grayhaven was a fortified manor. As Jane watched, the slim dark figure vanished into the shadow of the wall and did not reappear.

Jane started to run. There was a gate in that section of the wall; Megan must have gone through it, and once she was on the hillside it would be hard to see her. Tall weeds, brambles, and trees formed a mosaic of light and shadow, capable of concealing a troop of infantry. She could not imagine where Megan was going. That she had some specific destination in mind seemed clear from her quick, purposeful walk, but there was nothing in the hills except forest, wild and untended.

The gate swung open. Megan had not bothered to close it. The stream had been shrunk by drought into a feeble trickle, no problem even to a woman in thin shoes and long skirts. But had Megan crossed it? Jane was about to look for footprints when a movement high above caught her eyes.

She jumped the stream and began the ascent. She knew she could easily catch Megan; she knew the hills, and in her loose dress, unencumbered by stays and petticoats, she was as agile as a boy. Yet she hung back, staying just close enough to be sure she would not lose sight of her quarry. It had occurred to her that Megan might be walking in her sleep. Waking a sleepwalker could induce fits or hysteria or worse.

Before long Jane came upon a narrow path. Gradually the trees closed in around her till she was walking in deep shadow. Once she stumbled over a root, but for the most part the path was remarkably clear and well defined. She had lost sight of Megan, but felt sure she could not have left the path; tangled boughs and brambles formed a barrier as impenetrable as a wall. The night was filled with little rustling, creaking sounds, as if the old beeches were shifting their roots, or leaning over to whisper to their neighbors.

At last she saw a glimmer of moonlight ahead, signifying a glade or clearing. She came to a stop. Now she remembered. Now she knew where she was. She knew why the path was so smooth and well trodden; and she knew why Megan had come.

One slow step at a time, as if she approached a dreaded ordeal, she went to the edge of the clearing.

She had been here before. How long ago was it? She had had little time for rambling in the past years, and no reason to remember. Now memory returned, so vividly that the shadowy dimness before her was replaced by a brighter picture, an image eight or nine years old.

A day in spring, bright and warm; sunlight, dazzling bright after the green gloom of the woodland path. Oak trees, old as Time, and twisted branches of thorn formed a living wall around the glade. The hawthorn was in bloom, and under the trees the white bells of lily of the valley swayed on slender stems. The grass was brilliant emerald, smooth and even as a lawn. Clear as liquid glass, a small spring bubbled from a heap of tumbled stones. And the animals . . . a doe, with one dappled fawn, a brown hare, nibbling the grass, a big russet fox, squirrels. . . . The doe had glanced in her direction and returned to her grazing, unalarmed. The other animals had not stirred.

There were no flowers now. The glowing daylight colors had faded into shades of gray and black. But the grass was still lush and thick, the stream still whispered over the rocks; and on the opposite side of the clearing was the stone Jane remembered. It was as high as a tall man, pierced by a roughly circular opening. Megan was kneeling before it. She went down on all fours and crawled into the hole.

One part of Jane's mind—the waking, sensible part—found the act pitiful and grotesque. Another, deeper segment of consciousness acknowledged the ritual and found it fitting.

Megan emerged on the other side of the stone. When she stood up she caught her foot in her skirt and made a soft sound of annoyance. Then she saw Jane. Brushing off her dress, she came to meet her.

"Lizzie told me," she said calmly. "The women come here from all over the parish. Farther, even."

"I know. They call it the Toman stone. They believe . . ." Jane could not finish.

"Yes, that's just it—don't you understand? They believe."

"Oh, my dear. . . ."

"Are you going to tell Edmund?"

"No, Megan."

"I've tried everything else," Megan said, in that same cool, remote voice. "You don't understand, Jane. You are sweet and loving, but you don't understand." She made a strange, formal gesture, that took in the stone and the quiet glade.

"We must go back now," Jane said, in the tone she would have used to a small child. "It is very late."

"Yes, of course."

The path was so narrow they could not walk side by side. Jane followed Megan, holding her by the shoulder. Her teeth were set so hard that her jaw ached; she had the feeling that if she relaxed that one set of muscles, all the others would fail and she would start shaking.

The Toman stone was visited by barren women. She could have accepted Megan's sudden and unexpected descent into the grossest of pagan superstitions; desperate needs produce desperate acts. What frightened her was Megan's unearthly calm.

When they came out of the wooded part of the path and

started to descend the hill, Megan said abruptly, "I hope you don't despise me, Jane. I know it was foolish, but it can't do any harm."

Her voice was so normal and her comment so sensible that Jane could hardly believe the change. Cautiously she ventured, "You don't really think—"

"That a dirty old rock with a hole in it can help me conceive?" Megan laughed. "It's rather like throwing salt over one's shoulder."

"I do that myself," Jane admitted.

"I know you do." Megan gave her a quick affectionate hug. "I suppose you thought I was up to no good, creeping out at night like a burglar. How did you happen to see me?"

They discussed the subject fully as they descended. Megan was her old self, mocking her own folly and making jokes about what Edmund would say if he ever heard of her escapade. Jane was reassured. If the mad performance had made Megan feel better, as it obviously had, who was she to decry it? Yet she could not entirely dismiss the feeling that something significant had happened—that she and Megan had not been alone in the moonlit glade when Megan paid homage to the Toman stone.

Chapter Three

THE MOMENT the quarantine period was over, Jane bolted. She did not ask Edmund for permission, fearing he would produce some new excuse for waiting. He had said one week, and one week was what she had given him.

The groom made no objection when she asked him to saddle her favorite horse, a placid gray mare— "just the sort of dull, plodding animal I would expect you to favor, Jane." Like her mistress, Molly disliked rapid movement, but this morning she started out with alacrity, as if she too had been bored during the long weeks.

As they approached the park gates, Jane saw that some sort of construction was in progress. The man in charge of the workers tugged off his cap and approached when she reined up.

"What is going on, Hal?" she asked, recognizing one of their tenants.

"It's a new gatehouse, Miss Jane."

The old one had fallen in ruins years before. In her father's time the gates were always open, and he had felt no need for a gatekeeper.

"I see," she said. "Well, Hal, open the gates, please."

He hesitated, looking in every direction but at her. "Would you be going to the village, miss?"

"Yes. Is there a message I can carry for you?"

"No, miss—thankee. . . ."

Normally Jane would have waited patiently until he made up his mind whether to speak. But freedom, long withheld, beckoned her; after a moment she said, "Well, then;" and, with a shrug, Hal went to open the gates.

Once through them, Jane looked about with gloating eyes. The landscape, undistinguished and long familiar, had all the charm of novelty; no exotic foreign scene could have thrilled her more. She urged Molly into a trot, the quickest pace that staid old matron permitted. The first scattered cottages came into view.

Jane's hands released their grip on the reins, and the mare stopped. She felt like the man in the folktale who had been carried away by the fairies and returned to find that a century had passed in the outside world. It was not so much the physical changes, the inevitable shabbiness produced by time and weather, but the atmosphere. A deadly quiet hung over the street. There were too many people about—too many men, who ought to be at their work this time of day. Gaunt, silent men, sitting idle on the front steps or leaning against the fence. She recognized some of them. Joe Barlow, Tom Moxon, Charlie Garnet—Charlie was one of their best weavers. When he saw she was looking at him, he went inside the house and closed the door. Several other men quietly slipped away. The others stared, their faces dull and hostile.

Jane's first impulse was to follow Charlie and ask what was ailing him. But the blank-faced, silent men intimidated her. She had never met this sort of thing before and did not know how to deal with it. Lifting the reins, she urged Molly to go on.

The old village looked much the same, except for the expected signs of heat and drought. Mrs. Miggs's shop had not changed—and there was Mrs. Miggs on the same old stool, with what appeared to be the same strip of bright blue knitting. Hearing the shop bell, she looked up. Her eyes and her open mouth formed matching circles of surprise.

"I don't blame you for being startled," Jane said, smiling. "But I assure you, Mrs. Miggs, it was not lack of inclination on my part that kept me away so long. I am so glad to see you are well. And Granny Miggs—I suppose she is in her own house now—how is she?"

Mrs. Miggs replied that her mother-in-law was indeed in her own house—God be praised—and that the old lady had survived, out of sheer perversity, the pestilence that had struck down so many of the young and beloved. Leaning against the counter, Jane prepared for a comfortable chat, like many another she had had with Mrs. Miggs. It was not long before she realized her companion was suffering from the same peculiar ailment that afflicted the mill workers. Her responses to Jane's questions were brief and awkward; her eyes kept slipping away, toward the door. Finally she mumbled that it looked like rain, and was there anything special Miss Jane wanted?

Miss Jane, somewhat taken aback, mentioned several items, all of which Mrs. Miggs procured with an alacrity as uncommon as her offer of assistance. Jane lingered, turning over the piles of merchandise and watching Mrs. Miggs' nervousness grow. No one came in the shop, and that, too, was unusual. She knew it would be futile to ask for an explanation. Mrs. Miggs might be a "foreigner," but she shared the villagers' reticence. If she had anything to say she would say it; if she chose not to speak, nothing could persuade her to do so.

Finally Jane gave up. She paid for her purchases, asking that they be sent, and left the shop. Instead of returning home, she rode on down the street. She had a small sum of money she wanted to give the vicar, to dispense to those in need. Perhaps he could explain the alteration in the town.

St. Arca was not really a market town; most of the farmers preferred to take their produce to the larger village of Northgate. Presumably a weekly market had been held at one time, or the Market Square would not have earned its name, but it could never have been a sizable affair, for the square was not very large or very square, only a wide space surrounding the spot where several roads met. The largest building fronting the area was the inn, a modest little structure so old that it appeared to have grown like a mushroom instead of being created by human hands. Like all old buildings, it had settled over the years until there was not a straight line or a right angle anywhere in the whitewashed facade, and the inn sign, commemorating some long-forgotten monarch, had faded until only the dim outline of a crowned head could be seen.

A crowd had gathered in front of the inn, spilling out across the square. Most were men—the men she had seen in the mill town, waiting for this very event? As she came closer, she heard a voice rising and falling in formal oratory. The speaker stood on the carriage block, but even with that addition to his height his shock of gray-streaked, unkempt hair was barely visible over the heads of the crowd. His voice belied his meager stature; it rang with a metallic fervor that carried quite a distance.

"Will you stand for injustice, brothers? Will you let the heel of the tyrant grind you into the dust? You ask for bread and they give you a stone! Are you curs cringing under the lash of oppression, or freeborn Englishmen who are not afraid to fight for their rights?"

The first to see Jane was the landlord, who was leaning against the gate, his arms wrapped in his apron. With a guilty start, he stepped forward and caught the speaker by the arm. "Here, now, that's enough o' that. This ain't Speakers' Hall."

As the crowd became aware of Jane's presence, a growing murmur arose. A few of the listeners edged away, their caps pulled down over their eyes, as if anxious to avoid recognition. Others shifted uneasily, opening a path that gave her a clear view of the man on the carriage block.

The words "dwarf" and "hunchback" came into her mind, and were dismissed; he was neither, yet his limbs and body were subtly misshapen, as if stunted by disease. From the twist of his narrow shoulders rose a head as noble and commanding as that of an antique conqueror, a Caesar or Pompey. The fierce hawk's eyes focused on Jane, and the chiseled mouth curved in a grimace of hate. She had never seen him before in her life.

The landlord had prudently disappeared. The crowd swayed like a field of grain in a strong wind. Then from somewhere in the front ranks of the spectators an arm reached up and tugged at the speaker's coat sleeve. He turned an angry glare on the newcomer, who was hidden from Jane's view. After appearing to expostulate for a time, he shrugged and got down off his makeshift podium. The crowd broke up. Knots of people drifted off in one direction or another, giving Jane a wide berth, except for one man who came directly to her and grasped Molly's bridle.

At first she did not recognize him. He had been clean-shaven before; the dark beard and sideburns altered the character of his face, and the cap pulled low over his forehead hid his eyes. Before she could object to his unwarranted liberty he spoke—and his voice she did know.

"Miss Jane, this is no place for you. Come out of it, quick."

"Sam!" He put his finger to his lips, and she obediently lowered her voice. "Oh, Sam, I am so happy. . . . Where have you been? Why did you go off without a word to me? What in heaven's name is happening? Has everyone gone mad?"

He had turned the horse and was leading it back in the direction from which she had come. He chuckled softly.

"You haven't changed, Miss Jane. Still asking questions too fast for a man to answer."

"I have so much to ask—"

"And I'll answer. But not here. Look scornful at me and stop your smiling; there's spies and blacklegs everywhere."

"Blacklegs?"

"Best go back to the shop. You'd want a rest and a cup of tea, like, after your fright at being carried off by a desperate rough-looking stranger. I'll join you there."

Not once had he raised his eyes to her face. He did not do so now, only slapped the mare sharply on the rump before he walked away.

Instead of moving faster, the mare gave him a look of pained reproach. She had known him immediately, and had not expected such treatment from him.

When Jane reached the shop, Mrs. Miggs was standing in the doorway. "Lord forgive me, miss, I ought to've warned ye—"

"There was no cause for concern, Mrs. Miggs." She followed the woman inside. "I am to meet—"

"Hush." Mrs. Miggs gestured toward the back of the shop.

Jane went through the curtain into Mrs. Miggs's parlor. It was as cluttered as the shop, but a great deal neater. Sam was waiting; he stood pressed against the wall by the back door, where he could not be seen from the window.

"If anyone comes in the shop, you'll just be resting here by yourself," he said, holding a chair for her. "I'll be out the back—and you haven't seen me, nor no one."

"I am about to scream with exasperation," Jane said crossly, as she sat down. "What is wrong with everyone? Even Mrs. Miggs acts like a conspirator, and—"

"You'll have to let me do the talking, Miss Jane," Sam said, with a faint smile. "We must not take much time, and I've a deal to tell. You cut yourself off from us—"

"Not by my own choice, Sam."

"I know that. Some others aren't so sure. I left here sudden-like because—well, mainly because Mr. Mandeville had taken against me, and I saw I would never get on where I was. That time at the house, when he spoke so sharp—it wasn't the first time I had stood up to him in a way he didn't like. May be he has other reasons—but that one would be enough for him.

"I've been working in Birmingham. 'Twas there I met Jackson—the man you heard speaking. He's a union man, and so am I, Miss Jane. I don't hold with all Jackson's ideas. He's a violent man, Jackson; and if you knew his history you'd understand why. I'd never go so far as he wants to go. I'm for changing the law, not breaking it. But without unions we haven't got a chance."

"Father never approved of unions."

"In his day, may be there was not the need for them. But the old ways aren't always the good ways, Jane, and times change."

She did not notice his use of her given name; it sounded quite natural. "Then Mr. Jackson is stirring up our men? To what, a strike?"

"It must come, if your brother goes on as he began. Oh, he's not broken the law. That regulates the hours we work, but not the pay we get. If he lowers wages and raises rents, the men have no choice but to take it, they've homes and families here, and no savings to keep them while they look elsewhere. And there's the childern. Your dad wouldn't take 'em under thirteen, but the law says nine years—and what's a year or two, more or less? They earn less, for they're not as skilled, so the men get laid off to save wages. When the cholera struck and many were too sick to work, he brought in folks from Birmingham and elsewhere, packed 'em in ten to a room in the tenement he built down by the railroad station. Mostly our men are idle now. It takes the heart out of a man to sit at home by the fire while his wife and children are out earning. The enclosure coming at the same time made matters worse, for those that lost their livelihood by that had no place to find work. They're dry tinder, Jane, and Jackson's the man who can put the torch to it."

"We must do something," Jane said. It never occurred to her to doubt his word, or his assessment of the situation.

"There's naught you can do. I know how you're placed. I've been near frantic trying to find a way to get word to you —to warn you—"

"Of what? I don't believe any of our men would do us harm."

"Not any one of them, no. But there's a spirit in a mob that's worse than all the separate parts of it. When people are in trouble they look about for something to put the blame on. I read the word once. . . ."

"A scapegoat?"

"That's right. And there's another thing—"

The jingle of the shop bell interrupted him. Jane heard a man's voice. She did not recognize it, but apparently Sam did; the back door opened and closed without a sound, and he was gone.

"Miss Mandeville?"

Jane looked around. The man standing in the doorway was someone she had never seen before. Ginger-pink hair and whiskers framed a face as doughy and soft as suet pudding, pitted with smallpox scars.

"Yes?" she said.

"You won't know me, miss; I'm Ballantine, one of the foremen from the mill. Saw you there by the inn and took the liberty of making sure you was all right."

Jane was about to ask why she shouldn't be all right when she remembered Sam's hints.

"I was a trifle upset," she said wanly. "That man—that rough man who took my horse—"

"Did he say anything, miss? Was he rude or threatening?"

"No, it was only his manner—so brusque and peremptory. But I am better now. Perhaps I ought to go back to the house."

"Yes, miss, I think you had."

Respectfully he stood back to let her pass.

Jane urged Molly to a speed that resentful animal was not accustomed to. Even after she had left the village she kept glancing apprehensively from side to side, and starting at every rustle of foliage. The world had turned topsy-turvy and she had turned with it, imagining hidden perils in the old secure places, playing conspirator with a slyness alien to her nature. Ballantine might be just what he claimed—a faithful employee, concerned for her safety. Or he might be —what was the word Sam had used?—a blackleg. She could guess what it meant. She had no way of knowing for sure. In this insane new world people and objects were no longer what they appeared; like the shape changers in the old legends, the enchanted animals and disguised princes, a dark glamour hid their true natures.

She could not talk to Edmund about the danger of a strike. She had lost the power to persuade him of anything, if she had ever possessed it. Besides, she couldn't reveal her knowledge without raising questions as to how, and from whom, she had obtained it. I am as bad as the rest, she thought sadly; in order to live in this world, I must change my shape, too.

The only possibility that occurred to her was to consult Mr. Trumbull. It might be a vain endeavor, but it could do no harm. As soon as she got to her room she wrote a letter, and put it on the table in the hall with the rest of the outgoing post.

Edmund's demeanor at dinner that night told her he was vexed about something, but he said nothing in front of Megan, waiting until he could take Jane aside.

"I understand you went to St. Arca today."

So Ballantine was a blackleg. Jane said, "Yes, I did. You might have warned me, Edmund."

"Of the danger of rude stares and uncouth people? Your tastes are so peculiar, Jane, I assumed you enjoyed such things."

Obviously it had never occurred to him there was a chance of physical danger to himself or anything that belonged to him. Jane was inclined to agree. Sam's vague remarks about mob spirit had made little impression on her; she could not imagine being afraid of the men she had known all her life.

"It was very unpleasant," she muttered.

"If such things disturb you, you can avoid them by not going there again. I never go myself; the place has nothing to attract a person of refinement."

"Perhaps you are right," said the new Jane meekly.

She expected he would leave her then, but instead he said casually, "Did I hear of some rude fellow who spoke to you and led your horse away? I won't have that sort of thing. What did he look like?"

"He had a black beard and sideburns," Jane said readily. "A large, tall, burly man, rather shabbily dressed—blue trousers and a checked jacket with a scarf knotted around his neck."

"And his voice?"

"He didn't speak. In fact, he seemed ashamed; he did not so much as look me in the face. Perhaps he only meant to get me out of harm's way."

"There was no danger," Edmund said irritably. "He was impertinent to approach you. I want to track him down. He is one of these labor agitators—incendiaries, no less. I won't have them around."

Jane said nothing. Her silence seemed to worry Edmund. Looking closely at her, he added, "Father did not believe in unions, you know."

"I know. Edmund . . ."

"Yes?"

"I am afraid. We are surrounded by anger, dislike, even hate. . . ."

"What are you afraid of? There is nothing they can do except grumble. I hope you won't express these irrational fears to Megan. I don't want her upset."

"As if I would!"

"Oh, and by the way. . . ." Edmund reached into his pocket and took out a letter. "There is no use your writing to Mr. Trumbull. He has gone abroad and will be absent all summer."

"How dare you examine my correspondence!" Jane snatched the letter from him.

"I happened to see it on the table and thought to spare you time," was the cool reply. "But I am not surprised you should be unjust to me, Jane. It has become your habit."

An inspection of the letter assured Jane that her seal was unbroken. Perhaps she had been unjust. Nothing was simple any longer; every act had a dozen different interpretations.

Glumly she followed Edmund into the drawing room, prepared for another dull evening. She would have preferred her own sitting room, where she could kick off her shoes, curl up on the sofa, and read in peace. Edmund didn't object to her reading, but he was always interrupting to read aloud some excerpt from his book or newspaper. And he expected a response.

That evening was no exception, but she did not mind the interruptions so much since she was unable to concentrate on her book. Her mind kept returning to what had happened that day; she was concerned about Sam, who was walking a dark and dangerous road; about the workers; about Megan and herself; about Edmund. . . . He, too, walked his road alone. She seemed to see his solitary figure moving deeper and deeper into shadow and pushing aside the hands that reached out to help him.

When Edmund finally put his paper down, Megan said hopefully, "Shall we have some music, my dear?"

"Not this evening. You may go up to bed, if you like; I have work to do."

Megan's face fell. "You work so hard, darling. I wish I could help you."

"Thank you, Megan. I know things have been dull for

you; perhaps it is time we had a house party. In a fortnight, let us say."

He was already on his way to the door and would have proceeded without further comment if Megan had not stopped him.

"Who—whom do you mean to ask, Edmund?"

"There will be ten in all."

Megan's hands clenched, crumpling the delicate silk kerchief she was embroidering. "Who, Edmund?"

"No one you know. Except, of course, the Astleys."

"I thought you had severed your connection with that precious pair," Jane exclaimed. "You said they were false friends, hypocrites—"

"It was a temporary misunderstanding," Edmund said. "I came to the conclusion that I had been mistaken—or perhaps misinformed."

His eyes moved to Megan's face. She met his look with one as steady—challenge countering challenge, defiance answering accusation.

"I detest both of them, as you know," Jane said. "But if you insist—"

"I do insist," Edmund exclaimed. "Good God, what a house! A man is not master in his own drawing room!"

Megan completed the ruin of her embroidery by jamming it into her workbag. "I believe I will retire now. Good night, dear Jane."

She followed Edmund out.

Jane slumped back in the chair and pressed her hands against her temples. Her head felt swollen to twice its normal size, bulging with secrets and mysteries and perils and unsolved problems. This latest difficulty between Megan and Edmund—it must concern Lord George and his sister, but those meaningful glances and heavily significant comments suggested something more serious than a wife's jealousy of a former love. It's too much, Jane thought despairingly; I cannot stand any more problems!

There was another problem, the most pressing of all; but Jane was not even aware it existed. It was not surprising that she had failed to note the urgency in Sam's manner when he referred to it, for his warning had been interrupted by the shop bell. And even Sam did not realize until it was almost too late that the danger he feared would be the determining factor in the crisis that was almost upon them.

Chapter Four

THE DAY the visitors were to arrive Jane woke early. Freeing her limbs of the tangled bedclothes, she padded to the window and looked out. The sun was barely above the hills, but already the air was close and hot. Would the heat wave never end? The crops must be suffering badly from lack of rain; tempers certainly were. She felt as cross and tired as if she had had no sleep. Lord Henry and Lady Georgina would be a fine addition to a family already at odds with one another. Sighing, she prepared to face the day.

Later in the morning she carried Ta-chin to the stable, whither the cat had been exiled for the duration of Lady Georgina's stay. Jane didn't believe for a moment that Ta-chin would remain out of the house, but in this minor matter she was willing to obey Edmund's express orders. There would doubtless be other, more serious areas of conflict that she could not or would not avoid.

The stable was no hardship to Ta-chin; the cat spent a lot

of her spare time there, bullying the stable cats and observing the horses and grooms with the patronizing sneer of a superior species. She and Molly, the gray mare, had developed a relationship that could hardly be called friendship, since it consisted of indifference on one side and contemptuous exploitation on the other. Molly's broad hindquarters made a comfortable warm sleeping place, for a cat.

As Jane was leaving, she saw a groom leading out Megan's spirited white stallion. She went at once to the front of the house, where she found Megan in riding costume.

"Where are you going?" she asked.

"Riding, of course. What do you suppose?" She indicated the horse, which the groom had just led up to her, and got nimbly into the saddle.

"The guests will be here shortly," Jane said.

"I will be back before they arrive. And I don't care if I am not. I need to ride off my evil humor, Jane. Don't try to stop me."

"Megan, wait—"

It was too late. She was gone, at a gallop.

Perhaps it was not such a bad idea, Jane thought. She wished she could gallop off and not come back until the weekend was past. She had meant to warn Megan to avoid the village; but after all, what did it matter? Megan probably wouldn't notice the things that had disturbed her, and she wouldn't recognize Sam even if she happened to see him. Jane had heard nothing from him since their chance encounter, and she had been afraid to make inquiries. She hoped and believed he had left the district. His recent activities could only lead to trouble with Edmund.

Having learned to expect the worst, she was not surprised when the Astleys appeared before their time. Megan had only been gone half an hour when Jane heard the carriage; with some confused idea of shielding the runaway, she hurried to join Edmund in receiving them.

The first courtesies had barely been exchanged when Lady

Georgina asked, "And where is Mrs. Mandeville? I am longing to see her in her new role; I'm sure she does it to perfection."

"She has gone for a ride," Jane said, adding, as Edmund's brows drew together, "You are too early."

Lord Henry broke into a hearty laugh. "You are right to scold us, Miss Mandeville. If there is one thing I cannot stand, it is guests who arrive early. It is all my sister's fault. She has been trying to reform my bad habits, and I fear she has overdone it."

Edmund frowned. "I am sure Jane did not mean—"

"Let me show you to your rooms," Jane said. Tact was all very well, but she was cursed if she was going to allow Edmund to apologize for her.

"A canter before luncheon sounds just the thing," Lady Georgina said. "You know how I admire your stable, Edmund. And perhaps we will meet Mrs. Mandeville somewhere in the park."

Jane handed the visitors over to Lizzie and went to change. She had not been invited to ride with the others, but she had no intention of letting Megan face Lady Georgina alone on their first meeting since her marriage. She only hoped Megan would appreciate the barely veiled spite in Lady Georgina's pronunciation of "Mrs. Mandeville."

When the party was mounted, Edmund led them toward the main entrance. He was desirous of showing off his new gatehouse, which had been finished so expeditiously that Jane was sure it must be badly built. Edmund was delighted with the result, which followed his own plans; it had so many miniature turrets and quaint gables that there was little space left for the business of living. He seemed intent on pointing out its beauties; but he was the first to see the horse on the road beyond the gates, and remark, "Here she is."

Not until the animal emerged from the shadows of the trees could Jane make out anything beyond a slowly moving, light-colored shape. When she saw the rider, she found herself on the ground and running, without any recollection of how she had dismounted.

Megan's bright hair tumbled over her shoulders, framing a face streaked with dust and perspiration. Her hat was missing. Though she sat upright, back straight and head high, she had lost the reins. They were held by the man who walked beside her, leading the horse. His head was also bare. A defiant plume of black hair stood up like a banner.

Edmund recognized him immediately in spite of the beard. "What the devil are you doing here?" he cried angrily.

"It is a public road, sir," Sam said. "Mrs. Mandeville has had an unpleasant experience, and should—"

"I will decide what my wife should do." Edmund snatched the reins from him.

"I daresay she was thrown," Lady Georgina murmured. "It does happen. . . ." But not to me, her tone implied.

"This is no time for a debate," Jane exclaimed. "She should go to bed at once. Edmund?"

She hoped Edmund would go, with the others, and leave her to exchange a private word with Sam. But, like herself, Edmund had concluded Megan was more shocked than hurt, and he was determined to have his say.

"Freeman, I know the sort of scoundrel you are, and I won't have you on my property. If I find you trespassing again, I shall have you taken in custody."

Sam was at no loss for a reply, but after a glance at Megan he closed his mouth so tightly it disappeared into his beard.

To Jane, that look, so fleeting and yet so revealing, was like a window opening into a world whose existence she had never suspected. She only hoped the others had not noticed; but she did not like the smile that curved Lady Georgina's lips, as she watched from the superior height of her mount like a spectator in a theater box.

"I'll go—sir." The last word almost choked Sam, but

he got it out. "Only you should know what happened, it was—"

"I told you to get out."

The air was so charged with potential violence that Jane was afraid to speak; an imploring look and a quiet gesture had the desired effect, however; after a moment Sam turned and walked away. She knew why he had given in so easily, but Edmund squared his shoulders and smiled, like a pugilist who has just knocked his opponent down.

"That's the way to deal with such rabble," Lord Henry remarked, in a voice that was clearly intended to carry. "Well done, Mandeville."

"The rest of you can stand here and talk as long as you like," Jane snapped. "Give me the reins, Edmund, I want to get Megan to bed."

For the first time Megan seemed to be aware of her surroundings. "I do not need to be put to bed," she said clearly. "And I was not thrown."

Jane persuaded the other three to continue their ride. She wanted to talk to Megan alone—but she was illogically infuriated with Edmund when, after a perfunctory protest, he allowed himself to be sent from his wife's side.

Megan refused to take to her bed, but she consented to let Jane help her change her tight, crumpled dress for a loose gown.

"I ought to have warned you," Jane said remorsefully. "We are not popular in the village these days, but I never thought—"

"I didn't go to the village. At least, not to the Market Square. I meant to cut through the mill town and come home by way of the bridge. I didn't hurt the child, Jane, truly I didn't."

"Oh, curse it," Jane muttered. "What happened?"

"It had no business in the road anyway," Megan said. "What sort of mother would allow a tiny tot to wander out of the house? A filthy, ragged little thing—I could not tell whether it was a boy or girl. Hero was walking; he did not so much as touch the child, it tripped and fell in the dust and began bawling. I was about to dismount, to make sure it was not hurt, when people came rushing out of the houses—men and women both—and before I knew what was happening they were screaming and cursing at me. One old woman, with hair standing up like an angry cat's fur, actually threw a missile—just a clod of dirt, I think—but it struck Hero, who had been rendered nervous by the shouting and the crowd. I was so taken aback I lost control of him. . . . Well, one woman did go sprawling; I hope she was not hurt, I think she only threw herself aside to avoid his rush, but . . ."

She had begun her narrative in a controlled manner, but as she went on, her voice began to waver.

"It was not your fault," Jane said. "Don't think about it. Where did you meet Sam?"

"I lost my hat," Megan said querulously. "I don't know where. I let Hero run until we were well away, and then I stopped him, for I was beginning to feel a little faint. I don't know how long I sat there in the shade of the trees, catching my breath and my nerve. . . . All at once he was there, and somehow I wasn't afraid any longer, though that horrid beard confused me at first. . . . Jane, why do they hate me so? I have never done anything to harm them. It wasn't the curses or the things they threw, it was their hate that frightened me."

"It has nothing to do with you," Jane said. "It has to do with the mill and the cholera, and perhaps even the heat. Try to forget it."

Scapegoat. Sam had used the word, and now she understood its appropriateness—or rather, she thought she did. It was not her fault that she missed the real significance of the word, and of the episode. Sam had tried twice to tell her and had been prevented, but he assumed she would learn the truth from Megan and would comprehend the danger. He failed to take several factors into account. For one thing,

Megan had not understood the words that had been shouted at her, distorted as they were by anger and by the local accent; nor is it likely that she would have known what they meant even if she had understood. Jane might have known their meaning, but even she would have underestimated their importance. She was now too far removed from the world in which such ideas still lingered, passed on from father to son and mother to daughter, fading slowly with the passage of the centuries, but ready to leap up like a smoldering fire when fresh kindling is added.

So she said, "Try to forget it," and promised herself she must attempt to reason with Edmund, futile as it would probably prove. Perhaps he could be brought to see that his own interests would best be served by a reversal of the methods that had bred such discontent.

ii

THE WEEKEND brought no opportunity to speak to Edmund, but it was not the utter disaster Jane had feared. After cultivating the London nouveau riche and the scholarly middle class, Edmund had turned to the county gentry; many of the guests were known to Jane. One day the men took out their guns, accompanied by Lady Georgina, who bagged more game than any of them.

Jane hoped Edmund would talk to the other men about the troubles he was having at the mill. Though she did not know what they talked about over the port, when the ladies had withdrawn, she decided he had actually said very little, probably because he didn't like to admit he was incapable of dealing with the matter. There were a few references to poaching, and other intrusions into the privileges these gentlefolk insisted upon; their nearest neighbor, Sir William Gilbert, mentioned that he had been forced to hire extra gamekeepers to patrol his grounds.

"Why not try mantraps?" Sir Henry suggested.

Bluff old Sir William gave him a glance of open dislike. "They happen to be illegal, your lordship. No, no; a good thrashing, when a feller is caught, gets the point across."

"They poach because they need food," Jane said. "And if the harvest is as bad as I expect, after the dry summer, matters will get worse this winter. Your thrashings and mantraps will not stop a father who sees his children crying with hunger."

"Always lecturing, Jane," Edmund said, with an angry laugh.

"That's the proper role for the ladies, bless 'em." Sir William came to Jane's defense. "Where would we rough fellers be if they didn't remind us of our Christian duty, eh? Humph, yes. You're right, Miss Jane; up to you ladies to organize some kind of relief, eh? Soup. Good nourishing soup. You'll see to it. And Vicar, eh?"

"Yes, indeed," Mr. Higgins said readily. "I am at Miss Mandeville's command—and that of the other ladies."

Most of the guests took their departure on Tuesday, but the Astleys stayed on. "How much longer?" Jane demanded, when she had an opportunity to speak to Edmund alone.

"As long as they like. His lordship is assisting me on certain matters. You are at liberty to leave the house, Jane, if you don't care for the company."

"What matters?" Jane asked. But Edmund had left her.

By resorting to methods as near spying and eavesdropping as her conscience would allow, Jane managed to acquire a few clues. Edmund was disinclined to go out on his errands; he preferred people to come to him. He had an unusual number of callers in the next few days. Mr. Gorm, the mill manager, was frequently with him. Jane did not recognize any of the others; some were men of a class she instinctively disliked, rough, furtive-looking persons with hard eyes. One was a young officer whose insignia she recognized as that of the fusiliers who were stationed at Coventry.

Edmund had indeed been forced to admit that there

was danger, but he underestimated its strength and did not expect it to boil over as soon as it did. He and Lord Henry were in the billiard room that evening—with, of course, Lady Georgina. Jane sat with Megan in the drawing room. The windows were open to the warm summer night, but Jane was reading aloud, so they did not hear the footsteps approaching. The first warning they had was a peremptory pounding on the door.

No casual visitor would knock like that. The noise brought everyone out into the hall, Lord Henry still holding his billiard cue. Edmund's outflung arm stopped Jane as she started impulsively for the door, so she was forced to wait until Barkens, the butler, performed his proper task.

The old man was sent staggering back as a man forced his way into the house. A profane exclamation burst from Edmund, and Lord Henry laughed and remarked, "By God, it's the gallant rescuer. What now, young Lochinvar?"

Jane ducked under Edmund's arm and ran to the newcomer.

"What is it, Sam? Are you hurt?"

Dried blood traced a line from his forehead across his cheek, but he shook his head, struggling to find the breath to speak. His chest heaved up and down like that of a horse that has been ridden too hard, and his sweat-soaked shirt clung to his body.

"They're coming," he gasped. "Not far behind. Two hundred or more. . . ."

"Who? What?" Jane demanded.

Edmund knew the answer. "You have the effrontery to come here, after stirring them up to riot and rebellion, and pretend. . . . Got cold feet, did you, Freeman? I am not stupid enough to be deceived by this. By heaven, I'll have you transported—or worse."

"Not me," Sam said, a little more easily. "Never mind, I came to warn you—she must go. She's the one they're after —and you, of course—sir—but you're a man and you've brought this on yourself. . . ."

His breath gave out. This time no one replied. They were staring incredulously at Megan, for Sam's gesture had left no doubt she was the one he referred to.

She was as bewildered as the others. "Me? You must be mistaken, Sam. I haven't done—"

"No, no, of course you haven't," Sam said, half in a groan. "You still don't understand. Jane, didn't she tell you? He'd never have done it—you know who I mean, Jane—he couldn't have stirred them up to this without the other thing—I don't excuse them, but they've suffered so much and are so afraid, they aren't thinking straight. It was old Granny Miggs that began it, with her talk of curses. It's since *she* came that the troubles began—that's what they say, and they think if she goes away—or is taken. . . ."

"Dear God," Jane gasped. She was beginning to understand. Half-forgotten childhood memories—certain of Lizzie's folktales, bowdlerized for childish ears but retaining a hint of the pagan barbarities that had spawned them. . . .

The others were still in the dark. "What are you raving about?" Edmund demanded. "Here—Barkens—call the footmen. I'll have this scoundrel under lock and key at any rate, and then we'll deal with—"

He stopped when he realized no one was paying any attention to him. Sam went on speaking to Jane. "I'll talk to 'em, I think I can turn them back if I tell them she's not here—get her away, Jane, for the night, at least. For God's sake, hurry—they are here."

Through the open door Jane saw them—a darkness sparked by flaring torches and accompanied by a wordless animal roaring.

"I will," she said. "Sam, go; you can't talk to them, they'll call you traitor if they see you here."

She turned to Megan, but Edmund was before her.

"No one is leaving this house," he said. "Jane, are you mad? I will deal with this, and with him—"

But Sam was gone. The door gaped empty and the roar of the mob was closer.

Jane didn't waste time arguing. She caught Megan by the wrist and dragged her unresisting up the stairs. As they went she heard Lady Georgina say coolly, "We are three guns, Edmund, if it comes to that."

Jane didn't wait to hear Edmund's reply. Without pausing, she towed Megan along the passageway to the back stairs of the west wing. She was not in the least afraid. Excitement sent the blood coursing through her veins and gave her an illusion of competence and strength.

"I don't understand," Megan said breathlessly.

"No; but I should have. Yet who could suppose in this day and age. . . . Hurry, Megan."

Down the last flight and along the corridor to the tower. It was the quickest way to the stable yard. Mounted, Megan would be safe. Then straight across country to the high road, and south to Lydford Abbey, Sir William's home.

She was neither surprised nor alarmed when a dark shape materialized out of the shrubbery and fell in beside her.

"I'll see you away," Sam said. "Then I'll go back—"

"No. No. If your former friends don't shoot you, Edmund will. He's sent for the troops, I think."

It was when she realized that the stables and courtyard were utterly deserted that Jane felt the first stab of real fear. If their own servants were involved in the riot—people she had grown up with—then the world had indeed gone mad, with no solid ground left to stand on. She glanced at the man beside her, and as if feeling her look, he gave her a quick smile. Not everyone had failed her. There were still solid sections of ground amid the quicksand.

Sam did not comment on the desertion of the grooms. He had apparently expected it. "We must move fast," he grunted, wrenching open the door to the room where the tack was kept.

Megan had not spoken for some time. Now she said calmly, "I'll get Hero," and went to do so. When Jane opened the door of the mare's stall, she was received by a low grating growl which, after the first start of surprise, she recognized as a greeting.

"You had better get out of sight," she said, removing the cat from Molly's back and urging the latter to move. As she led the mare out, she saw that Sam had already begun to saddle Megan's white.

"That is a man's saddle," she protested.

"Then she must ride astride," was the reply, as Sam turned back to the tack shed.

There were no lanterns in the stable area, for fear of fire; but the moon and stars gave enough light to enable Jane to see dimly. She saw Megan lift her skirts and fumble with the tapes that held crinoline and petticoats in place. She didn't doubt that Megan could use a man's saddle, her sister-in-law was a fine horsewoman; and her cool acceptance of danger was admirable . . . but she wished Megan would say something. Her responses had been those of a machine, performing the correct action when the correct lever was pressed.

She caught the bridle Sam threw her and buckled it in place while he tossed the saddle on to the mare. The voices had died to a murmur, like that of waves on the shore. Over it a single voice rose in strident oratory. Jackson? She knew the carrying power of his voice, she had heard it the day he spoke at the inn.

Jackson's voice was interrupted by an explosive crash that echoed across the valley. A moment of utter silence followed; then an outburst of screams and shouts, mingled with a second and third shot. Cursing under his breath, Sam struggled with the girth. He got no cooperation from the mare, who resented being aroused at such an unseemly hour. Finally he accomplished the task and, grasping Jane by the waist, tossed her into the saddle.

From her elevated position she saw the torches before the others did. The fusillade had dispersed the crowd, but not all of them had gone home. Others had been more interested in loot than principle from the beginning; scattering, they made for the outbuildings.

"Mount!" Jane cried to Megan, who was standing quietly to one side. "Hurry; they are coming!"

"I will wait for Sam to help me," Megan said sweetly. Then she saw the men approaching—and the torches they carried.

It was some time later before Jane found out why Megan acted as she did. The memory had been long suppressed—a fire set by an aggrieved servant at a country estate in France, the screams of the horses, the curses and tears of the men who came too late to help. . . . Megan's eyes dilated. Before Sam could reach her, she darted back toward the stalls. She had opened half a dozen doors before he caught her. By that time a raucous shout showed that they had been seen.

"This way—it's them, it's the witch. . . ."

Sam scrambled into the saddle and dragged Megan up with him. It happened too fast for Jane to do anything but watch; she realized Sam had forgotten about her, he was intent on one thing and one thing only. As he turned the white horse toward the entrance to the stable yard, Jane was close behind him. It was the only way out. None of them had thought to unbar the gate on the other side.

He rode straight at the men, who scattered, crying out in alarm. Jane closed her eyes, dug in her heels, and followed.

She lost the others almost at once. Outraged by the noise and the change in routine, the mare took off at her own sweet will. She even jumped a fence or two, which was not a custom of hers. Jane made no attempt to stop or guide the indignant animal; when she finally stopped, she was high on the hillside north of the house.

That place suited Jane as well as any other. There was nothing near her but night and silence. Far below, cupped in the hollow, Grayhaven Manor lay like a doll's house in a museum exhibit. She was too far away to hear the cries of inquiry and indignation that were undoubtedly ringing through its rooms, but she could see everything. The house was ablaze with light. The grounds in front were deserted—not even a crumpled doll-sized shape on the graveled drive. The attackers had taken their dead and wounded with them when they retreated.

Jane winced. That Edmund had fired the first shot she did not doubt. "We are three guns, Edmund, if it comes to that." To what? Nothing less than a direct, murderous assault on the house and its inhabitants could excuse killing. But Edmund would view the trespass onto his land as tantamount to assault.

As she sat there, her hands loose on the reins, Jane felt quite calm and detached from the doll's house below. A sudden gust of wind lifted the horse's mane. The trees sighed and waved leafy arms. On the horizon, over the crest of the opposite hills, a dark mass of cloud stretched out shapeless tentacles. The air felt cooler.

The last time she had been out so late, the moon was a half-circle, guiding Megan toward the glade and the Toman stone. Somewhere on the ridge just opposite. . . . For a moment she fancied she saw a glow of pale silver among the dark outline of the trees; but it must have been imagination, no lantern or candle could cast such a light, and when she blinked her eyes, it was gone.

She ought to go back to the house. Edmund would be worried. . . . Be honest, she told herself. Edmund would be furious—with her. Megan would not have run away if she had not led her. As matters had turned out, they would have been safe at the house. But Jane didn't regret her decision. She had done what seemed sensible at the time. Things might have turned out differently. The surest way of ending the blight brought on by a curse was to shed the blood of the witch who had cast the spell.

The breeze felt delightful, cool, with an unmistakable

feeling of dampness. Perhaps the long-awaited, badly needed rain was on its way at last. How pleasant it was to be here, in the quiet, with no one talking, no one shooting angry, hateful looks.

In a perverse way, Jane could understand the superstitious folly that had driven the mob to their door. She only wished she could find a simple, obvious explanation—a scapegoat— for the miseries of the past year and a half. It was dreadful to feel you were the helpless tool of vast, indifferent forces. And it was something of a coincidence that the changes had begun when Megan came. Poor Megan—poor, harmless girl, no one could possibly blame her. . . .

Jane sat unmoving until the moon dropped low, and finally the soldiers came, riding in a furious gallop down the drive. She picked up the reins and urged the mare to move.

As dawn was breaking into a sky streaked with angry clouds, Megan came home. She walked into the drawing room, where the rest of them were assembled, waiting for news from the searchers who were scouring the countryside for her. Her muslin dress hung limp around her, moist with dew and streaked with dust and other stains.

"I'm so sorry you were worried," she said serenely, in reply to the chorus of inquiry and expostulation that burst around her. "I must have fallen asleep. I was perfectly safe, in a little meadow, on the crest of the hill. You know the place, Jane."

She smiled at Jane—a smile so radiant, so glowing, that the latter felt a stab of uncomprehending envy that was as sharp as pain.

The storm broke a little later. It rained all day, soaking the parched fields and dusty plants.

Chapter
Five

MEGAN'S CHILD was born the following June. It was a healthy boy, with the coarse dark hair and unfocused blue eyes common to most newborns.

ii

EDMUND WAS beside himself with delight when his wife announced she was pregnant at last, and his treatment of her was tenderly devoted. He lavished gifts on her, sending all the way to London for exotic food and hothouse flowers, until Megan laughingly protested that she really had no taste for lobster salad. No guests were invited to the house unless she expressed a desire to see them. Needless to say, this did not include the Astleys.

That winter the weather was perfect—for winter—not the unhealthy and unseasonable warmth that brought on sickness, but mild enough to allow some winter crops to flourish. This mitigated to some extent the food shortage Jane had accurately predicted; thanks to her efforts and those of the other ladies of the parish, the worst cases of need were relieved. Edmund graciously contributed to the funds collected for this purpose. His temper was so good that Jane even plucked up enough courage to ask him to be gentle with the rioters. He agreed that they had suffered enough. No one had been killed, though several men and one woman had sustained minor wounds. There had been a certain amount of unfavorable comment in the press, for naturally the affair could not be kept quiet; and it might have been dislike of publicity as much as compassion that made Edmund agree to press the matter no further.

On one point, however, he was stubbornly resistant to Jane's pleas. The ringleaders, who had unfortunately escaped unhurt, must be arrested. He had sworn out a warrant against Jackson, on the charge of inciting to riot; but Jackson had gone into hiding and had not been seen since. Jane's attempt to defend Sam was a failure. Edmund was convinced he was as guilty as Jackson. He had also disappeared from the district, and flight, Edmund declared, was tantamount to a confession. Jane had not mentioned Sam's part in their escape from the stable yard, knowing this would only make matters worse. Megan had also remained silent about that incident, insisting that she had got lost and spent the night alone in the woods.

In the new year, when Megan's body began to change, Edmund stopped entertaining altogether. He spent more and more time alone. Megan did not appear to care what he did. Pregnancy became her; her skin took on a smooth sleekness, and her face had a look of placid contentment. She spent hours sewing and embroidering the finest white lawn and muslin clothes for the baby. Though she spoke little, she liked having Jane with her, and Jane was happy to oblige. After the first of the year she seldom left the house, taking a vicarious pleasure in Megan's pregnancy. As soon as it was warm enough, the two women spent a good deal of time out of doors in the garden; and in late spring Jane was relieved of one fear, hidden but never forgotten, when a gift came from the women of St. Arca.

Lizzie brought the parcel to them one morning when they were sitting in the rose garden. Megan, increasingly lethargic, asked Jane to open it. When Jane held up the garment it contained, she let out a cry of surprise and admiration.

It was a christening robe—pure white, long enough to cover several babies laid end to end, and covered entirely with lace and hand embroidery. Jane and Megan examined it, wondering at the work that had gone into it and at the originality of the designs. Flowers and waving stalks of corn, so naturalistically rendered that one could almost feel the breeze that stirred them; birds and butterflies, and the forms of small animals cunningly hidden in the grain.

Ta-chin roused herself and put out a paw toward a dangling ribbon. The cat had changed her allegiance to Megan that winter, following her from room to room and curling up at her feet or beside her. Edmund refused to countenance her presence in the bedroom, but he was no match for Ta-chin; she would slink in with one of the maids and hide until he fell asleep, whereupon she would leap onto the bed and lie down next to her new idol. Megan had become rather fond of the animal; few people can resist the appeal of abject devotion.

Jane lifted the dainty garment out of the cat's reach. "I have never seen anything so beautiful," she exclaimed. "Who brought it, Lizzie?"

Lizzie eyed the christening robe with a sour expression. She is jealous, Jane thought, smiling to herself; she doesn't want outsiders showing favor.

"It's the women of the village," Lizzie said finally. "As if we couldn't give Master Edmund's son everything a child could want."

Jane folded the garment into its wrappings; Ta-chin would have that ribbon yet if she continued to dangle it.

Megan's pleasure in the beauty of the work and the thoughtfulness of the givers was as great as hers, but Jane sensed the gift had a deeper meaning. It was a wordless apology and recantation. They had chosen this way to say they had been wrong.

Megan mentioned the christening robe to Edmund that evening. Jane was curious to see if he would recognize its significance, but he expressed only mild interest. She had not really expected him to understand. He had only laughed incredulously when she tried to convince him that Granny Miggs was as culpable as Jackson in starting the riot.

As Megan entered the last months of pregnancy, her lassitude increased. She was not very entertaining company; Edmund teased her about her tendency to doze off, and even when she was awake her contributions to the conversation often consisted of nothing more than a sleepy smile. Edmund had gone back to his antiquarian interests. There was little else for him to do, and he was reluctant to leave the house on extended trips. He was working in the cellars again, and had found more tombstones, in the room next to the one containing the brass.

"I hope you don't intend to extend your investigations any deeper," Jane said one afternoon, when he was telling them about his recent discoveries. "Antiquarian studies are all very well, but grave-robbing—"

"Hardly an appropriate term," Edmund said sharply. "However, you will be relieved to hear that Higgins shares your views; he tells me the crypt is consecrated ground, like any Christian cemetery, and that church law prohibits excavation of the graves."

Mr. Higgins had found this out while attempting to satisfy Edmund's desire to hold services in the chapel. He had begun to press the matter earlier in the year, and when the cholera broke out and the manor family stopped attending services at St. Arca's, the conscientious little vicar felt obliged to discover an alternative method of worship. He learned that the chapel had in fact been used for religious purposes as recently as the early part of the century, and since it had never been desecrated or misused, there was no reason why services should not be resumed. Edmund had had the room cleaned and redecorated, with pews taken from a church in Warwick that was being demolished, and the household staff made quite a respectably sized congregation, so poor Mr. Higgins came to the house every Sunday before rushing off to conduct services in the parish church.

Having her brother constantly about the house was not Jane's idea of comfort, and she urged him to visit neighbors or spend a few days in London. This he would not do, saying he had enough to amuse him at home. He had gone back to his painting; one day he proudly showed Jane his latest masterpiece.

His technique had improved, but he had no more talent for figures than for landscape. The full-length portrait of a young woman in long robes, with fair hair flowing down over her shoulders, had an insipid prettiness, but that was about all that could be said for it.

"It is very nice," Jane said. "Who is it meant to be, one of Sir Walter Scott's heroines? I know—the Lady Rowena, from *Ivanhoe.*"

"Your suggestion is interesting," Edmund said. "Rowena was a Saxon princess, was she not? I had in mind a representation of our ancestress, Ethelfleda. But I think it has rather a look of Megan."

So Ethelfleda had become "our" ancestress. Suddenly Jane felt rather sorry for her brother. Young, wealthy, handsome, intelligent—what weakness made him so unsure of himself that he had to invent spurious sources of pride? She did not think the painted girl had a look of Megan. There was no resemblance except that both had long fair hair and slim figures.

At any rate, Edmund was pleased with it, and it soon appeared in the gallery, next to the plumed cavalier.

Edmund had been with difficulty dissuaded from engaging the Queen's own physician to attend his wife when her confinement took place. He was finally persuaded that Sir James had other things to do. Lizzie disapproved of doctors in general; having a man around at such times was indecent, no less. They finally compromised on a well-known physician from Birmingham, and he was engaged to come a week before Megan was due. That date was almost a month away when Lizzie took Jane aside.

"Miss Jane, if you're still set on having the medical gentleman, he'd best be sent for. Miss Megan will never go another month."

"Are you sure, Lizzie?"

"I know the signs." The old woman nodded stubbornly. "A week, maybe less."

Jane didn't take this assessment seriously. Lizzie was always trying to prove she knew more than any doctor.

"I'll speak to Edmund," she said. "But you said yourself, Lizzie, that there was no need to have the doctor ahead of time—that first babies take a while to be born, and we would have ample time to summon him."

"I myself said there was no need for him at all," Lizzie grumbled. "The midwife from Northgate was what I would have had; but you know Master Edmund, he'll take on if he doesn't get his way, and I won't have it be said that I failed in me duty."

When questioned, Megan replied placidly that she felt perfectly well, except for a slight increase in pressure in the lower part of her body. "But," she added, in the same calm tone, "I am counting on you and Lizzie to tell me what to expect, Jane; I have not the least idea myself."

Jane duly reported the housekeeper's diagnosis to Edmund. Like her, he was inclined to discount it, but a messenger was dispatched to Birmingham. The answer came that evening; Dr. Winters had gone to Scotland for a few days, but his locum was taking calls in case of an emergency.

Lizzie was the only one who was not surprised when Megan went into labor three days later.

It was the old nurse's time of triumph, and she made the

most of it. Her first move was to get rid of Edmund. Expectant fathers could be a great nuisance, and she did not want him pacing the halls and bothering her with questions. At her suggestion Edmund set off for Birmingham to fetch the doctor, though Jane pointed out that it might be more sensible to send one of the servants. Edmund was not unwilling to be out of the house. He had been surprised and disconcerted by Megan's reaction to the onset of labor.

Megan was as surprised as Edmund at what was happening to her, and she was not at all sure she liked it. Jane was almost as ignorant, and somewhat uneasy, for if Megan's calculations were correct, the baby was almost a month early. Premature children were often sickly and frail; it would be terrible if their hopes were to be dashed to earth after such joyous anticipation.

She kept her worries to herself and settled down at Megan's bedside, prepared to read, talk, or do whatever was required. Megan was no coward; at first she did not cry out when the pains came, but by midafternoon they were only minutes apart, and Jane knew, from Lizzie's increasing air of concentration, that matters were progressing more rapidly than she had expected.

However, she was reassuring when Jane managed to get her away from the bed long enough to whisper a question.

"It'll be a while yet. Don't fret, child, worse comes to worst, I know what must be done. It's a woman's business after all. But, Miss Jane, I think you'd best go. A birthing is no place for a young lady."

Jane had no intention of leaving, but as the day wore on, she wished she could. Megan had given up playing Spartan. With each contraction she cried out and drew herself into a knot of tightened muscle. Perspiration streamed down her face and soaked her tangled hair. Lizzie kept the fire blazing and refused to allow Jane to open a window.

At Lizzie's insistence, Jane withdrew to a corner, from which she could not see what Lizzie was doing under the tentlike draperies that concealed Megan's body. She sensed that Megan was aware of her presence and wanted her there; but sitting with folded hands, in helpless stupidity, was a habit she was not accustomed to. At least she had not been accustomed to it until Edmund came home and stripped her of responsibilities, leaving her as useless and idle as any other woman. . . .

She cringed and clenched her hands as Megan shrieked. Almost as hard to bear was Lizzie's flushed complacency. Lizzie actually seemed pleased that Megan was in pain. No doubt she hoped it would all be over before the doctor came, so she could boast of delivering Master Edmund's heir all by herself. How in heaven's name could she look so smug? How could women go through this awful ordeal, not once but time after time? Perhaps it wasn't so bad after the first time. Perhaps it was easier when one knew what to expect. Megan's screams held as much surprise and outrage as pain.

It shouldn't be like this, Jane thought rebelliously. If I could only do something—help her somehow. I should have tried to find out about it; at least I could have prepared her for what was going to happen to her.

Jane had had more experience than most women. She had seen Ta-chin and the farm animals give birth. But cats didn't scream for hours. Cows didn't appear to mind that much. Why, why, had she complacently assumed it was the same for women? She ought to have known better; after all, she had read about the Queen's taking chloroform when Prince Leopold was born. Her eighth child—she, the highest lady in the land, had experienced this screaming torment seven times before Sir James, the royal physician, had bothered to call in a specialist—that same multitalented Dr. Snow, who had worked on the control of cholera. However, most doctors disapproved of anesthesia. They quoted the Bible— "In sorrow thou shalt bring forth children" —and insisted that the suffering of childbirth created love for the child. I wonder if they would feel that way if they had to bear the children, Jane thought, as Megan's voice rose again, and Lizzie exclaimed gleefully, "That was a good one, my dearie, just a few more now. . . ."

Because she was listening anxiously for them, Jane was the first to hear the approaching footsteps. She ran to the door.

The doctor was fashionably, almost foppishly dressed in top hat, frock coat, and striped satin waistcoat. He dismissed Jane with a glance and started to address Lizzie, but his voice was overcome by Megan's scream. The doctor looked pleased.

"I see I am in good time." Taking off his hat, he handed it to Jane. "Here, hang this up."

When he advanced toward the bed without even taking off his coat, Jane exclaimed, "Aren't you going to wash your hands?"

"Who the devil are you?" was the reply.

Lizzie muttered in his ear. His frown deepened. "Miss Mandeville? I beg your pardon; but I did not expect to find you here. Be so good as to leave at once, if you please."

Jane had no choice but to obey. However, she did have the satisfaction of seeing the doctor turn toward the basin and towels Lizzie had provided. He might not have bothered if she had not reminded him.

She sank down onto a bench on the landing and buried her face in her hands. Apparently there was no cause for alarm; the doctor shared Lizzie's satisfaction with the progress of the patient. But if this was a normal birth, then she was not anxious to assume the joys of motherhood.

She was still sitting there several hours later when the sound of a mellow baritone humming presaged the appearance of the doctor. He broke off when he saw her, and smiled in quite an amiable fashion, but when she started to question him, he shook his head teasingly.

"I admire your sisterly devotion, Miss Mandeville, but I would be remiss if I told you anything before the lady's husband has received my report. Where is Mr. Mandeville?"

Jane had been wondering too, but had not been inclined to find out. Edmund was not far away; hearing the doctor's loud tones, he came out of the drawing room and looked up. He held a glass in his hand and his voice was a little slurred.

"Well? Is the child born? Is it—is it a boy?"

"Congratulations, Mr. Mandeville." Adjusting his cuffs, the doctor started down the stairs. "It is a son, a fine, healthy child. Your wife is doing nicely."

iii

EDMUND'S REACTION to the infant was that of any young father —immense pride in the idea of a son, and visible consternation in the presence of the actuality. When Lizzie first presented it to him, it was so swathed in blankets and caps that its tiny scarlet face was barely visible. Edmund's own face fell when he got a closer look. Presumably he had expected something on the order of Lina's wax doll, perfectly formed and exquisitely pale. When the baby started to cry, he backed away and Lizzie laughed heartily.

She guarded the baby jealously even from its Aunt Jane, and that affectionate new relative was seldom allowed the privilege of holding it. Lizzie delighted in exposing Jane's ignorance; when she commented on the child's mop of black hair and pretty blue eyes, Lizzie was quick to inform her that most babies had blue eyes and dark hair. The latter might change color and the eyes almost certainly would. "Let's hope they're a lovely soft brown, like his papa's."

The christening took place in the chapel, Edmund overruling Jane's suggestion that the village church was more appropriate. She could not have explained why this seemed so important to her, but she was disappointed when Edmund refused. He would not have the child exposed to the air. It might take cold.

So Edmund John Albert Mandeville assumed his name

within the walls of his ancestral home, and Jane, as god-
mother, was finally allowed to cuddle her nephew. He protested bitterly when the devils flew out of him, and Sir
William, the co-sponsor and father of six, laughed heartily
and said it was a good sign. He then presented his godson
with an ivory teething ring and a silver cup and, tickling him
under his chin with a blunt, knowledgeable finger, added,
"By Gad, if he's not the dead spit of your dad, Edmund. He
had the Freeman look, from his ma, and so does this young
feller."

"Not at all," Jane said quickly. "He is the image of his
papa, aren't you, darling?"

In fact, she couldn't see that resemblance or the other one
Sir William had suggested. The baby's minuscule features
were as formless as wax. She had spoken without thinking,
prompted by the strange look that had come over Edmund's
face. She took it for offended paternal pride; it was many
months before she would look back on the incident and see
a deeper significance in Edmund's expression.

His heir having been duly delivered, Edmund gradually
took up his outside interests and duties. He was more often
away from home, and the joking comments of neighbors
informed Jane of the purpose of some of his trips—he was
calling on friends to brag about his offspring. He came back
from one of these expeditions in a vile humor, which lasted
for several days. Jane suspected he had called on the Astleys.
They always had that effect on her, and she could imagine
that their congratulatory comments would have the usual
leavening of envy and sarcasm.

However, when Megan came down with a bad summer
cold, Edmund was quick to summon the doctor. That gentleman's bland diagnosis to the contrary, she had had a difficult
time with the birth and had never fully recovered her
strength. Edmund's delicate consideration for her was the
talk of the household; not only had he refrained from returning to the connubial bed, he had even taken himself to
another room, one of the baronial bedchambers in the Tudor

wing, which had been refurnished to suit his taste. Jane deplored the fact that this was so much talked of, but it could hardly be otherwise, and she admired Edmund's forbearance.

As soon as Megan began to sniffle, he ordered her to bed. He gave another order that was not so dutifully received. Jane found Megan in tears that afternoon when she came to see how her sister-in-law was feeling.

"He won't let me see the baby," Megan sobbed. "Oh, Jane, I miss him already—and how will he get on without me?"

Jane knew what this euphemistic question referred to. Megan had insisted on nursing the baby, and the doctor had supported her. Motherhood was back in fashion; modern medical opinion had decided that the old habits of baby-farming and wet nurses were deterimental to mother and child alike. They both had to battle Lizzie, who thought no lady should suckle her own baby. When the doctor agreed that it might be better for the child to be kept away from possible infection, a wet nurse was procured with such speed that Jane suspected Lizzie had had one laid on. It was only too easy to find a mother whose baby had recently died.

"Lizzie has the situation well in hand," Jane said evasively. "You wouldn't want him to catch your cold, Megan —just think how terrible it would be to have a cold with a nose the size of his."

Megan was not amused. "Lizzie wants him all to herself," she said sullenly. "She would hardly let me hold him before. I don't believe in all this nonsense about infection."

"Then rest and take care of yourself so you will soon be well."

Instead of getting better, Megan got worse. The cold settled in her chest, and the doctor was sent for again. He was inclined to scoff at Edmund's fears, but he left medicine that he said would help Megan get the rest she needed. It certainly had that effect, which was not surprising, since its basic constituent was the popular soporific laudanum.

Megan slept like a dead woman that night, but her breathing was as ragged as ever, and Jane, who was sleeping on a trundle bed in Megan's room, found herself lying awake waiting for Megan's next painful breath.

However, by the following evening she began to think Megan was a little better. She administered the medicine with a careful hand and saw Megan slip into a stupefied but easier sleep. Edmund came in shortly after that, and agreed matters had improved.

"You are the one we must think of now, Jane," he said affectionately. "You have worn yourself out. I will send one of the maids to take your place tonight. Bess is to be trusted, isn't she?"

Jane had to acknowledge that she was too tired to be a fit nurse. Bessie had had some experience in tending the sick and was completely trustworthy, so after giving orders that she was to be called immediately if there was any change, Jane went to bed.

She woke next morning feeling quite restored and much more optimistic. After several days of chilly rain the sun had come out, and the blue skies seemed like a promise of hope. Knowing Bess would have summoned her if there had been need, she took her time about dressing before she went to Megan's room.

Bessie was not there. Edmund was sprawled in the arm-chair next to the bed, sound asleep. At her exclamation he stirred, rubbed his eyes, and muttered, "Is the sun up? I must have dozed off."

"Where is Bess?" Jane went to the bed. Megan's head was turned away. She appeared to be resting quietly.

"I could not sleep, so I decided to take over the night watch," Edmund explained. "I sent Bess to bed; there was no reason for everyone to sit up. But I am tired; now you are here, I think I will lie down for a while."

"Yes, do," Jane said.

After Edmund had gone, she reached for the bottle of

medicine. It was time for the next dose. But perhaps Edmund had already given it—the level of the liquid in the bottle was lower than she remembered, and Megan's slumber was uncommonly sound. She put her hand on the girl's cheek and drew it back with a gasp. She was burning with fever.

Jane jerked back the covers, which had been drawn to Megan's chin, and turned her lax body over on its back. She was breathing quietly—too quietly and too slowly. Long seconds passed between each inhalation, and instead of the rasping in the throat she had heard before, Jane now heard a lower, more remote grating noise with every breath.

She tugged on the bellpull, then reached for the water bottle, meaning to bathe Megan's hot face. The bottle was empty. Again she pulled on the bell, and finally there was a response.

The doctor's surprise and distress at the change in his patient's condition was apparent, but when Jane demanded an explanation, he could only look at her sympathetically.

"One never knows what course an illness may take, Miss Mandeville. And a lady so delicate, with such a weak constitution—"

"She is much stronger than she looks. She never had a moment's illness. . . ."

"You have nothing to reproach yourself with," the doctor said, thinking he understood her distress. "You did splendidly this morning, before I came; though some believe a fever patient should be heavily covered, in order to induce sweating, I am of the opinion that the fever ought to be brought down, if that can be done without danger of chilling. You were quite right to bathe her face and hands with cold water."

"I only did it to make her more comfortable," Jane said.

"She had perspired—her nightgown was still damp. Do you think she took a chill from that?"

"No, no. If you will excuse me, I had better get back to her."

His kindness comforted Jane, but she still felt guilty, as if she had neglected something. Believing Edmund would feel the same, she went in search of him and found him in the library. She saw that he had already spoken to the doctor. He stood with his arm resting on the mantel and his head bowed upon it, in a pose of utter dejection.

"Don't feel bad, Edmund," she said, putting an affectionate hand on his shoulder. "It is not your fault. The same thing might have happened if I had been there, or Bessie."

Edmund raised his head. There were no signs of tears on his face, but his eyes were rimmed in fiery red and they held a wild, hot glare.

"Fault?" he repeated, as if the word were unfamiliar to him. "Jane—do you believe in premonitions?"

"No," Jane said forcibly.

"I do. I have a premonition, Jane, that she will die."

"And I am equally sure she will live. Don't give way, Edmund. God will not take her from us when we love her so much."

"God doesn't listen to prayer," Edmund said. "He has never listened to mine."

iv

MEGAN DID not die. When the weary, triumphant doctor told Edmund his wife had passed the crisis he turned and went hastily from the room, but not before Jane saw tears spring to his eyes and course down his cheeks. She did not follow; she felt he needed time to himself to adjust to the joyful news. When he returned, several hours later, he was able to express his gratitude with suitable fervor.

Jane expected it would take Megan some time to recover, but as the weeks dragged on and Megan continued to spend most of her time in bed, or resting on the chaise longue in her room, she expressed her concern to Edmund.

"The doctor says she has made a full recovery, but she is not at all like the girl I used to know. All her radiance and energy are gone."

"I am only too well aware of the change," Edmund said. "We must resign ourselves, Jane. She will always be an invalid."

"Perhaps if we did not encourage her to rest and refrain from normal activities—"

"I assume that reproach is meant for me," Edmund said with a sigh. "Be just, for once, Jane; do you suppose I prefer this languid, drooping woman to the girl I married? You must admit I have accepted my deprivation far more gracefully than most men."

Jane knew what he referred to. Embarrassment made her cheeks burn, and she withdrew in some confusion. All the same, she wondered if Megan was really that much of an invalid, and whether the estrangement between husband and wife had been her doing. The girl had doted on Edmund, always touching him, leaning against him, seeking physical contact. But perhaps the pains of childbirth. . . . Jane was unable to pursue that idea to its inevitable conclusion. Physical love was a mystery to her; she had no experience on which to base a judgment as to how it might be altered by circumstances.

She would like to have spent more time with little Edmund, but between Megan and Lizzie she was given few opportunities to play with him. So she turned her attention to Lina, whose pretty little nose had been put badly out of joint by the arrival of the baby. Lizzie had banned her from the nursery after she caught Lina methodically dropping building blocks onto little Eddie. Quite an imposing edifice had been constructed before his howls summoned assistance.

Jane took Lina with her on her next trip to the village. She had resumed her visits, without incident. No one had the bad taste to refer to the recent unpleasantness, but the old ease was gone. People were polite but reserved. Mrs. Miggs only stared blankly if Jane asked about Sam or made any reference to the mill; inquiries about Granny Miggs reduced her to such a state of stuttering incoherence that Jane did not have the heart to pursue them.

As the pony cart drew up before the shop, Jane noticed that there had been a change in one of the houses down the road, near the square. There was a sign over the door, which she was unable to read because of the distance, and people were going in and out as to a shop or office. She would have gone to see, but Lina's desire for sweets would not wait, so she let the child drag her into the shop.

While Lina rummaged in the piles of goods, she asked casually, "What has happened to the Babcocks' house?"

Mrs. Miggs's knitting needles clashed stormily. "They do say that's one of them cooperative stores, Miss Jane. A wicked cheat on honest tradesmen, I calls it."

"Cooperative!" Jane went to the window and stared.

She had heard of these enterprises, the first of which had been established in a small town in Yorkshire. The movement had spread rapidly, for it provided honest merchandise at low prices, and was owned by the workingmen who founded it, instead of by a single merchant whose sole aim was high profits. The original founders had been followers of the mill owner Robert Owen—one of Sam's idols.

"Who is in charge?" Jane asked.

"Why, no one, miss," said Mrs. Miggs with awful sarcasm. "That's the idea; they's none o'they be master, they's all equal together."

She continued to knit furiously, her face set in a disapproving scowl, but Jane was not deceived. Stepping close to the counter, she said in a low voice, "If a certain person is involved in this enterprise, as I think possible, he ought to be reminded that this parish is not safe for him. There was a warrant out—"

At that interesting juncture Lina came running up with a rusty mechanical toy she had discovered under a heap of men's shirts, so Jane had to let the subject drop. However, she hoped her warning had not been in vain.

Megan dined in her room that evening, as had become her habit. Jane and Edmund were alone at the table in the empty, echoing Hall, where he insisted on being served. He seemed to be in a fairly affable mood, so Jane decided to risk a question.

"Have you seen the new cooperative store, Edmund?"

"Naturally. I am not so unaware of what is going on as you think, Jane."

"Why must you always. . . ." She checked herself. "I was only curious, Edmund. What do you think of it?"

"What I think is beside the point. I cannot order the place closed; the Act of '52 gave such organizations full legal status, and the house in question is not my property."

"I had the impression that the cooperative stores were somehow connected with the union movement."

"That is correct," Edmund said, taking a sip of wine. "How well informed you are—for a woman."

"I seek to be better informed," Jane retorted. "And if it is unwomanly to ask questions—"

"That's the old Jane!" Edmund laughed. "You have been so meek and mild of late, I hardly know you; and to be truthful, I miss the impertinent creature who used to hurl rude questions and accusations at me. What is it you are after now?"

"I want to know whether you have changed your mind about the unions," Jane said, encouraged by his smile. "They are legal—if I understand the law—and some employers feel that forbidding them only exacerbates labor problems."

"There is some truth in that opinion."

"Why, Edmund! I never thought to hear you say that."

"I am not impervious to reason, Jane. I want the mill to prosper. That is only common sense. And if you are of the opinion that a union would increase prosperity. . . ." He shrugged and raised his glass to his lips.

"I am," Jane said eagerly. "I have given the matter a great deal of thought, Edmund. Father did not approve, but I wonder if he would not feel differently if he were alive today. Times change, and the old ways are not always—" She checked herself, with the feeling she had heard those words somewhere before.

"Perhaps you are right," Edmund said. "At any rate, one ought to accept gracefully what one cannot change. As you so rightly point out, there is no law against unions—as such."

The footman came to take away their plates. "I promised Lina I would go up to say good night," Edmund said, rising. "Thank you, Jane, for your care of her; I am afraid I have been neglectful of late."

Jane sat in a daze until the footman's apologetic cough reminded her she was late in leaving the table. What had come over Edmund? It was not really change, though, it was the old Edmund, the brother she had loved. She ought to have been more patient. She ought to have realized that time would bring maturity, and that her dear brother would survive his disappointments to mellow into a fine man.

V

EARLY IN 1857 the British army in India was issued new cartridges for their Enfield rifles. Heavily greased with animal fat, the casings had to be ripped open with the teeth in order to free the powder before they were rammed into the guns. Some soldiers were of the Hindu faith, which considered cow's fat an abomination; others were Muslims and had been taught to regard pigs as unclean. When Colonel Smyth, commanding the garrison at Meerut, ordered the men to use the new cartridges, the Indian regiments refused, starting a conflagration that spread like wildfire across British India. The cartridges were only an excuse, the last of many violations of age-old custom by the conquerors; the result was the most bloody military mutiny in history. Reaction in England rose to a pitch of fury when Cawnpore surrendered to the mutineers on June 27, and the women and children of the garrison were brutally massacred.

Like everyone else in England that summer, Jane snatched up the newspaper as soon as it came into the house. Since they took the London journals, she was not particularly concerned when the local newspaper failed to appear in its usual place on the library table, but after three days had gone by she asked the footman whose duty it was to distribute incoming mail and parcels. The newspaper had arrived, he assured her. Perhaps Mr. Edmund . . . ?

It had not occurred to Edmund that the London papers would report a provincial story. Most of them did not, but the *Times* had an ambitious local correspondent who sensed potential drama. The London editor was not so sure, but he gave it a few lines on a back page.

"Labor Agitator Arrested. Incitement to riot, trespass, abduction. . . ."

It was the last charge that left Jane doubting the evidence of her own eyes. The story was infuriatingly skeletal; no names were mentioned except Sam's. Her first impulse was to order her horse brought around, to jump into the saddle and ride. . . . Where? Sam was being held at the county seat, but it would do no good to go there, she would probably not be allowed to see him without permission from a magistrate. Sir William Gilbert was one of the justices. And Edmund was another. . . . He had been appointed the previous autumn.

He had gone out, and it was several hours before he returned. By the time he came, Jane had convinced herself there must be some mistake. Edmund would set it straight.

He had been so reasonable the last few days. . . . Perhaps the journalist had mistaken the name, or an overzealous constable had acted on the old warrant, not realizing it could not hold. There were a dozen witnesses who could prove that Sam Freeman's actions on the night of the riot were blameless.

However, she was too upset to settle anywhere, so when Edmund entered the house, she was lying in wait for him.

"Edmund, I must talk to you at once."

Edmund brushed past her and started up the stairs. "I hope you don't mind if I change first. I have been in the saddle all afternoon."

Jane followed him. His face was calm and untroubled, his manner casual; but for some reason she could not have explained, that moment was the beginning of realization. She had difficulty keeping her voice steady. "It can't wait."

"Oh, very well." He glanced at her obliquely. "I see you are in one of your moods. Where is this confrontation to take place?"

Jane gestured mutely. She needed the comfort of familiar surroundings.

Edmund opened the door of her sitting room and stood back with exaggerated courtesy to let her precede him. Picking up the newspaper, she held it out to him. "What is the meaning of this?"

"It is written in plain English, I believe."

"Then it was you. . . . I can't believe it."

"I told you I was determined to put an end to violence of that sort."

"But you know the truth. You know he came to warn us."

"Jane, Jane, you are hopelessly naive. It is time you learned to stop taking people at face value."

The last doubt, the last hope, died as she studied his face. "Yes, you are right," she said finally. "I have been naive. You encouraged the union and the cooperative shop, didn't you? You hoped to lull him into a false sense of security and then you had him arrested."

"I don't intend to explain my actions to you." Edmund turned toward the door.

"You cannot succeed, Edmund. I can stop you, and I will. Never doubt that."

"What do you mean?" Edmund spun around.

"You must be mad!" She struck her hands together, unable to comprehend what she had heard. "If you believe these charges, you are insane. If you know them to be lies, you are a villain. Do you think I will keep silent while you swear his life away? My word is as good as yours, though I am a woman."

Calculation replaced the anger on his face as he stood staring at her. She realized he had not expected such a reaction from her, and she did not know what appalled her more, his overwhelming egotism or his indifference to the feelings of others.

"You can't do that," he said after a while.

"I will do it! How can you prevent me?"

She had thought herself completely undeceived, with no illusions left, but she was wrong; she was still ignorant of how far Edmund had gone on the long dark descent. When he raised his hand she didn't even try to avoid the blow. Until it actually landed, she could not believe he would do it.

Chapter
Six

WHEN JANE came to her senses, Edmund's arms were holding her and his voice was murmuring in her ear. "You brought it on yourself, it is not my fault; if you would only stop tormenting me!"

The words stripped away almost twenty years of time. She was a child, four, or perhaps five—a demanding, irritating child, always tagging after her adored big brother and teasing him to make him pay attention to her. The stone really hurt when it hit, and for a minute she thought she was going to be sick. But Edmund was really sorry. It was her own fault. . . .

". . . leave me alone, stop trying to interfere . . . never meant to hurt you, you should not have made me angry. . . ."

Jane opened her eyes. Edmund's face was close to hers, but when he saw she was conscious he stepped back.

"It won't be long," he said, retreating. "A week—perhaps two. I'll see that you have all you need."

"Edmund—"

"I'll be back." He reached for the door handle. "It won't be for long. It is for your own good, Jane."

The door closed. After a moment she heard the metallic scrape of a key turning in the lock.

The door was low and arched, darkened with time. The surface on which she lay was hard and lumpy at the same time; the sour stench of mold and dust made her nostrils contract.

Still disoriented, not so much from the force of the blow as from the fact that Edmund had delivered it, she was slow to realize where she was. Somewhere in the house, surely; there had not been time for him to carry her far. But it was not until she turned from the door to the wall opposite that she recognized her surroundings. Its curve defined the chamber as circular, the symmetry broken only by the straight line of the wall in which the door was located. The house had a number of towers and turrets, in addition to the large North Tower, but only one was isolated enough and ruinous enough to qualify as a prison. The Lovell Tower— named after a fifteenth-century lord of the manor who had been confined there by an ambitious and unscrupulous uncle. After spending ten years in solitary confinement, the unfortunate young man had hanged himself with his lacings.

Jane sat up, arms hugging her bent knees. The stone walls gave off a damp chill, but her fit of shivering was not induced by cold or by superstitious fear, though the barren, gloomy room was eerie enough to justify the servants' terror of it. They never came here. They believed Lord Lovell still walked the path his restless feet had worn so long ago, back and forth across the small space that had been his universe, his black and bloated face always turned toward the door. Sometimes on winter nights his cries could be heard in the lower corridors of the Tudor wing.

Edmund could not have found a more secure prison. The only part of the old wing that was inhabited was the long corridor at the front. This room was at the far end of the same wing, cut off by several doors and a flight of narrow, twisting stairs. She could scream and pound the door till throat and fists were raw, and even if a servant heard a distant cry he would not come to investigate; he would run away as fast as his legs could carry him. The windows were small and high, so thickly encrusted with the grime of centuries that sunlight scarcely entered.

But the strongest bars on the prison were impalpable. They were created by Edmund's unassailable position and unquestioned authority. She could not imagine what excuse he would invent to account for her sudden disappearance— a message from a dying friend, a sudden whim to travel? He might even profess ignorance as to her whereabouts and set the servants to searching the countryside. It didn't matter what he said. No one would question his word.

Her nerve did not break till darkness came. In the meantime she had explored the room in the forlorn hope of finding a way of escape. There was none; even the windows were sealed shut by rust, their thick, uneven panes scarcely more translucent than the leaded frames that held them. In addition to the bed, a big four-poster with rotted hangings fringing its top, the room contained only a table and two broken chairs, a few rough, chipped earthenware bowls, and a broken candlestick without a candle.

The first trickle of terror invaded her mind while she was walking up and down and heard each footstep echo faintly, as if an invisible companion kept pace with her. Only an echo—of course—but she scrambled up onto the bed with more speed than dignity. At least its headboard was against the wall. There were, she supposed, rats. . . .

As night crept in and deepened, she realized there were worse things than rats. The creatures of darkness entered into their kingdom; goblins and demons, the pale wraiths of the restless dead, every monstrous creature from every folktale and legend she had ever heard crowded around the bed, gibbering and leering. The barriers of rational skepticism went down before that diabolical assault. Huddling against the carved headboard, Jane sobbed and screamed for help like the madman who had once inhabited the chamber. Her incoherent cries were addressed to Edmund. God had nothing to do with this; the Powers of Light seemed infinitely far away.

Sheer exhaustion finally reduced her weeping to long, gasping sobs, and slowly, so slowly that she was scarcely aware of when it began, she realized that something was aware of her need and was responsive to it. It had no name and no dimension. It was simply there, and in its presence the leering shapes shrank back. Jane's tense muscles relaxed. Her head drooped. She was asleep.

When Edmund finally came, she was still sleeping. His movements roused her, but when she opened her eyes she was conscious of only one thing. Light. Beautiful, comforting, wonderful light. She sat up, brushing the tangled hair from her eyes.

The lamp, which Edmund had placed on the table, was one of hers. Its clean modernity, and the flowers painted on the base, looked utterly incongruous here, but its glow banished the demons.

"There," Edmund said, indicating a heavy basket. "Food and drink and a few other necessities. It should last several days, but I expect to return tomorrow night at the same time."

A wave of fresh disbelief swept over Jane. His calm, matter-of-fact tone was that of an innkeeper attending a guest.

"You can't hope to succeed in this," she said. "How long do you think you can keep me here before my absence is questioned?"

"It won't be long. A week, perhaps two."

"He will come to trial as soon as that? I assume that is your reason for this—this criminal act—to keep me from testifying."

"If you were not so disloyal and treacherous, it wouldn't be necessary."

"But, Edmund . . ." The weaknesses in his position were so apparent to her she could hardly believe they needed to be voiced. "I am not the only one who will speak for him. You can't abduct all the witnesses."

"The others will be reasonable. You have already proved, a hundred times over, that you cannot accept my authority."

"What is to prevent me from going to the magistrates even after the trial? Or do you plan to silence me permanently?"

"How dare you?" Edmund cried angrily. "Can you think me capable of such villainy?"

His indignation was genuine. This was what it must be like to reason with a lunatic, Jane thought.

Edmund resumed, in a quieter voice. "I am deeply hurt, Jane. But that is nothing new. You have wounded me to the heart more times than I can count. When I think how often, how passionately I longed for home and a life of peaceful happiness—and how tragically everything I yearned for has failed me. I will not give in to the unfairness of fate. I will overcome adversity and achieve the happiness I deserve. Oh, Jane, if you would only help me! Life could be so wonderful."

His pleading look and voice, his outstretched hand would have moved her once. Now she felt only numb dismay. Seeing her expression, he shrugged and let his hand fall.

"Perhaps a few days of quiet meditation will change your mind. I have not given up hope of you, Jane. You are not evil, only misguided."

When he reached for the lamp, Jane found she was not as strong as she had thought. "Please, please, Edmund—don't take the light!"

"Very well. If you want it, you shall have it. You see, I am doing my best for you, Jane. Is there any other small comfort you would like?"

Jane let out a strangled gasp of laughter. The desolate, ruined room was so lacking in even basic necessities that his question had a kind of ironic humor.

"Blankets and mattress, cleaning materials, fresh clothing, a bath," she began.

Edmund made it clear that he considered these demands unreasonable, but he promised to bring some of the things she wanted the following night. He was in a hurry to be gone, and Jane was equally anxious to be rid of him. His presence had become a horror worse than any imaginary demon.

The light made all the difference. Or perhaps her fit of weeping had exhausted fear; she remembered her strange fancy, of someone listening to her pleas, with a sad smile and a shake of her head. How glad she was that Edmund had not heard her frantic cries! They would not have moved him, and pride was the only thing she could cling to now. He was guiltless of one crime, though; he had not deliberately deprived her of light. Having no imagination himself, he could not realize the dreadfulness of the dark.

The basket contained a bizarre mixture of practical and luxury items—cheese and bread, a jar of preserved strawberries and a bottle of wine; a pair of high-heeled satin slippers, which she had never worn, and an old flannel dressing gown, among other things. Jane put on the dressing gown and forced herself to eat some of the bread and cheese. She had no appetite, though she had not eaten since lunch, but she knew she ought to keep her strength up.

After brushing the worst of the dust from the bed, she wrapped her gown around her and lay down, her eyes fixed on the comforting glow of the rose-painted lamp. But she had the feeling that even if it were taken away she would never feel the same degree of terror. She had reached the abyss and come back; she would not have to pass it again.

ii

THE FOLLOWING days tried her patience and her strength to the utmost. There were a few incidents of incongruous humor, verging on the farcical; one was the sight of Edmund's look of fastidious dismay when she gravely presented him with the vessel she had been forced to employ as a chamber pot. He hadn't thought of that—though how anyone, even Edmund, could have ignored it she could not imagine. His response was typical. When he returned the following night, he brought a servant with him. The man was a stranger to Jane, who would never have employed such a villainous-looking creature; grossly and unhealthily fat, with little piglike eyes and unshaven jowls. He performed the functions for which Edmund had fetched him with nervous alacrity and retreated without once having looked directly at Jane.

"I will be away for a few days," Edmund said. "He will come in my place."

"That disgusting creature?"

"If he does anything to disgust or offend you, he will be severely punished. He knows that. In fact, he has been forbidden to speak to you, so don't waste time trying to bribe or cajole him into letting you out."

Naturally, Jane did try. But she found her jailer, whose name she never learned, as impervious as Edmund had claimed. He was afraid of her; his sidelong glances and fumbling movements made that clear, and at first she could not comprehend why. One blow from his hamlike fist would have crumpled her like a sheet of paper. Finally she understood. Edmund must have told him she was mad—described fits of gnashing, scratching, biting insanity.

She assumed Edmund had gone to attend Sam's trial, but the more she thought about it, the more incomprehensible the situation became. How could a prisoner be brought to trial so quickly? The offenses with which Sam was charged were very grave. He could be transported, even hanged, if he was found guilty. Did the local court of quarter sessions have jurisdiction over such cases?

At first she could not believe Sam was in real danger, but as she went over Edmund's seemingly irrational plans, she began to realize it was she, not her brother, who was out of touch with reality.

The Astleys, Megan, Barkens the butler, perhaps a few of Sam's union friends—like Jane herself, they were witnesses to Sam's real motives the night of the riot. However, when she started to break the list down, she realized the frailty of Sam's defense. The Astleys didn't count. Cynical and corrupt themselves, they probably agreed with Edmund's interpretation of why Sam had come that night, and even if they believed Sam innocent, they would support whatever Edmund chose to say. Poor old Barkens probably had not understood half of what transpired that night; he would never contradict his master; and even if he did, his word would carry no weight against Edmund's. The same applied to Sam's friends. The only person who might be believed was a member of the same class as Edmund and his fellow justices.

Megan was his only hope. When she comprehended that, Jane's heart sank. Megan would speak out, if she had the chance; Jane did not doubt her integrity or her sense of right and wrong. But she would not have the chance. Edmund did not have to imprison her physically, she was cut off from the world by her semi-invalidism and disinterest. She never read a newspaper, she said the ghastly stories of the Mutiny upset her. The servants had been told to keep distressing news from the mistress. And even if, by some chance, she heard of Sam's danger, she lacked the strength and the will to act.

Edmund had not been stupid after all. She, Jane, was Sam's only witness, and once he was condemned it would be almost impossible for her, a woman, to convince the magistrates that justice had not been done.

Sickness like sour bile rose in her throat. That was the real root of her helplessness. She was a woman. She had been slow to comprehend this because her father had never treated her as an inferior. To all intents and purposes, however, she was a member of a lower class, almost a lower species of humanity—without legal rights, without control over her surroundings or even her own body. If she accused Edmund of swearing away a man's life and of imprisoning her against her will, he would simply say she had lost her mind; and the great male-dominated outside world would support his cause and accept his word. She hated them—all of them—curse their smug, complacent, narrow minds! Even her father had done her no service when he allowed her privileges she could never claim as rights. And Edmund had been a sweet, lovable human being before he turned into a *man.*

The realization born that day was never to leave her. It would become one of her most deeply held convictions. But as her anger faded, she knew she was wrong about Edmund, at least. For months she had made excuses for him, and tried to understand what had changed him. He had not changed. He had always been selfish and self-centered. Utterly charming, when he got his way—and he always got his way, from fawning servants and adoring little sister and indulgent father. It had taken the inevitable frustrations and tragedies of adult life to bring out his true nature, but the seeds of corruption had always been there. Only her own uncritical affection had kept her from seeing them. She should have known—if not before, then on the day the shabby, desperate girl had forced her way into the house with Edmund's baby in her arms. Edmund had rejected child and mother; it was his father, not he, who had offered little Caroline a home and provided the mother with enough money to make a new life for herself.

A few slow, hot tears trickled down Jane's cheeks as she mourned the death of a boy who had never lived, except in her own mind.

Resolutely she brushed the tears away. Sam was her main concern now—another man! If it had not been for Sam. . . . But that was too outrageous; her sense of humor, battered and bloody but still alive, would not allow her to entertain resentment of Sam. She laughed and said aloud, "There must be a few good men. So many billion human beings can't all be wicked. And now I'm talking to myself. A few more days of solitude and I'll be as mad as Edmund claims."

Knowing that Sam's time must be running out, she made her last effort to bribe the jailor that night. Every other means had been explored and found wanting. She had torn her nails and bruised her knuckles on the stones looking for hidden doors; on hands and knees she had gone over every inch of the floor. Balancing dangerously on the rickety table, she had finally worked one of the leaded panes of glass out of its enclosure. It fell without a sound, the impact muffled by the grass below. For hours she stood looking down at the rhododendron and azaleas on the lawn; when, at last, the foreshortened figure of a housemaid in white cap and apron appeared, she put her mouth to the opening and shouted at the top of her lungs. The girl didn't even look around.

When the jailor finally came, Jane was ready for him. She had little to offer, only a pair of plain gold earrings and a brooch with a twisted braid of hair—Edmund's and her father's. For the first time she regretted her simple tastes. But when she held out the pathetic trinkets she saw a flash of greed illumine the dull, porcine face.

"I have more," she said quickly. "In my room. My jewel box is there, and some money. You can come with me, close behind me."

For a moment she thought she had him. But he was not as stupid as she had thought, or else Edmund was paying him a princely retainer. She had also underestimated the terror felt by the uneducated for insanity—they still thought in terms of demons and possession. When in her eagerness she took a step toward him, he stumbled back, extending his fingers in a gesture older than the Druids.

The key scraped in the lock. Jane sat down on the bed, holding her rejected treasures. So that was that. The last hope had failed.

And the wretch had neglected to bring oil for the lamp. It would scarcely last the night, and she would have none for the hours of darkness before he came next night—if he came. She had frightened him badly. What a pity she did not have the power he feared—the Evil Eye. "I would have dropped him in his tracks and then gone after Edmund," Jane thought viciously.

Best to save as much oil as she could. She turned the knob that lowered the wick and lessened the flame. She had not meant to turn it off completely, only dim it, but her fingers continued to twist, quite independently of her will, until the last spark flickered and died.

Jane scuttled up the length of the bed to her old refuge against the headboard. It was the first time she had been in the dark since the initial night of her imprisonment, but the assault she feared and expected did not come. Wincingly, as a tongue probes an aching tooth, she sent out an exploring tendril of thought, tapping the reservoir of fearful memories. The Hag, the Black Dog, the ghost of Lord Lovell—are you there? Where are you? Nothing answered. The dark night was empty.

She must have stretched out and closed her eyes, but when the dream began it seemed to her that she was still sitting upright staring into blackness broken by a single point of light—one star, framed in the space left by the missing pane of glass. The lights blossomed and multiplied. The opening was expanding. That was when she knew she must be dreaming, for she felt no surprise, only gratification as the walls melted into air and the broad starry sky arched over her. It was the same sky she knew, with the constellations she had learned to read in childhood—the Great Bear,

Sagittarius the Archer, Cassiopeia on her glittering throne. At first the landscape, silvered by a full moon, was unfamiliar; there were no walls or gates or buildings, only an empty clearing enclosed by forest wilder and more tangled than any she had seen. Then she saw the hills. Their shapes had altered, but not beyond recognition. A shining ribbon of river flowed down one dark slope and vanished, to reappear at the edge of the clearing.

With no sense of transition or movement she found herself standing on a grassy surface starred with small white flowers whose scent filled the air with sweetness. She was facing the center of the clearing. There was something there —something angular and unnatural. Its shape was hidden by a pale, luminous mist, like curdled moonlight.

Jane started to walk toward it. The mist wavered and blew away, together with whatever shape it had concealed. She was on a dim path whose surface glimmered, unsubstantial as water, and the path was moving. She was carried with it, passing through trees and shrubs as if they were shadows. Strange objects began to appear along the path, lumpish and unformed. Gradually they took on human shape—men and women and the smaller forms of children; a Roman soldier in breastplate and cuirass, a woman in a rough homespun robe like the one she had worn to the ball; all quiet and motionless as life-sized painted statues.

Faster and faster the path carried her past them—or were they rushing forward and gliding by, while she stood still? She could not tell; she could no longer distinguish the details of faces and clothing, though one white-robed image, surmounted by a gleam of golden hair, reminded her of Edmund's painting.

She sensed that she was coming to the end of the strange journey. Something waited for her there in the shadows; she could see a dim outline, featureless but oddly familiar. She had felt no sense of fear, but now a vague horror seized her, not of the thing itself, but of what it meant. Struggling in vain to free herself of the dream, she was carried remorse-lessly on till she saw it plain, its face twisted and rotted by the primeval sin, its bloody hands stretched out to greet her. Covering her eyes, she came gasping back to consciousness in the musty dark of the tower room.

Book Three

MEGAN

Chapter
One

THE PLOT devices of real life are never as appropriate as the ones invented by novelists and playwrights. Megan should have learned of her lover's peril from a breathless messenger galloping hell-for-leather across the country, and arrived at the foot of the gallows in the nick of time. Instead she heard the news from a gossipy old woman whose violation of her master's express orders was prompted by prurient curiosity instead of zeal for justice.

Lizzie had no doubt Sam was guilty. Master Edmund had said he was, and that was fact. She and the other servants had accepted Edmund's original explanation of Megan's absence the night of the riot: she and Jane had lost their heads, as women were inclined to do, and had gone running out into the night instead of staying safe at home. Yes, Lizzie was genuinely shocked and surprised when Master Edmund told her the truth and warned her to make sure her mistress was not upset by the news of Sam's arrest. Sam didn't seem like that sort of man. He had been a limb of Satan when he was small, like all lads, and she had often threatened to take a stick to him when he teased her. She hadn't approved of Miss Jane's friendship with him and the other village children either. But there had been no harm in him. She had rather liked the young rapscallion.

It just went to show what happened when a boy got above his station and read all those books.

Edmund had not attempted to conceal Sam's arrest from the servants. They were bound to hear about it from friends and relatives, since the local paper had carried the story. But the charge of abduction was one of his mistakes. Inciting to riot was a serious crime, but it did not necessarily carry the ultimate penalty; Edmund wanted blood, not a few years in prison. It never occurred to him that Lizzie, like all virtuous women, would be irresistibly titillated by the implications of the word "abduction." Since she could not stoop to discuss it with the lower servants, her curiosity boiled for three days before she finally succumbed.

Megan was in the nursery with the baby that morning. As she sat on the hearth rug tickling young Eddie's nose with a feather, she looked almost like the girl who had come to Grayhaven two years earlier. The baby was the only thing that could rouse her from her dreamy lethargy. A pity there would be no more, Lizzie thought sadly. She didn't know why she was so sure of that, but she was. And Miss Jane looked to be a spinster all her life, she never did flirt with the young men. Maybe she would meet some gentleman in London. At the least she would buy some handsome new clothes. She hadn't taken hardly a stitch with her.

It was very sad. Miss Jane practically an old maid and Miss Megan—not that she was good enough for Master Edmund anyway—and now not really a wife at all, just a mopey little thing, wasting away . . . not long for this world.

Lizzie sighed. Absorbed with the baby, Megan paid no attention, so Lizzie sighed again, louder.

"What is it, Lizzie? Tired, already? It is just the start of the day."

Master Edmund had told her to make sure none of the servants mentioned the subject to their mistress. That didn't apply to her, not really. Besides, she wasn't exactly bringing it up, she had to answer if her mistress asked.

The feather stopped moving as Megan listened. The baby's fat, fumbling fingers closed over it. Mechanically, without looking, Megan pulled it away before he could stuff it into his mouth.

Lizzie was disappointed by Megan's calm reception of the shocking news, but she was also reassured. She hadn't done any harm in telling the girl; Master Edmund was just fussy, like all men.

"I was that shocked, you can't believe, ma'am," she concluded. "Why, you must have been frightened to death. Did he—er—did he harm you, ma'am?"

"No."

"Or say something—well—rude?" Lizzie persisted.

"No."

"Oh," Lizzie said flatly. "I'm that glad to hear it."

Megan rose. "Thank you, Lizzie."

She didn't even say good-bye to the baby, Lizzie thought, as her mistress moved to the door. Poor young thing, she's failing every day.

Megan sat down, very carefully, in her favorite chair. Dressed in the height of fashion, with every curl in place and gems glittering at neck and wrists, she was a modish, elegant little figure, and her face had the remote doll-like expression Victorian gentlemen favored in their ladies. Beneath the calm look her mind was racing.

Edmund couldn't know. He must have his suspicions,

though, for nothing less could have driven him to invent that final, fatal charge. She was ready to acquit him of deliberate fabrication on the other charges; it would be like him to assume that ignoble motives underlay Sam's attempt to warn him. But the other. . . . Oh, no, he knew she had not left the house under duress. If he had not believed her own carefully censored report, Jane would have told him.

Jane. That was another thing. Jane was gone. . . . Fretfully, Megan rubbed her head. She had been in a fog for so long, her brain felt paralyzed. The medicine didn't seem to be doing her any good. Perhaps she should stop taking it.

Jane had gone to London. Megan had thought it curious, when Edmund told her, that Jane had left so suddenly without a word of farewell. And to London, of all places. Jane hated London, as she hated all cities.

Perhaps Jane had gone to the court, or the trial, or whatever it was—gone to tell the truth, to help Sam. It was a reasonable idea, and for a moment it comforted Megan. Another vague, uneasy memory raised fresh doubts. Jane had been gone a long time—two days, perhaps longer. If only she could remember! Long enough, at any rate, to give her evidence and return. Edmund was still away, though. Perhaps he, too, was at the trial.

She could not count on Jane. When she had time, she would begin to worry about Jane. But not until she had done something else.

Rising, she went to the wardrobe and opened the door.

Edmund had not told the grooms she was not allowed to ride. It had not occurred to him that she would try. The head groom, a trusted old servant, did try to expostulate with her. He had heard she was ill, and she certainly looked odd—a kind of wild glitter in her eyes and skin stretched tight as a drum over her cheekbones. She replied in a tone he had never heard her use, and he limped off to do her bidding.

It was midafternoon before Megan reached her destination, after a series of misadventures that would have reduced a woman less obsessed to tears or despair. She had no idea where she had to go, or how to get there. Inquiries in the village gave her some of the necessary information, but Mr. Higgins delayed her a good half hour, arguing and fussing, after he had learned the reason for her questions. Finally she just stood up and walked out. She got lost, not once but several times.

Despite her anxiety, she found an unexpected pleasure in the ride. She had not been on horseback for months; now she wondered how she could have moped in her room so long, only half alive, while spring blossomed into summer. The sunshine and the breeze were like a balm, warm to her troubled spirit.

Her conscience was not at peace. She had done Edmund a grievous wrong, and she was prepared to spend the rest of her life making it up to him—and that would be penance enough for her sin. That night on the grass beside the Toman stone she had learned what rapture really was. Never to know again that passionate tenderness, that sense of utter security. . . . If the real torture of damnation is absence from the loving presence of God, then she would truly be in Hell—and if that was blasphemy, she couldn't help it. She was prepared for the sacrifice. She had wronged her husband and hurt the Holy Mother. . . . But it was Edmund's anger that concerned her. She had a feeling the Holy Mother would understand, and She would certainly be quicker to forgive.

Megan entered Warwick by the new bridge over the Avon and promptly got lost again. A kindly passerby directed her to the Shire Hall. The imposing neoclassical building was so much bigger than she had expected that she was momentarily disheartened, foreseeing another period of aimless wandering and questioning. She had lost so much time already. . . .

She was not as late as she feared. The progress of justice was leisurely in the extreme, for the justices saw no reason to shorten the dinner hour for the convenience of prisoners who had nowhere to go but the jail, just around the corner. The hearing had only recently reconvened when Megan found the room she wanted.

She got in by the simple expedient of pushing past the gaping attendant and opening the door. The scene wasn't as intimidating as she had expected, just a few men sitting around a table . . . and Sam. After the first quick identifying glance, to make sure she was in the right place, she didn't look at him again. Nor did she look at Edmund, who had leaped to his feet and was staring at her in mingled fury and disbelief.

The other men rose too. Sir William's jaw dropped till his chin completely vanished into the folds of his old-fashioned neckcloth. The sight of his bluff honest face made Megan feel more at ease. He had always been kind to her.

"Gentlemen," she said clearly. "Please forgive the interruption. I have come to give my evidence."

Edmund's face was the color of port—no, not so dark—a nice light claret, rather. He is not very quick, she thought coolly. It should not be difficult to outwit him.

Recovering himself, Edmund turned to his fellow justices and spoke in a low mumble. He is telling them I am ill or out of my mind, Megan thought. He is so obvious. . . . She stood waiting and knew her appearance, cool and quiet and calm, gave the desired impression. Sir William kept glancing at her, and finally he broke into Edmund's speech with a loud "Come, come, man, we can't keep the lady standing there. What's the harm in letting her speak?"

"Thank you, Sir William," Megan said. She began to strip off her gloves.

Sir William left his judicial seat to place a chair for her with his own hands. "Now then, my dear, just say your piece," he said.

Megan glanced around. "Should I not take my oath first?"

With some fumbling a Bible was produced, and she repeated the words in a clear voice.

"I protest this—this irregularity," Edmund said thickly.

"The witness is under oath," said the other justice, a thin, gray-haired gentleman wearing spectacles. "You know the procedure, Mr. Mandeville."

Megan was allowed to tell her story without interruption. She had had plenty of time in which to plan what to say, especially the conclusion.

"Naturally I cannot testify with regard to Mr. Freeman's connection with the organization he is supposed to have been a member of; and I certainly would not commit the impropriety of attempting to explain his motives in warning us. My husband is much wiser than I; I do not contradict any of *his* interpretations, gentlemen. That he has leaped to an erroneous conclusion about certain other occurrences of that night is probably my fault; I should have been more explicit. I came here to correct that error, and to assure you that Mr. Freeman did not . . . abduct me. I left the house of my own accord. I was so frightened I lost my head and infected Miss Mandeville as well. I was the one at fault; she only followed because I made her."

She stopped at that point and gazed limpidly at Sir William. She was not sure what story Sam had told and did not want to contradict him.

It was the third justice, the gray-haired man, who said, "The story is not complete, Mrs. Mandeville. We have witnesses who swore they saw Mr. Freeman pull you onto a horse and ride away with you."

"Witnesses? Drunken ruffians, you mean," Megan exclaimed. "The fact is correct, the interpretation is wholly false. Mr. Freeman did join Miss Mandeville and myself in the stable yard, as we were trying to saddle our horses. We intended to come to you for protection, Sir William." She smiled at him, and he gave her a fatuous grin. "The grooms had run away, and we were having a difficult time. Without Mr. Freeman's help we would never have succeeded in saddling the horses. He had barely finished the task when we saw several men—horrid, rough drunken men—running toward us, shouting and cursing. Again I lost my head. I ran. Had not Mr. Freeman pulled me onto the horse and ridden away, I would have been subjected to insult, if not bodily harm. As soon as we were away from the house and I had regained my composure, he left me."

Another lie, she thought, but what does it matter? I have so much on my conscience now. . . .

Edmund had tried several times to interrupt, but had been squelched by his fellow justices. Now he said in a strangled voice, "Well, gentlemen, this pathetic fantasy is surely evidence of Mrs. Mandeville's state of mind. Have you tortured her enough? May I take her away now?"

"It doesn't have the ring of fantasy to me," Sir William said. "And it fits the other evidence we have heard. I never trusted those rascals who testified to seeing Freeman snatch your wife into the saddle; what the devil were they doing in the stable yard anyway, where they had no business to be? Jones, you're the legal feller. What's your opinion?"

The lawyer cleared his throat. "I have seldom heard a clearer or more sensible statement. Mrs. Mandeville appears to be well acquainted with the laws of evidence, particularly the ones concerning hearsay and unwarranted assumptions." He glanced meaningfully at Edmund.

"Well, we can hardly convict the feller of abduction if the abductee denies it, can we?" said Sir William cheerfully. "I say he's innocent."

"Sir William, you are not following the correct procedure," the lawyer exclaimed. "It is not our duty to decide on the defendant's guilt or innocence, only whether. . . . Oh, dear, this is most irregular. Mrs. Mandeville, thank you for coming. You are excused."

Megan walked to the door. She was careful to avoid Edmund's furious gaze, but she could not resist one last look at Sam. After all, she would probably never see him again.

He seemed to be in a stupor of disbelief. He wasn't even looking at her. She wished he would smile, so she could carry that picture of him in her heart; but she dared not linger. Her head high, her face composed, she left the room.

Too restless to sit down, she walked back and forth along the hall until finally the door opened and Sir William burst out. He came directly to her and took her arm.

"Let's be off, my dear; give Edmund's temper a chance to cool. A man doesn't like to be called a liar by his wife, especially when she's right and he's wrong."

"Then—"

"Yes, yes, it's all settled; no prima facie case, none at all, no reason to hold him for trial." Sir William towed her toward the exit. "Edmund is off for home, but I persuaded him you had better stay overnight; my good lady will be pleased to have your company. She is here with me, at our town house." He bundled her into his waiting carriage and, still talking animatedly, waved one of his footmen to attend to Megan's horse. "Never believed it, you know; known the boy for years, he's a good lad, though he's picked up some strange ideas from all that schooling. Don't approve of schooling. Gives people strange ideas. Look at Edmund. Strange, very strange, some of his notions."

ii

THOUGH GRATEFUL for the Gilberts' hospitality, Megan would have preferred to be alone that evening. However, Lady Gilbert was one of those people who think of solitude as a curse and would never be guilty of afflicting such discourtesy on a guest. She and Megan were sitting in the drawing room after dinner when Sir William came in.

"Someone to see you, Mrs. Mandeville," he said with a grin. "Hope you feel up to it—just a few minutes. Quite right and proper of him to come and thank you."

Megan rose, but she felt sick and weak. To see him again, after she had said a silent, eternal farewell; to keep up the pretense of cool indifference in front of Sir William. . . . However, as the latter ushered her into the room where Sam was waiting, he remarked, "Got some things to do—you'll excuse me, won't you, Mrs. Mandeville? Don't keep her long, Sam; not that you were ever much of a talker, eh?"

As soon as the door had closed, Megan walked straight across the room and into his arms. He held her close for a moment, his cheek resting on her tumbled curls, and then, almost roughly, pushed her away.

"Not here—you've risked yourself enough for me today."

"There was no risk," Megan said. "I'd do more if I could, you know that—"

"I must talk fast, he'll think it strange if I linger. Megan—I asked you once to come away with me."

"And I said yes."

"I couldn't let you. You weren't yourself, and I was wrong to ask it, I knew that as soon as I spoke. Now—now it's changed. I'm asking you again. Will you come?"

It was a bizarre interchange; Sam had backed away, twisting his cap in his hands as he shot out the brief, brusque sentences. She saw how he trembled, and the old warmth, the certainty of safety and peace filled her. How different from the childish infatuation she had felt for Edmund!

"I cannot," she said steadily. "There is the child."

"Can you believe I forgot?" Sam said after a moment. And that, too, was like him, she thought; no argument, no debate, only an unwilling acknowledgment of fact that turned his face, in an instant, into the haggard countenance of a tired old man.

"You couldn't forget him if you had ever seen him. He is so sweet—growing every day—he smiles now when he sees me, I know he does, though Lizzie says it is only wind—"

"Megan—don't."

"My darling—"

"Don't, I said." He put out a hand to halt her advance

toward him. "You're right again. I must go. Promise me you'll take care."

"For what?"

"Yourself. Guard yourself. There are so many dangers—accidents—"

"Walking in the rain and catching a chill," she said, fondly mocking what she took for a lover's excessive solicitude. "My dearest, I will. And you—you promise too?"

"I promise."

There was nothing more he could say. As he left the house, emerging into the soft rain of an autumn night, he searched for a means of protection for her, and found none. He couldn't even warn her; it would only frighten her, and she probably wouldn't believe him. No one would believe him—not Sir William, not Jane. But he was not unacquainted with violence. He had seen the look of murder before, and that was the look he had seen in the courtroom on the face of Edmund Mandeville.

Chapter
Two

SIR WILLIAM insisted that Megan accept the loan of his carriage to take her home. If the day had been fine, she would have preferred to ride, but a gray mist hung low over the fields, so she endured the long, jolting journey, her white horse tied behind the carriage. She had fought her way back to calm after a sleepless night; but she was not looking forward to seeing Edmund.

It wasn't as bad as she expected, perhaps because Jane was with him. She came running forward and threw her arms around Megan.

"I am so glad you are back," Megan said, returning the embrace warmly. "Did you have a good time in London? Did you bring back a lot of beautiful new frocks?"

There was an odd little pause. Then Jane said, with a glance at Edmund, "Not a stitch. You know how I am. Edmund gave me such a scolding."

"And now it is Megan's turn to be scolded," Edmund said.

"I thought you had taken leave of your senses, my dear, to do such a wild thing, in your delicate state of health. You could have spared both of us inconvenience and embarrassment if you had only told me the whole story in the beginning."

"I am sorry," Megan stammered. She had been prepared for angry resentment. His mild, affectionate tone disarmed her completely. It did not seem possible that the handsome, smiling face could belong to the same man who had been choleric and incoherent with fury the day before. She would almost have preferred anger. Rational, fond forgiveness only increased her sense of guilt.

"Well, it is over and done with." Edmund turned away. "I only hope you have taken no harm from your adventure. Excuse me now, ladies; I have work to do."

"Come with me while I change," Megan said to Jane. "Now that you are home again, I realize how much I missed you."

"Gladly." Jane linked arms with her and they started up the stairs. "I feel as if I had been gone for weeks instead of days. The change in you is astonishing! You look so much better."

"I feel much better. I do believe that medicine was doing me harm instead of good. I shan't take any more of it."

"Medicine," Jane repeated slowly. "Not the laudanum?"

"Some kind of tonic, I believe," Megan said carelessly. "The doctor told Edmund I ought to go on with it, but I'm sure I don't need it any longer. Jane—I must tell you—"

"Yes, I want to hear. But come in and close the door. Now then. . . . Was it Lizzie who told you? Edmund reduced her to hysterics last night, after he came home."

"Poor Lizzie." Megan began to unbutton her crumpled gown. "I am glad she disobeyed him. When I think what might have happened. . . ."

"I admire you more than I can say, Megan."

"You would have done the same if you had been here.

And," Megan admitted, with a rueful laugh, "it was no last-minute reprieve, or anything of that sort, Jane; only a preliminary hearing, with the possibility of a trial to follow."

"I know," Jane said in a remote voice, as if she were talking to herself. "I realized that after a time; and that is why I cannot understand. . . ." She checked herself and sat in brooding silence for a few moments before continuing, "Pay no attention to me. You know my habit of talking to myself. What were you saying?"

"That I might just as well have waited and consulted with you—and Edmund, of course—before rushing off."

"No. No, you acted rightly."

Neither of them had mentioned his name. Megan nerved herself to do so. "Sam came to thank me, last evening. He looks well—he . . ." She could not think what else to say. "He told me to remember him to you."

"That was kind," Jane said.

She had dropped into a chair and sat with bowed head and hands clasped. Impulsively Megan bent and kissed her on the cheek.

"Your holiday does not seem to have agreed with you, Jane. How thin you are! Have you been eating properly?"

"No," Jane said, with a little laugh. "Not properly."

ii

EDMUND NEVER again referred to Megan's testimony. She had not expected such magnanimity; few people can forgive an injury, fancied or real, without endless reminders of their nobility of soul. She renewed her private vow to be a dutiful, fond wife. Perhaps Edmund, too, had determined to turn over a new leaf. He gave up jeering and taunting her; he invited her to participate in some of his hobbies. They were closer than they had been since the first months of their marriage, except for one thing—Edmund did not assert his rights as a husband. This bothered Megan less than it ought to have done. She had the satisfaction of being physically faithful to the man she secretly wanted, without the onus of rejecting the man who had the legal right to her love.

Their quiet hours together in the library came to be a source of considerable pleasure to Megan. Edmund was pursuing his investigation into the history of the house and its previous owners, and some of the stories he unearthed were as fascinating as any novel. To his great disappointment, however, he found no secret passages or priest's holes.

"You are a hopeless romantic, Edmund," Megan said teasingly. "What would you do with a priest's hole if you found one?"

"Shut Higgins up in it when he annoys me," Edmund replied. "If he continues to cast sheep's eyes at Jane, I will have to take steps of some kind."

Edmund's next suggestion was that the girls learn how to shoot. Their exclamations of disgust made him laugh. "I know you are both too squeamish to kill game," he said. "I was thinking of target shooting. But if guns offend you, what about bow and arrow? Archery is an old and honored English art, and if Her Majesty practices it, it must be considered suitable for ladies. It ought to attract you, Jane; you always claim you can do anything as well as a man."

"I never made any such claim!"

"Oh, very well, if you are ready to concede your inferiority. . . ."

Jane rose to the bait like a trout to a fly, and Edmund had butts set up on the lawn. To see Jane, hair clubbed back and sleeves rolled up, squinting to find her point of aim, was a sight that never failed to amuse her brother, yet she developed considerable skill and drew a surprisingly heavy bow for one of her size. Megan was not so ambitious; but both admitted they derived a good deal of pleasure from the exercise, especially because they shared it with Edmund.

He was so affable, so considerate, so like the old Edmund, that both girls stopped exchanging glances of surprise when he did something accommodating. One evening at dinner, when he made an announcement he knew would displease them, his manner was almost apologetic.

"I feel I must warn you well in advance so you can take steps to revenge yourself on me," he began. "I have invited three of the people you most dislike to visit. Promise you will defend me, Megan, if Jane loses her temper; you know I am in deadly terror of her."

Jane could not help laughing through her frown. "You needn't tell me the names. The Astleys and Mr. Belts?"

"I assure you, Jane, you need not fear any undue familiarity from Belts," Edmund said earnestly. "Our acquaintance is one of business. I have no more desire than you to be connected with him intimately."

"And what is the business?" Jane asked.

Once Edmund would have haughtily denied her right to question him. Now he said mildly, "We are in the same trade, we have common interests and common problems. In fact, Jane, you ought to commend my present intention. I hope to persuade Belts to give up his prejudice against a labor union."

"You astonish me, Edmund," Jane said. "I thought you had the same prejudice."

"As I told you once before, I have reconsidered. I am counting on you, Jane, to put up with Mr. Belts's crude habits for the sake of principle; will you not consent? To mitigate your suffering, I will invite Sir William and Lady Gilbert, and your admirer, Higgins."

He had to go out that evening, so after dinner the two girls retired to Jane's sitting room. After much grumbling Jane had finally consented to employ her skill in making a party frock for herself. Megan insisted on supervising, to make sure Jane would not alter the elegant pattern she had helped to select. This evening marked the occasion of the first fitting. Jane circled slowly, at Megan's direction, and the latter laughed merrily at the contrast between the charming look of the sprigged taffeta and the sulky face above it.

"It becomes you," she said.

"No doubt Belts will think I am making myself fine for him." Jane's lower lip went out another half inch.

"It needs a deeper dart here. Let me pin it. . . . Now take it off and I will help you whip the frills." She went on more soberly, "If Belts bothers you so much, Jane, take to your bed while he is here. I will swear you have the vapors or the ague."

"If you can endure the Astleys, I can stand Belts. Megan —do you mind very much?"

Megan took her time threading her needle. She knew what Jane meant, and wanted to reassure her, but she could hardly explain to Edmund's unmarried sister that she no longer cared what Edmund did or whose bed he shared.

"I don't believe Edmund cares for her any longer," she said truthfully. "I don't know why he goes on seeing them, unless it is because he is trying to impress them with something. . . . His happiness, perhaps, or his success. But I am not jealous, Jane, believe me."

"I am so glad you feel that way. I agree with you. He has changed, hasn't he? And you are happy, Megan? I am sure he loves you; he has been so affectionate, so caring."

Megan bowed her head over her sewing to hide her face. Dear, innocent Jane! She must know that Edmund still occupied the bedchamber in the Tudor wing; did she really believe that married love consisted only of smiles and courtesy? Well—perhaps she did. For all her down-to-earth manner, there was something essentially virginal about Jane. The words "spinster" and "old maid" didn't really suit her, for they suggested frustrated hope and dried-up emotions. Jane suffered from neither of these, at least not visibly.

Megan rubbed her aching knee as she tried to think of something noncommital and comforting to say. Jane looked up from her work.

"I noticed you were limping. Have you hurt yourself?"

"Some careless housemaid left a patch of grease or oil on the library steps this morning. I managed to catch the railing when I slipped. I count myself lucky to have only a sprained knee."

"I should think so," Jane exclaimed. "I told Edmund that cast-iron spiral staircase was dangerous when he installed it. I hope you gave the maid a sharp lecture."

"Edmund did, I believe. He was very angry. But it is nothing, only a bruise."

Jane had apparently forgotten her question. Megan was glad she had not been forced to lie. She was sorry she could not speak freely to Jane; they had once been so close. There were too many forbidden subjects now.

For instance, her suspicion that Edmund was sleeping with one of the maids. It would not be surprising if he was; such things were only too common, and if Edmund preferred a servant to his wife, there was nothing his wife could do about it.

It had unquestionably been a woman's voice she heard that night when she had gone late to the nursery, worried because the baby had appeared to be starting a cold. A faint light in the corridor where Edmund slept had caught her attention as she returned. It was only a soft glow, quickly fading; but she had immediately thought of fire. When she ventured into the corridor, the light was gone, and there was no smell of smoke. Passing Edmund's door, she had heard a woman laughing, softly. Something in the quality of that laughter had sent her tiptoeing away, her face hot with embarrassment.

Certainly she was in no position to complain. But she felt sorry for the girl.

And certainly it was not the sort of thing she could discuss with dear, innocent Jane. She glanced at Jane's absorbed face, bent over her work. At least the reticence and the reservations were all on one side. Dear innocent Jane had no guilty secrets.

iii

WATCHING EDMUND with Lady Georgina, Megan felt sure she had been right about his feelings for the lady. He was civil, but hardly more than that; in fact, she caught a look of faint disgust cross his face on several occasions when Lady Georgina was more than usually coarse or rude. She treated him with the same proprietary insolence, but she also devoted some attention to George Belts. One could hardly call her ladyship's technique flirting, it was too unsubtle, but Belts responded with elephantine gallantry.

He had not given up hope of Jane, however, and Megan was sometimes hard pressed to hide her amusement as she watched her sister-in-law's two admirers vie for her attention. Mr. Higgins' soft brown eyes followed Jane's every movement with doglike adoration. If she dropped a skein of silk or a book, he was out of his chair before the object touched the floor. Once he collided with the footman, who was intent on the same errand. Megan laughed with the others, but felt guilty immediately afterward. The unfortunate young man was really devoted to Jane, and his suit was hopeless. Jane would never care for him, and doubtless Edmund had higher ambitions for his sister.

Belts was obviously making an effort to avoid offense. Only once did he break the unwritten rule in regard to discussing business before the ladies, continuing an argument that had begun over the port and that he was unwilling to abandon. As the men entered the drawing room where the ladies were sitting by the coffee tray, he exclaimed, "Nay, nay, Mandeville, you don't know a domned thing about it.

These domned cooperatives have spread over Yorkshire like plague sores on a mon's face—" He took the coffee cup Megan handed him, nodding his thanks, but before he could continue, Edmund said coldly, "Moderate your language, I beg. There are ladies present."

Jane's ears had pricked like those of a little gray fox. "Mr. Belts's language is rough, but his subject interests me very much. Go on, Mr. Belts."

It was one of the few times she had addressed him directly or shown any interest in what he said. Belts swelled with pleasure. "I told you the lass had raight good sense for a female," he informed Edmund. "May be she'll see what you don't—these shops run by t'workers take profits from us. It's not only t'shops, mind—they're putting their plaguey hands into other kinds of businesses, grain mills, housing—and textiles. What d'you say to that, eh?"

"Even if I disapproved, I could not prevent them," Edmund said resignedly. "The law supports them."

"Radical scum, the lot on 'em," Belts fumed. "Union men and Owenites. . . ." Both words sounded like vile epithets as he spat them out. "That villain managing t'shop in your village—he's a bad 'un, I know of him. I wonder you allow him to hang about, after what he did to—"

With a neat twist of the wrist Jane poured her hot coffee into Belts's lap, bringing his tirade to an abrupt halt. Apologies and repairs followed, and the topic of cooperatives was not renewed.

Megan's start had passed unnoticed in the general confusion. No name had been mentioned, but she did not doubt that Belts had been referring to Sam. She had assumed he meant to leave the district; her hard-won resignation went down like a house of straw at the thought that he was so close, that she might see him any day. She resolved to avoid the village, at least until she had got used to the idea; but a hard seed of resentment took root in her mind. How could he do this to her? Didn't he realize he was making things more difficult? Maybe it wasn't difficult for him. Maybe he didn't care how she suffered.

When the harvest festival came around again, Megan tried to excuse herself. She put no stock in Mr. Higgins' ridiculous theories, but his remarks about pagan ceremonies and sacrifices had left an unpleasant aftertaste. Courteously but firmly Edmund insisted she take part. "The people expect it, my dear. It is their way of expressing their loyalty and affection for us. Since we were unable to participate last year, it is all the more incumbent upon us to be present on this occasion."

Mr. Higgins threw out so many broad hints that it was impossible not to include him in the party. Megan acknowledged that his presence helped make the ceremony less trying than she had expected it would be; it was impossible to be solemn about it with Mr. Higgins beaming and nodding and scribbling notes. Yet it seemed to her that there was a new gravity about the performance, and a more profound deference in the attitude of the workers toward Edmund. This pleased him and put him in an excellent temper, so it was a cheerful little group that returned to the manor. Mr. Higgins was ecstatic, in his genteel way; the chance to spend hours in Jane's company, and the confirmation, as he believed, of his scholarly theories combined to raise him to the heights of enjoyment. He spoke primarily to Jane, and Megan paid little attention, catching only a phrase here and there.

". . . that crude straw image . . . a primitive goddess of vegetation . . . Cybele and Attis, the divine mother and her dying consort, who is reborn. . . ."

Mr. Higgins seemed to be obsessed with pagan gods! His talk of divine mothers and resurrected gods struck Megan as decidedly unorthodox. The bishop would certainly not care for them; she hoped Jane would drop Mr. Higgins a gentle hint to keep his opinions to himself.

Her restless, unhappy mood intensified during the following days. She knew the cause of it. She had stayed resolutely away from the village, and had confined her walks and rides to the park, but she knew that sooner or later the meeting she dreaded must occur, and though she steeled herself to face it, she made little headway in combating emotions she had no right to feel. When the critical moment came, she was unprepared, for it took a form she had never dreamed of.

She and Edmund were in the library that evening, and Jane, who had declared herself curious about their discoveries, was with them. Edmund was teasing his sister about keeping such late hours, for the clock had already struck ten. When the footman entered and presented the note to Megan, she was sitting some distance from the others, in a chair whose high back and wings shaded her face. If it had not been for that, she would surely have given herself away. The handwriting aroused no emotion except curiosity; it was unfamiliar to her. But when she opened the note and read the few lines it contained, she thought she was going to faint.

"I must see you tonight. Come to the entrance to the maze at midnight."

There was no signature. None was needed.

"What a strange hour to send a message," Edmund said casually. "Who is it from, my dear?"

Megan's fingers closed convulsively over the scrap of paper. "I suppose the messenger lingered on the way," she said. "It is only—it is only from Mr. Higgins' housekeeper, asking for a recipe—that almond cake he enjoyed so much."

"I wonder she did not write to Cook, then," Edmund said. "However, it is of no consequence. Jane, would you hand me that small leather box? There are some old parchments and papers that may interest you."

Megan slipped the note into her bodice, where it burned against her skin. Though she knew nothing but extreme urgency could have prompted such a message, she felt degraded and angry. Mortal sin is a heavy weight on one's conscience, but it possesses a certain dark dignity. This had all the stigma of a common vulgar intrigue.

It never occurred to her not to keep the assignation. But when she crept out of the house, just before midnight, she was determined that it would be for the last time.

The maze was not one of Edmund's innovations. Its walls of tall, thick boxwood had been centuries growing. The quickest way to reach it was past the kennels, but Megan gave this building a wide berth. The hounds knew her scent and might not give tongue, but Edmund's new mastiff was quite a different matter.

He had brought it home a few weeks before, and even Jane, who loved all animals, recoiled when she saw the great brindled monster, big as a pony. The keeper who held its chain had to exert all his strength as it fought the lead, baring its long white fangs.

"We need a watchdog, Jane," Edmund had explained, when she expostulated. "You have ruined the other dogs for that task, with your petting and spoiling."

Jane had nothing more to say to that. Surreptitiously, however, she began visiting the dog and trying to make friends with it. "He is not really vicious," she said sheepishly, when Megan remonstrated. "He has only been trained to be that way. Promise you won't tell Edmund, Megan."

Megan had promised, of course, but she refused to join in Jane's visits. She was fond of dogs, but this one seemed more like a wild beast than a potential pet.

She passed the kennels without rousing the dogs, and breathed a sigh of relief when she reached the entrance to the maze unseen and unannounced. It was very dark in the shadow of the tall shrubs; the faintly unpleasant scent of the boxwood was strong around her as she stood with her hand pressed against her pounding heart.

She waited for what seemed a long time, her anger growing. Bad enough that he should demand this risk; to keep her waiting, like an infatuated servant girl. . . .

She did not see the dog until it was almost upon her. It had been trained to attack, not to warn. The air left her lungs in a wordless gasp of terror. There was nowhere to run. She was pressed against the prickly thickness of the boxwood, and even if she had known the twisting paths of the maze, the dog could easily track her into a cul-de-sac.

The mastiff came to a stop, only feet away, as if it had run into an invisible wall. Megan thought perhaps her frozen immobility had puzzled it; she stood motionless, hardly daring to draw a breath.

Then a voice said quietly, "Caesar. Good dog, Caesar. Stay."

Megan rolled her eyes to the side.

"Don't move, Megan," Jane said, in the same low, calm voice. "Good dog, Caesar. Come. Come to Jane."

The dog leaped, not at Megan, but at the diminutive figure that had summoned it. Whimpering, it dropped at Jane's feet. She knelt and rubbed its pale belly.

"Good boy. Jane's sweet baby. Jane loves you. Come along now and she will find you a nice bone. Such a good dog, Caesar. . . ."

She straightened up with the dog's lead in her hand. The mastiff continued to wriggle and rub against her while she examined the chain.

"The link is pulled open," she said. "It would take a stouter chain than this to hold him. Go inside, Megan. Come with Jane, good boy. A bone, or perhaps a leftover mutton chop. . . ."

Megan was unable to move at first. Her knees felt like water. She watched the two bizarre figures walk away across the garden, Jane with her hand on the dog's collar like a juvenile Christian martyr who had tamed his lion. Not until they disappeared into the shrubbery did she gain strength enough to obey Jane's order.

Early the following morning she found an opportunity to speak to Jane alone. "I must explain why I went out last night—"

"You were restless and went for a walk," Jane said. "It might . . . it might be wise if you did not do it again."

"I promise."

Jane dropped the subject. But Megan sensed that Jane's suggestion, as well as her own response, referred to something more serious than a late-night stroll.

Chapter
Three

WHEN MEGAN came down to breakfast a few days later, she was the only one at the table. She had slept badly and had little appetite; nibbling disinterestedly at her toast, she wondered how she was going to fill the long day.

The door to the pantry opened and Lizzie's head appeared. "Miss Jane? Oh, excuse me, ma'am. I see she's not back yet."

"Back from where?" Megan asked. But Lizzie had vanished. The housekeeper was still smarting from the effects of Edmund's scolding. Not surprisingly, she blamed Megan rather than Edmund, and had been excessively formal with her mistress ever since.

She never thought I was worthy of Edmund, Megan mused. I wonder if she did that on purpose, to arouse my curiosity and leave it unsatisfied. If so, she has succeeded!

She didn't want to ask Lizzie where Jane had gone so

early, for Lizzie was likely to roll her eyes and say she did not want to be accused of gossiping. Before Megan was tempted to lower herself to question the parlormaid, Jane came in.

She was dressed for riding, in one of the drab, narrow gowns she preferred. That in itself was unusual; early-morning gallops were not Jane's style. Upon seeing Megan, she smiled and murmured, "Good morning." Megan would have been less concerned if she had burst into tears; the smile was the most ghastly caricature of good spirits she had ever seen.

Before she could ask what was wrong, Lizzie's face reappeared. "I thought I heard you, Miss Jane. Is it as bad as they say? The store burned to the ground, and everyone with it? Black as a bit of burned toast, they say he was, poor Sam—"

The room spun like a top and tipped sideways. Megan slid out of her chair onto the floor.

When she came to her senses, she was lying on the chaise longue in her room. Jane sat in a chair nearby, her chin resting on her hand. As soon as Megan's eyes opened, she said, "He is not dead. He is hurt, but not badly. I have just seen him."

After a moment, Megan said, "How long have you known?"

"I did not know for certain until today. Sometimes, before . . . I wondered."

"Jane—I wanted to tell you—you must believe me—"

"Don't tell me. I don't want to hear. Except—was it the Toman glade?"

"Yes. You must hate and despise me, Jane."

"I don't hate you. Or despise you."

"Then you are kinder than I deserve. You have always been kind to me, Jane." She caught the hand that lay limply in Jane's lap and raised it to her lips.

Jane gasped and pulled it roughly away, as a healthy

person might recoil from a leper's touch. Her face was a death's head in dry stretched skin, her lips drawn back from her teeth, her eyes dull and staring. She was not looking at Megan; she seemed to be contemplating something invisible except to her own mind, something so monstrous that it had brought her to the brink of madness.

"That night, a few days ago, when the mastiff was loose —why did you go out, Megan? Was it the note you received earlier?"

"I can conceal nothing from you now, Jane," Megan said. "The note was from him—from Sam. He asked me to meet him. It wasn't what you think, Jane, it had never happened before—"

"What I think . . ." The words were as low and harsh as a groan of pain. "If you only knew, Megan, what I am thinking. I suspected it might be that, so I asked him. . . . Megan, Megan—didn't you wonder why he never came?"

"I thought of many reasons," Megan said quietly. "Delays, accidents . . . and then I thought perhaps he had changed his mind."

"You never wondered why the dog slipped his chain that night, of all nights in the year? And the grease on the staircase in the library—the medicine that made you so lethargic —the empty water bottle. . . . But you wouldn't know about that. . . . How many other accidents have there been that you did not mention to me?"

"I do seem to be rather awkward lately. I suppose I am distracted."

Jane raised her hands and tugged at her hair. The gesture would have been comical if her face had not been so wild. She got stiffly to her feet and walked to the window. Standing with her back to Megan, she muttered,

"How can I make anyone believe it when you do not? When I can hardly believe it myself. . . . I kept telling myself I must be wrong. That I could not be certain unless it happened again . . . and again. . . . Sooner or later he'll succeed.

Then it will be too late. And there is no way I can stop it. No way at all."

The agonized, incoherent monologue filled Megan with alarm. She struggled up and ran to Jane.

"You are not yourself, Jane. It is my fault, I have upset you. Please come and lie down. What can I get you?"

She put a tentative hand on Jane's arm, fearing another rejection. Jane's withdrawal had been understandable—but, oh, the pain of that gesture of loathing and disgust!

Instead Jane turned and clasped Megan's hand in hers. Her face was still pale, but it had lost its look of wild dismay. "I frightened *you*—forgive me. I am indeed concerned about something, but it is not what you think. I must deal with it myself."

"I wish I could help you, Jane."

"I know you would if you could. Now sit down and I will tell you what happened last night. I know you are anxious to hear, but are ashamed to ask."

Megan's cheeks grew warm. "I must say one thing more, Jane. I did wrong, I know I did. I intend to spend the rest of my life making it up to Edmund. I don't understand how it happened. I never meant it to happen—"

"I understand," Jane said. "Better than you think."

Megan could contain herself no longer. "Tell me, Jane. How badly was he hurt? Was he burned in the fire? How did it happen? Why was I not told?"

"I did not hear of it myself until early this morning. No one knows how the fire started; it completely destroyed the shop and damaged an adjoining building before it was brought under control. No one was burned. The two men who lived behind the shop got out in time. One was stupefied by the smoke. Sam dragged him out; in doing so he was struck by a falling beam and suffered a broken collarbone and a number of bruises."

"You—you have seen him, you said."

"Edmund and I went to the village when we heard," Jane

said. "It was a shocking sight—nothing left but scorched foundations and blackened beams. Edmund was very upset. He has offered a sum of money to help rebuild."

"That is good of him."

"Yes."

"He was sincere when he said he had changed his mind about the shop and the union," Megan said. "And he feels a personal sense of outrage, no doubt."

"I asked about Sam," Jane continued, as if she had been interrupted in the middle of a memorized recitation. "Mrs. Miggs has taken him in. The doctor has already been to see him, and he is resting comfortably."

Abruptly she turned toward the door. "I think I will have some breakfast. There was no time earlier."

Megan wanted to hear more; but the questions she yearned to have answered were the ones she had no right to ask. "How did he look? Does he suffer much? Did he ask about me?" It was up to Jane to offer what details she chose, and Jane was undoubtedly right to cut the discussion short. So she said humbly, "Thank you, Jane."

"What for?" Jane said, and went out before Megan could answer.

ii

MEGAN'S AFFECTION and gratitude toward her sister-in-law increased a hundredfold in the following days. Jane seemed intent on demonstrating that the disclosure of Megan's crime had not lessened her fondness; she was constantly with Megan, from early morning until they said good night. Her attention verged on the maternal; she fussed over Megan's food, checked on the way the maids cleaned her room, and inspected her wardrobe. There were times when Megan found the constant supervision a little oppressive, but appreciating the delicate sensitivity that prompted it, she never protested.

She was able to repay Jane, in a small way, by supporting her against Belts, who had become a constant visitor. It was not Edmund's fault that the Yorkshireman annoyed Jane with his attentions; he scowled angrily every time Belts paid Jane one of his heavy-handed compliments. Belts was impervious to scowls or sharp answers, which were the only kind he ever received from Jane. The ruder her remark, the louder his laugh and his admiring "By Gar, I do like a lass that speaks her mind!"

One morning in early October, when they met at breakfast, Edmund was in an excellent humor. Glancing around the table, he said cheerfully, "Well, Jane, you will not have to endure Belts's attentions any longer. I have informed him he must look elsewhere. Shall I confess how I rescued you? Don't be angry; I intimated that your affections and your person were engaged elsewhere."

"I hope you didn't suggest that the lucky man is Mr. Higgins," Megan said, laughing. "Jane is as indifferent to him as she is to Mr. Belts."

Jane did not laugh. "You have sold the mill, haven't you, Edmund?"

Edmund concentrated on his creamed fish for a while before answering. "Why do you say that, Jane?"

"Let's not fence," Jane said wearily. "You tolerated Belts and forced me to tolerate him when you hoped to gain something from him. Now you have what you want, and you have dismissed him."

Edmund put down his knife and fork and met her look with one as steady. "Very well, I won't equivocate. I have sold the mill. The final papers will be signed in a week or two, after the lawyers have finished drawing them up. You can't stop it, Jane. You have a half-interest, and you will receive your share of the money, to do with as you like; but you do not have control. If you doubt me, ask Mr. Trumbull."

"I don't doubt you."

"Try to be reasonable, Jane. The mill has brought me nothing but trouble, and matters will get worse in the future; government regulations make it very difficult to run a business with profit. On the other hand, there has never been a better time for agriculture. I mean to put the money into the estate —improve cultivation methods and buy more land. I foresee a steady rise in food prices over the next ten years, and—"

"And it is the proper occupation for a gentleman."

"Is there anything wrong with that? Our father wanted his son to have advantages he lacked. I hope to give my father's grandson greater advantages than I have had."

It was an odd way of putting it, Megan thought.

Jane rose unsteadily to her feet, her napkin crumpled in her hand. She was very pale. "Excuse me. . . ."

"I will go after her," Megan said, as Jane ran from the room. "She is very distressed."

"She will have to get used to it," Edmund said, picking up his fork. "It is for her own good, after all."

After some searching Megan found Jane in her favorite part of the garden. It was no formal French or Italian arrangement, but a wonderful confusion of native blooms growing in random loveliness. Crimsoning Virginia creeper veiled a stone wall, and the Michaelmas daisies formed clumps of purple and lavender bloom. Jane sat huddled on a bench, her knees drawn up and her hands clasped.

Megan sat down beside her. "I am so sorry, Jane. I know how you hate this. Perhaps if I speak to Edmund—"

"It would do no good and you know it."

Megan bowed her head in acknowledgment. After a moment Jane went on, "Have you ever thought, Megan, that we are little better than the unfortunate slaves in America? We have no more control over our lives than they. They cannot go where they like; neither can we. They are bred like cattle, to the mate their master chooses; so are most of us. If they are abused, they have no appeal. Neither do we."

"Surely you exaggerate, Jane."

"I do; I admit it. There is a difference between outright, honest slavery and the kind of ownership men have over women. Not all women suffer the injustices I have mentioned, but if they have freedom of choice it is a freedom bestowed on them by the men who own them—a privilege, not a right. And how limited those privileges are! All professions and trades are closed to us, except the lowest and most degrading—heaven help you, you know more of that than I. We have no possessions, not even the clothing on our backs—they belong to the man who owns us."

Megan couldn't see the justice of Jane's complaints; the abuses she described did not apply to her, for she had money of her own. And any man, including Edmund, who attempted to force Jane into marriage would be sorry he tried! She attributed Jane's wild exaggeration to distress, and gently put her arm around the narrow, shaking shoulder. "My dear, do come inside; it is chilly, and you are cold."

"I am not cold. I am afraid."

"Of what, dear Jane? Surely not of men; you resent Edmund now, but one day you will fall in love and marry—"

"Marry." Jane spat the word out. "Do you realize, Megan, that if Edmund beat you or imprisoned you or struck you, there is not a court in the land that would defend you from him?"

"Jane, you are talking so wildly! You would never marry a man like that—and Edmund would never beat me. He is not that sort of person."

"No, you are right. He is not that sort of person." A violent shudder passed through Jane's body.

"I insist you come in, Jane. You are having a chill. Come with me to see little Eddie, he will make you smile again."

Jane allowed Megan to raise her to her feet. "Yes, little Eddie. Does Edmund spent much time with him, Megan?"

"Men don't care for babies of that age," Megan said lightly. "As soon as he can sit a horse and hold a cricket bat, his papa will take a greater interest in him."

Jane stood staring at her with such a peculiar expression that Megan felt herself flushing. "I know what you are thinking, Jane. I have vowed to conceal nothing from you, so I will answer the question you are too considerate to ask. *I don't know.* I cannot possibly be certain. Oh, it sounds so dreadful!"

"It doesn't matter," Jane said. "Not to *me.*"

Megan noticed the stress on the last word. "It is what I would expect you to say. Please come now."

Jane followed, unresisting. She muttered something under her breath.

"Two places at the same time?" Megan repeated. "What are you worrying about now?"

"The same thing," Jane said. "Twice over. Oh, pay no attention to my mumbling, Megan."

iii

THE FINAL papers for the sale of the mill were to be signed at the end of October, and Edmund decided that the occasion should be celebrated by a house party. He did not describe it that way to Jane. Instead he suggested that since Belts must be present, other guests might make him easier to bear.

"Ask anyone you like," Jane said. "It is a matter of complete indifference to me."

Megan almost wished Jane would express her feelings in her old way, by stamping and shouting. Jane's rages were soon over, and she usually seemed the better for them. This new Jane, silent, pale, and haggard, was painful to see, and some of Jane's remarks were so strange that Megan actually began to fear for her sanity. On one occasion she broke into a speech about Eddie's increasing beauty, intelligence, and strength to ask abruptly, "Do you believe in prayer, Megan?"

"Why, yes, of course," Megan said, startled.

"To whom do you pray? No, that was a silly question. To God and our Saviour, I suppose—and Mary, do you still pray to her?"

"Sometimes," Megan admitted.

"And the saints?"

Megan decided to humor her. "I used to. It is sometimes easier to confess one's human failings to an intermediary who once was human, than to a great impersonal Being so far away—"

"A male Being," Jane interrupted, with such disgust that Megan didn't know whether to smile or be shocked at her blasphemy.

"Perhaps that is why Our Lady is favored by Catholics," she said. "And the female saints—I remember deciding when I was very small that I would choose Saint Agnes as my patron, because of her lamb."

Jane brushed this frivolous comment aside. "Do you believe our prayers are answered?"

"How serious you are today, Jane."

"I believe they may be. If we ask for the right thing—and if we address our petitions to the appropriate Power."

"Jane, what is troubling you? I am worried about you."

"Nothing." Jane forced a smile. "Perhaps I will turn Catholic and find a saint who will listen to me. Saint Arca would be suitable; she must have been a local girl, and would understand my problems."

"It would be wise to find out who the lady was, and what her attributes are. You wouldn't want to adopt the patron of thieves or beggars."

"That is a point worth considering," Jane murmured.

iv

THE DAY before the guests were to arrive Edmund was much occupied. He took pride in his talent for entertaining, but on this occasion he was determined that every arrangement should be as perfect as possible. Megan thought she understood; this was the first demonstration of his new status as a landowner and gentleman of leisure, with the hated stigma of the mill at last removed.

Sir William and Lady Gilbert were to be among the party— "For I know they are favorites of yours," Edmund said, addressing Jane and Megan impartially. "I had great difficulty persuading Sir William; at this time of year he goes out shooting almost every day, and he was reluctant to give up his sport. I had to promise we would allow him a chance at our partridges and pheasants. Now don't glower at me, Jane; you know I don't favor blood sports. I hope you will give Sir William a demonstration of your skill at archery. When I mentioned it to him, he scoffed, not only at the sport itself, but at the idea that a lady could excel."

"We will prove him wrong, won't we, Jane?" Megan said.

Jane appeared unenthusiastic; but Sir William's jovial teasing the following afternoon roused her to accept the challenge. When the party assembled at the butts she performed with such skill as to win the admiration of all beholders. One of Sir William's daughters, a young lady who had just attained the dignity of putting her hair up and her skirts down, clapped her hands in delight and expressed her intention of taking up the sport. Edmund kindly showed her how to hold the bow; after several failures she managed to get an arrow into the target.

"There, Papa," she said, with a laughing glance at Sir William. "You see I can do it; when you arrange a practice ground for me at the Abbey, I will work at it every day."

"Well, well," Sir William grumbled. "I suppose I might; it is a nice ladylike kind of game."

"If you think it is so simple, why don't you try a shot?" Edmund said, offering Sir William his bow.

The unsuspecting old gentleman squared his shoulders and stepped confidently up to the line. After pinching his thumb in the bowstring and seeing several arrows drop ignominiously at his feet, he flung the bow aside and declared it was a silly occupation for a grown man.

Edmund went on baiting him all that evening. It was good-natured, but Sir William's vanity had been sorely offended by his failure, and his temper began to heat up under the pricks. "What's the point of it, Edmund, tell me that?" he demanded. "Punching holes in bales of straw—"

"Why, sir, what a way to speak of the noble art that won the battles of Crécy and Agincourt and fed our ancestors for centuries before the invention of gunpowder. I grant that to take a deer by means of bow and arrow requires more skill than shooting—"

"Oh, does it?" The old gentleman was red as a turkeycock. "Would you care to arrange a test?"

"I was about to suggest it," Edmund said, smiling.

"And a little wager, eh?"

"By all means."

To the amusement of the other guests the two solemnly proceeded to set up the conditions of the wager. The first to make a kill would proceed to the house, where the others, the judges, would be waiting. Wagers were laid; the ladies favored Edmund, and the gentlemen, to a man, declared Sir William must win. Belts refused to risk "good brass" on the enterprise, which he declared was all nonsense anyway.

Everyone assembled next morning for an elaborate breakfast. It was during the meal that somehow or other a fault in the conditions of the wager was discovered.

"We ought to have a more precise method of noting the moment of the kill," Edmund said. "In my case the judges won't even hear a shot, and if I am some distance away, so that it takes me longer to retrace my steps—"

"Are you implying that I would lie about the time?" Sir William demanded fiercely.

"My dear Sir William, quite the contrary. I am suggesting a signal to mark the precise moment."

One of the gentlemen facetiously suggested smoke signals, in the American Indian style. After some debate it was decided that the winner would fire two shots in rapid succession, to be followed, after a specified interval, by a third.

"That means I must carry a gun," Edmund objected. "I insist on a bearer, then. Jane, Megan—will one of you act as my squire?"

Several of the other ladies clamored to join the party, but Edmund laughingly declined. "This is a serious wager, ladies, not a walking party. I will have only skilled assistants, who understand the art of toxophily."

"You know Jane's feelings," Megan said, with an affectionate glance at Jane, whose countenance displayed a glum sobriety quite at variance with the cheerfulness of the others. "She cannot bear to see anything hurt. So if my services are acceptable, Edmund . . ."

She hoped to please Edmund and spare Jane by her offer, and Edmund's nod and smile proved she had accomplished the first of these aims. Jane exclaimed, "You hate it as much as I do, Megan, you know you do. Edmund, don't ask her."

She was overruled by the others, however, and the parties prepared to set out. Edmund's tall figure was seen to great advantage in a green-and-white-checked coat and striped trousers, with matching shoes. With a languishing glance Miss Gilbert said he only needed a cap with a long feather to be the image of Robin Hood.

"And here is Maid Marian," Edmund said, indicating Megan, whose gown was of the same green as his jacket.

"Off we go then," said Sir William. "I'll be back in a twinkling, ladies and gentlemen, with a fat buck to my score."

"I'll get my quarry before you get yours," Edmund replied. He offered Megan his arm, and they set off in the opposite direction to Sir William.

"Where are we going?" Megan asked, as they walked toward the wall south of the house.

"As far away from Sir William as we can get," Edmund replied. "He is in such a temper, he will blaze away at anything that moves."

"You are in a merry mood, Edmund."

"And why not? Today is the beginning of a new life for me."

The stream was running full, for there had been much rain that season. They crossed it by means of an ancient stone bridge east of the gate and began to climb. The slope was moderate and the trees soon closed in around them.

"You must tell me what to do," Megan said, breaking a long silence. "How do we know where to find the deer?"

Edmund laughed and took her hand to help her over a rise. His face was flushed. "There is a clearing farther up the hill where I think they come to graze. I found spoor there the other day."

Megan's step faltered. Edmund's fingers tightened over hers. "Keep walking. We don't want to be beaten."

They had not followed the path she knew, and she had lost her bearings since they entered the woods. Perhaps Edmund had another clearing in mind. But the Toman glade was the sort of place animals might frequent—secluded, with fresh water and ample grass.

She let Edmund lead her on. He kept her hand in his, his grasp painfully tight. She was scarcely aware of the pain as she fought to face what lay ahead. She had not returned to the glade after that night. To see it now, in Edmund's company . . .

Before they had gone much farther, they heard a crashing below and behind them, like a large animal charging toward them. Edmund dropped her hand and turned. The sunlight sifting through the brilliant fall leaves made him look like a saint in a stained-glass window.

"What is it?" Megan whispered. "It is coming straight toward us."

A figure emerged from the dappled gloom—a little figure all in brown—gown, hair, and tanned face, like a creature out of an old legend of enchantment.

"I changed my mind," Jane said. She was breathing quickly. "I will be your squire today, Edmund."

"What the devil—" Edmund began.

"Megan is the lady of the house, she should be with her guests. I will close my eyes when the poor deer falls—but Megan would have done that too. You don't mind, Edmund? There is no reason why I should not do as well as Megan—is there?"

"I suppose not," Edmund said ungraciously. "Well, Jane, you have certainly thrown all my plans awry—"

"Have I?"

"But since you are here, you may as well come along."

"Let me carry the gun for you, then."

Edmund handed over the shotgun. "Be careful with it. Hurry, now; you have wasted too much of my time already." He walked away.

Megan was limp with cowardly relief and renewed gratitude. Jane's sensitive kindness was beyond belief; she must have realized where Edmund was going, and intervened to spare Megan the shame and pain of returning to the scene of her crime with the victim of it.

"Jane, dear," she began in a low voice.

"Hush." Jane gestured. "Hurry back, Megan. Go straight back, don't wait for us. Do you promise?"

"Of course. But why do you—"

"No more. Go now." She started after Edmund and did not look back.

V

SIR WILLIAM won the wager. As she retraced her steps, Megan heard several shots echoing across the little valley. It was hard to count them or even determine their original direction; but when the agreed-upon signal came, just after she had crossed the bridge, there was no mistaking it, or the direction from which it came. Megan frowned. Edmund would be put out at losing, and Sir William would not be a graceful winner.

His stout little figure came strutting across the lawn shortly after she had changed and joined the others. He accepted their congratulations and compliments with a smug grin, but he could hardly wait for Edmund to return so he could crow over him. He cast increasingly impatient glances at his pocket watch and finally exclaimed, "Curse the feller, he must have heard my signal. What's keeping him?"

"If he can bag his deer, he may feel less embarrassed at losing the wager," one of the other men suggested with a chuckle. "I know I would hate to face you with empty hands, Sir William."

"That wasn't the agreement," Sir William grumbled. "Ha —I think I see someone coming now. He took his time about it."

For all his skill at shooting, his eyes were not as good as he believed. When Megan turned in the direction he indicated, she recognized the approaching figure as Jane's. She was alone, and she walked very slowly, with a perceptible pause between each step.

A sudden feeling of oppression and foreboding brought Megan to her feet. "Something is wrong," she said, and hurried to meet Jane.

Several of the men followed, infected by her alarm. Jane stopped when she saw them coming. She stood unmoving, her arms limp at her sides and her face as expressionless as a doll's. Megan caught her by the shoulders.

"What is it, Jane? Are you hurt?"

"Not I," Jane said. "There has been an accident. A fatal accident."

Her eyes closed. She slid through Megan's nerveless hands and lay in a crumpled heap at her feet.

Book Four
JANE

WAS MR. BELTS very angry when you told him you would not sell?" Megan asked.

"Oh, yes. But his ranting and cursing will have no effect. The papers were never signed, and since little Eddie is still a minor, the authority is mine."

"I suppose you intend to manage the place yourself," Megan said.

Jane smiled fondly at her. The somber black crepe of her mourning only made her look younger, like a little girl playing at widowhood. Indeed, the color was very becoming to her fair skin and soft golden curls.

"Oh, all the gentlemen have offered to assist me," she said ironically. "Sir William trotted out a nephew for my approval the other day—'quite a clever feller, knows all about figures—the mathematical kind, Miss Jane, heh, heh.' "

Megan smiled, but shook her head reproachfully. "You shouldn't make fun of him, Jane. He was so very kind to help us with—with the arrangements."

Jane looked down at the papers on the desk. "What else could he do? It fit so neatly with his preconceptions and prejudices; he always despised Edmund. He was not at all surprised that such an effeminate dandy would be inept enough to blow his own head off."

"Jane!"

"Forgive me."

"No, my dear—forgive me." Megan leaned forward, her blue eyes swimming with tears. "You saw it. I know the memory must be intolerable."

"Yes, I saw it." Jane turned away from Megan's sympathetic gaze. Sunlight streamed through the library windows, illumining the papers scattered on the desk. Jane itched to get to work at them. There were so many matters requiring immediate attention. Edmund had left no will, and there was no male relative to interfere with her; from now on she had a free hand. But she must remember to get a footstool. Edmund's chair was too big for her; her feet dangled several inches off the floor.

"I suppose you will marry Sam," she said. "Oh, don't look so scandalized, Megan, I don't mean tomorrow or next month; you will insist on the proper period of mourning. But someone will have to act as guardian for little Eddie and watch over his affairs. If you plan to marry again—"

"If I do," Megan said, blushing, "I hope you will always be a sister to me and manage everything just as you think best. But, Jane, you yourself will marry one day—"

"No. Would it be so tragic if I didn't?"

"Perhaps not," Megan said, after reflecting for a moment. "Perhaps marriage is not always the best for everyone. I only want what you want, Jane."

"I have everything I want. Almost everything—and what I don't have, I mean to get. Now run along, Megan, and let me deal with these papers."

After Megan had gone, her long black skirts and veils trailing gracefully, Jane leaned back in her chair. For the first time since it had happened, she deliberately let her mind retrace the steps along the dark path that had ended in the glade.

There was no beginning—no moment she could point to and think, "That was when he made up his mind to do it." It had come on so gradually, so insidiously, that probably Edmund himself had not made a conscious decision until the last hour of the last day, and only after a dozen other attempts had failed. Any one of them might have succeeded, but it was typical of Edmund that they had depended so much on chance. He was not a violent man, and he had, to a greater extent than anyone she had ever known, the power of self-deception. Even as his hand smeared the oil on the library steps or poured water over his wife's unconscious body before opening the window wide to the cold night air, his waking mind was absolving him of a charge of deliberate murder. At this very moment she could not be certain he had done those things, or others she suspected. There was no proof—no hope of convincing even the potential victim, much less a jury of his peers. That was why she had had to act.

Like Edmund himself, she had gone far down the dark road before she realized where it would end. The strange dream she had had that night in the Lovell Tower. . . . The figure at the end of the shimmering path had held out a murderer's bloody hands—but had the face been Edmund's or her own?

She had known him for what he was after he imprisoned her, yet she had been naive enough to believe his assurances, to trade her silence for a promise of kindness and tolerance he had never meant to keep. Besides, it would have done her no good to denounce him. No one would have believed her. They would have thought her mad. The vague, suppressed suspicions aroused by Megan's "accidents" were too incredible to be considered seriously—until the day she sat by Sam's bed and heard his white lips whisper of his own fears for Megan. He knew Edmund better than she, he was well aware that he risked his own safety by returning to St. Arca, but he had been unable to stay away. The final damning piece of evidence was Sam's denial that he had ever written to Megan. Only one person could have sent the note that took Megan out of the house into the path of a dog that had been trained to kill.

Once convinced, but well aware that she still lacked the power to convince others, she had stretched her wits to the limit to discover a way out. There was a path of escape for her. Once she got her share of the proceeds from the sale of the mill, she could leave—abandoning the home she loved, abandoning Megan. She could not take Megan with her. Sooner or later, wherever they fled, the law would track them down, and the law gave Edmund the right to force his wife to live with him. He would never sue for divorce; it was a humiliating, complex process.

I had to do it, Jane thought. There was no other way. Sooner or later he would have succeeded—and then it would have been the child—and Sam—and me, unless I kept silent and let him have his way. If he had shot me—if my blood, not his, had crimsoned the grass at the foot of the Toman stone—Sir William and the rest would have commiserated with him on his tragic loss, and he would have gone on to make sure of Megan—and Sam—and the baby. He would never have stood in the dock or spent an hour in prison. And how ironic that the very inequities of the system that drove me to do it should be my best defense. Dear old Sir William; it would never enter his stupid, kind, male head that Edmund's death could have been anything but an accident.

She began to sort through the papers. Edmund had left his desk in a frightful mess; accounts, bills, unanswered letters were all jumbled together. And here were some of the old papers relating to the house. One day, if she had the leisure, she would go on with the research Edmund had begun. The change in the name of the manor, for instance—it would be interesting to know when it was changed, and why.

She put the yellowing papers in a neat pile to one side. Letters here, bills there, builders' catalogs. . . . One last document, a scrap of crumbling paper with what appeared to be a prayer written out by a devout Catholic owner. Jane glanced at it before adding it to the other papers. Such strange, yet beautiful names they had for the Mother of God. . . .

> *Queen of Heaven, who inhabits the secret places of the woods, be propitious unto us. Mistress of life, white lady; shelter by spring and stone the sharers of thy peace. Virgin and Mother, sower of seed and bearer of fruit, accept our sacrifice so that we who serve you may be granted justice, and long life in the service of justice.*